DANGEROUS DESIRE

Yale came up behind Lexi and reached past her into the cupboard. For a moment there was only silence, and the faint sound of the wind moving through the trees outside. Then Yale heard a voice. It was, he realized with a start, his own. Words were spilling from his lips . . . impulsive words.

"Lexi, I've to go, but before I do, I have to ask you for one thing."

"What is it?" Her tone was hushed, as though she knew.

"I have to kiss you. Just once. Please, Lexi . . . it's been so damned long and I know nothing can come of it, but I have to kiss you."

Lexi turned slowly, and when she looked up, her gaze collided with his. And then she smiled a faraway smile. "One kiss, for old time's sake."

He swept her into his arms and his mouth swooped over hers. Her lips parted beneath his and she let out a soft whimper. She cupped his face in her hands, forcing him to deepen the kiss.

She wanted him the way he wanted her; he could feel her hunger as she pressed into him. She had pulled his shirt from the waistband of his jeans and her fingertips played over his bare back, sending delicious shivers over him.

He had to have her.

Now.

"Lexi," he whispered desperately. "Please . . . I don't want to stop. Please let me make love to you."

Her reply was a single, heated word: "Yes."

COMING SOON: ROMANCES THAT WILL MAKE YOUR HEART POUND

D·A·N·G·E·R·O·U·S

in collaboration with

Wendy Corsi Staub

PINNACLE BOOKS
KENSINGTON PUBLISHING CORP.

PINNACLE BOOKS are published by

Kensington Publishing Corp.
850 Third Avenue
New York, NY 10022

Pinnacle and the P logo Reg. U.S. Pat. & TM Off.

First Printing: July, 1996

Printed in the United States of America
10 9 8 7 6 5 4 3 2

To my mother and father—
For teaching me right from wrong;
and to women everywhere—
Thank you for making this world a better place.

Acknowledgments

My grateful acknowledgment to Wendy Corsi Staub, without whom this book would not have been possible.

Special thanks to my superagent, Mel Berger at the William Morris Agency for helping situate me at my new literary home.

Thanks also to Walter Zacharius, Paul Dinas, and Lynn Brown at Zebra for helping make the transition so easy.

As usual, thanks to my friend and business partner, Eric Ashenberg of Global Entertainment Management for his friendship and business guidance. Words can never fully express my appreciation.

Thanks to Janine Transon and Barry Sytner at C.M.I. for their help in looking after my various career matters.

Thanks as well to Bonnie Kuhlman, a wonderful person, and the best fan club president ever, whose tireless efforts in managing the Fabio International Fan Club, P.O. Box 827, Dubois, Wyoming, 82513 are astounding.

Special thanks to all my fans for their support & kindness. Bless you all.

Prologue

"Oh, God, help me . . . please . . . I'm dying . . ."

"You're not dying," retorted the nurse, a pretty but stern black woman who seemed to have perpetually pursed lips. "You're giving birth. And if you'd just concentrate on your breathing, you wouldn't be having such a hard time."

Lexi Sinclair, writhing on the bed in agony, moaned a single, mighty, all-purpose expletive.

She was cursing the all-business nurse, who bustled about the room as though Lexi were invisible; the anesthesiologist, who was so busy in the emergency room with a carload of accident victims that he couldn't come up to administer an epidural for Lexi; the doctor, who was too busy delivering a baby in the next room to be concerned with Lexi; and the woman who was having the baby in the next room and kept screaming at the top of her lungs, making Lexi even more terrified of what lay ahead.

And most of all, she cursed Emmett.

Emmett Bradigan.

The father of the child who, at the moment, was bent on forcing its way out of Lexi's swollen, unwilling thirty-year-old body.

"Oh, no . . . not again, no . . ." She sobbed as

another potent wave of pain descended upon her, seizing the core of her body and contorting it into an endless, excruciating cramp.

"Breathe!" barked the nurse.

"I . . . can't," Lexi gasped. "I . . . need . . . Emmett for . . . that . . ."

"Listen to me," the nurse said, parking herself on the bed and looking Lexi in the eye. "He's not here. I am. I'll help you . . . as long as you don't kick me again."

Did I actually kick her? Lexi clutched at the nurse's white sleeve and vaguely remembered that she had. It had served the woman right for telling her she wouldn't be able to get the epidural just as a monster of a contraction was starting. But still . . .

"Sorry," Lexi managed. "No . . . kicking. Promise."

"All right, then. Do what I do. Breathe like this . . ." The nurse began the rhythmic panting Lexi and Emmett had learned in Lamaze classes.

As Lexi struggled to imitate her, she dimly recalled how shocked she'd been a few months back when Emmett had actually agreed to go to class with her. Every Tuesday night the two of them had met at the doctor's office with the other round-bellied women and their nervous partners.

The first night, when they'd gone around the circle introducing themselves, all of the others had been married. When it was her turn, Lexi had said, "I'm Lexi Sinclair, this is my first baby, and I'm due on St. Patrick's Day, and this is . . . Emmett."

She had blurted that last part hurriedly, wondering if Emmett felt as uncomfortable as she did about the conspicuously missing phrase "my husband."

But he had simply waved and taken his turn, saying, in his shrugging, casual Emmett way, "Hey, everyone, I'm Emmett, obviously, the baby's dad."

And after that one sticky moment, classes had gone smoothly. Actually, Lexi had grown to look forward to those Tuesday night sessions, and thought that Emmett did, too, even though he grumbled about it a lot.

"Oww . . . owwww . . ." she wailed now as another contraction started only a moment after the last had subsided.

"Breathe, Lexi!" the nurse commanded. "Focus!"

She focused on Emmett, remembering how, at the childbirth prep classes, he had gamely learned to massage her lower back in just the right spot. He had practiced counting to ten at regular intervals so he'd be able to coach her when it was time to push the baby out. He'd sat cross-legged on the floor with the other fathers-to-be, he'd cradled Lexi's head and shoulders in his lap, and he'd even laughed at the instructor's corny jokes.

And when they'd seen an ancient seventies video of actual births, he hadn't made sarcastic comments about the participants' groovy clothes and flabby bodies, the way other men in the class had.

No, Emmett had watched the entire video in awed silence, and when it was over, he'd turned to Lexi and murmured, "It really is a miracle, huh, Lex?"

She'd been stunned to see tears in his eyes.

That was the moment when she'd actually

thought for the first time that things might turn out all right. That Emmett might have changed; that maybe he was ready, after all, to be a family with her and the baby.

Obviously, she'd been wrong.

"Where the hell *is* he?" she asked the nurse through clenched teeth as another contraction rode over her on the tail of the previous one.

"Don't worry about him right now. You're almost ready to push, and that's going to take every ounce of concentration you've got."

"But he said he'd be here!" Lexi wailed. "He *promised.*"

The nurse just shrugged, stood, and pulled on a pair of rubber gloves. She moved to the foot of the bed and bent over between Lexi's bent legs.

As the nurse's purposeful but gentle fingers probed her, Lexi winced, stared up at the ceiling, and whimpered again, this time just to herself, "He promised."

Emmett wasn't a man who made promises.

He had told her that, flat out, at the beginning of their relationship. "I don't make promises, and I don't lie—ever. Those are my rules."

But he'd broken his own rule one night not long ago, when they'd been lying in her bed after making love. He'd had his hand on her enormous belly, watching and feeling it pitch and roll as their child had changed position.

"Look, Lex! Look!" he'd exclaimed, as though she hadn't seen this a thousand times before. As though *he* hadn't. "Look how he's all over the place in there. He's so strong . . . he's going to be one of those kids who's walking when other kids his age are just learning to sit up," he'd said proudly.

"We don't know it's a he," Lexi said for the millionth time, not wanting him to be disappointed.

"But if it is, he'll be named after his old man. And we'll call him E. J. for Emmett Junior. Right, kid?" He patted a protruding bump—Lexi thought it was probably a knee or an elbow.

"What if it's a girl?"

"We'll name her after you. Alexandra."

Lexi made a face. "No."

"Come on, Lexi . . . Alexandra Junior—A. J. What do you think?"

"No," she'd said again, laughing at his expression.

"Then what?"

She shrugged.

They had been through this a thousand times. They couldn't come up with a name for a girl. Emmett liked "Debbie" and "Susie" and "Linda," which Lexi thought sounded like names for bouncy fifties cheerleaders in poodle skirts. She liked "Emily" and "Victoria" and "Charlotte," which he thought sounded like someone's eighty-year-old maiden aunt in a white lace collar.

So.

If it was a boy, it would definitely be E. J.

If it was a girl—well, it had better not be a girl, because they were stuck.

But Lexi had warned Emmett, "If it's a girl and you're not around when she's born, then I'll just pick a name myself."

"No way. I'll be there, Lex. Not just because I

don't want you to slap her with some crazy name. 'Cause I'm the dad, and I won't miss this."

"I've heard that before—about a lot of other things," Lexi had reminded him wistfully.

"This time it's different, Lex," he'd said quietly. "This time, I promise. *I'll be there.*"

And somehow, she'd believed him. He'd gone around wearing a beeper twenty-four hours a day just in case she went into labor when he wasn't around. She'd beeped him repeatedly when her water had broken right after her solitary dinner and she'd realized that the first contractions were far stronger than the false labor she'd had on and off for weeks.

Using her cell phone, she'd dialed his beeper number over and over during the wild cab ride down the West Side Highway, and as she filled out the paperwork at the hospital, and as she'd lain in the labor room, before the contractions had gotten too intense and she could no longer dial.

But he hadn't responded.

And he wasn't here.

Now, feeling a sudden, unbearably potent urge to bear down, Lexi heard herself sob his name pitifully.

Somewhere on the fringes of her awareness, she actually expected him to materialize. As she strained against the need to push, then went with it, as the nurse counted to ten over and over, then rushed to summon the doctor and another nurse to help with the coaching, Lexi kept looking frantically around the room.

Looking for Emmett.

Thinking she was going to see him sprawled in the "Daddy" chair by the bed, where she'd pictured him so many times before this night. Or standing over her, clutching her hand, locking eyes with her, and counting.

Instead, it was the stern black nurse who stood at one side and coached her, grabbing her bent leg at the knee and shoving it toward Lexi's shoulder every time she started to push. And it was a stranger, a young blond woman in aqua scrubs, who stood at her other side, where Emmett should have been, grabbing her other leg and holding it at her other shoulder and looking at the clock every once in a while as though she had other, infinitely more interesting things to do.

"One-two-three . . . that's it, Lexi, don't stop . . . four-five-six-seven-eight-nine-ten! Take a breath and start again, one-two-three . . ."

She fought to focus on the nurse's now-familiar pretty chocolate-colored face instead of longing for Emmett, struggled to remember to keep her bottom *down* as the nurse kept shouting reminders, labored to concentrate on what was happening—that she was bringing a life into the world—and not on what was missing.

Emmett . . .

"I can't do it!" she wailed in desperation, exhausted and tormented by the pressure between her legs.

"Yes, you can!"

"I need Emmett!" she shrieked at the nurse, as her body hurled her mercilessly into another bout of futile pushing.

"Who's Emmett?" she heard the doctor ask. It wasn't Noah Stein, her regular obstetrician—he wasn't on call tonight. This was a younger, cuter, more businesslike man named Gregory something-or-other, a total stranger who perched on a stool between her legs wearing a mask and a shower cap.

"Emmett's the father." The nurse tore her eyes from Lexi's long enough to exchange a look with the doctor. A look that said *Emmett is someone who obviously doesn't give a damn that his child is being born.*

"He does care!" Lexi screamed at the nurse. "He does!"

"Of course he cares," the nurse soothed automatically, turning back to Lexi and grabbing her leg again.

"Don't say it like that!"

The nurse ignored her and went back to counting.

Lexi groaned and wept and railed at these three strangers who were letting this happen—letting her body be agonizingly ripped apart by a baby who wouldn't be so eager to come out if it knew that its father was nowhere to be found.

"I can't do this," she told them in tears, but they ignored her.

This couldn't be happening. It was obscene, unreal, a nightmare.

"I can't do this. I can't . . ."

"Okay," the doctor called, suddenly changing his position and looking up at her expectantly, "if you want to have a baby, you can do it on this next push."

I don't want to have a baby! Lexi howled inside

her brain, too far gone to speak a coherent sentence aloud. *I don't want this baby because Emmett doesn't want it, and now he doesn't want me and he never did, he never wanted any of this; he never loved me even though he said he did, and I know he said he never lies, but he does because he never loved me, because if he did he would be here and he never meant it when he promised, and—*

"... eight-nine-ten, push, Lexi, there it is, the baby's coming out, push! One-two-three ..."

I have to make this stop right now, I have to tell them that I've changed my mind and I don't want this baby, because I'm going to lose Emmett, because he's not ready to be someone's father, just like he told me he wasn't ready to be someone's husband, and that was before we ever even knew about the baby, and I can't do this—I can't I can't I can't I—

"It's a girl!" the nurse announced breathlessly. "Lexi, you have a beautiful baby daughter. Congratulations, sweetie."

She lay back on the pillow, utterly exhausted, overwhelmed by relief. It was over. Nothing else mattered.

Then she heard it . . . the unmistakable sound she had, until now, encountered only in movies and in that Lamaze video.

The thin, high-pitched cry of a newborn child.

Her child.

"My baby," she murmured, opening her eyes just as the nurse gently laid a wet, bloody, squirming dark-haired bundle on her stomach.

"Here she is, Lexi, and she's beautiful."

"She's beautiful," she echoed softly, holding the warm, sticky little body against her and running a fingertip down the baby's bony arm.

The tiny girl blinked and stared into Lexi's eyes solemnly, as though she recognized her.

Tears streamed down Lexi's cheeks. "You know me, don't you? I'm your mommy, sweetheart. I'm your mommy, and I'll always love you and I'll never leave you. Never. Ever. I promise."

And the baby made a hushed sighing sound, as though she understood.

"Alexandra?"

Only one person in the world called her that.

Lexi looked up and saw her mother, Kathleen Nealon Sinclair, standing in the doorway of her hospital room.

"Mom!" She looked at the woman with new-found respect, suddenly feeling bonded to her by this recent rush of maternal understanding. "Come meet your granddaughter."

Kathleen stepped into the room looking characteristically nervous. She was a person prone to hand-wringing and lip-chewing, and she was doing both now. A scarf hid her thinning brown hair, and a bulky down coat hid her painfully thin body—both ravaged by the cancer and chemotherapy that had been a part of her life for nearly a year.

"I'm here, too, honey." Scott Sinclair followed his wife in. He also wore a down jacket and jeans, and his eyes behind his glasses looked unusually solemn.

"Here she is," Lexi announced, tilting the baby, swaddled in her receiving blanket, so that her parents could see her. "Come on, you guys can hold her if you want. They just brought her back from the nursery. They keep them there for the first few hours after birth, I guess to do tests and let the mothers rest. But I feel totally great . . ."

Physically, she amended silently. She had expected her body to feel trampled and battered after her ordeal, but it was her emotions that were shattered. She'd spent the last four hours staring out the window from her bed, watching the milky March sun come up over Manhattan and wondering how Emmett could have let her down. And it wasn't just *her* anymore. This was his daughter, too.

She imagined what she would say to him the first time he dared show his face to her after what he'd done. *You blew it, bud. This was your first test of fatherhood, and you flunked royally.*

Lexi realized that her parents were hovering just inside the door, looking oddly reluctant.

Could it be that they were suddenly having qualms about her unwed status, now that the baby was actually here? Both had been marvelously supportive these last nine months and had told their only daughter that they were thrilled at the prospect of becoming grandparents.

Only once had Kathleen tentatively asked Lexi if she planned to marry Emmett. Lexi hadn't dared tell her mother that she and Emmett had discussed marriage long before the baby had even been conceived. Rather, she'd attempted to discuss it, and he'd retreated emotionally, then physically.

He'd said he didn't believe in marriage—his parents were divorced, and so, it seemed, was the rest of the world. He loved her, yes . . . but he didn't want to be somebody's husband.

Somebody's husband.

Lexi wanted to tell him that they weren't talking about marriage in the abstract, about him being *somebody's* husband; they were talking about him being *her* husband. She wanted to argue and protest and beg. But thank God, she hadn't done any of those things. She had just let him go, swearing to herself that she'd never take him back.

And then, a few weeks later, she'd taken him back.

Because I love you, you jerk, she thought now, trying to shove thoughts of him away and focus on her parents.

"Alexandra . . ." her mother began, then seemed too choked up to continue.

Lexi rocked her daughter a little and smiled faintly. Her mother had always been the emotional type, especially lately, with her illness and Lexi's pregnancy.

Wiping at her eyes, Kathleen Sinclair crossed over to the bed. She sat carefully on the edge beside Lexi and peered at her granddaughter.

"Hello, my little precious," she said, sniffling and wiping at her eyes. "You're such a beautiful girl, aren't you? Look at you . . . oh . . ."

"Kathleen," Scott said as his wife wept, and came to stand by the bed. He patted Kathleen's shoulder, then Lexi's. He looked down at the baby, whose eyes were swollen into slits from the drops the nurses had put into them. "You had a lot of dark hair, too, when you were first born," he told Lexi, running his hand over her head.

Her long, black curls were matted into knots, she realized vaguely, looking from her father to her mother.

They both seemed so . . . subdued. Not how she'd have imagined them at their first meeting with the grandchild they'd so eagerly awaited. In fact, when she'd called them a few hours ago at their home in suburban Cady's Landing to tell them the news, they'd both seemed overjoyed. They'd promised to get dressed and jump into the car to come to the hospital.

"Would you mind stopping at my apartment first?" Lexi had asked. She'd forgotten, in her haste to get a cab, to grab the overnight bag that had sat packed and ready by the door throughout most of her third trimester.

Emmett had been the one who was supposed to be responsible for remembering to bring it. Emmett was supposed to be responsible for a lot of things.

"Oh, I almost forgot," Lexi said suddenly. "Her name—it's Emily Victoria."

"That's pretty," her mother murmured absently, running a bony finger along the baby's pink cheek.

"Emmett won't like it," Lexi told her parents. "But it's too bad. He missed out on his chance to be here to name her. He'll be lucky if I let him see her at all before she graduates from high school."

Her parents exchanged a glance.

"What?" Lexi asked sharply, looking from one

to the other. "You think I'm being too hard on him?"

"It's not that," Scott said, then hesitated.

Her mother pulled a crumpled Kleenex out of her coat pocket and wiped at her eyes. She was crying softly again.

A terrible feeling took hold somewhere in the pit of Lexi's stomach.

"What is it?" she asked, trying not to acknowledge the sense of dread that crept over her.

"Can I hold her, honey?" her mother asked, tucking her tissue away and holding out her arms.

"What . . . ?"

"The baby, can I—?"

Blankly, Lexi handed her daughter over, forgetting—or not caring—what the nurses had said about making people scrub their hands before touching the baby.

She was riveted on her father's face.

Scott Sinclair was handsome in a craggy sort of way, and his blue eyes seemed to be perpetually twinkling. But right now, they were filled with . . . concern. And something else Lexi couldn't pinpoint.

"Daddy?" she asked in a small voice.

He took a deep breath. "Lexi, when your mother and I stopped at your building just now, the . . . uh, the police were there."

She shook her head in denial, somehow knowing what was coming.

"They told us . . . ." He paused, swallowed, and took her hands in his.

"Noooo," she whimpered in a barely audible voice, shaking her head.

"They told us," her father went on hoarsely, "that there was a fire at Emmett's apartment in Queens last night . . . and . . . oh, God, Lexi, I'm so sorry. Emmett was killed."

One

"Who loves you, punkin? Who loves you? Your mommy does! That's right, Mommy does!"

Lexi lifted her six-month-old daughter over her head and the baby squealed with delight.

"Know what, Em? You're getting too heavy," Lexi said, lowering her and cuddling her dark little head against her breast. She planted a kiss on the silky hair that was just starting to curl up at the ends.

"Goo," her daughter announced, her big seafoam-colored eyes staring solemnly into Lexi's.

"Goo to you, too." Lexi got off the saggy couch and plunked her daughter in the padded bouncy seat she loved. She fastened the straps snugly around the baby's chubby tummy so she couldn't tumble out onto the hardwood floor. Lately, it seemed she'd gotten more mobile. In no time she'd be motoring around the apartment on her own two feet.

Just as Daddy predicted, Lexi thought wistfully, patting her daughter's head and then turning back to the cardboard boxes stacked in every corner. They were filled with everything she owned, and among them were a few sealed cartons of Emmett's things. He'd brought them over from his Queens apartment a few weeks before the baby's birth, telling Lexi he'd probably be spending more time there—"You know, with the kid."

She ran a distracted hand through her tangle of long black curls, then rolled up the sleeves on her oversized plaid flannel shirt. It had once belonged to Emmett. He'd given it to her long before he'd . . .

Died.

Even now, months later, Lexi found it impossible to connect that word with Emmett.

After all this time, she still woke every morning forgetting, for a blissful, fleeting second or two, that he was gone. In that brief moment of ignorance, the world was a wonderful place.

Then reality would crash over her and she'd remember that Emmett was dead.

Emmett—the man she'd loved. The man her daughter would never get the chance to love.

You never even had a chance to screw up as a father, she thought to herself, as she pulled the strip of packing tape off the nearest box and opened the flaps.

Or a chance to prove me wrong—to prove that you weren't going to screw up, after all. You were robbed, Emmett.

But I can't keep thinking about you.

I have to move on.

"Hey, Em," she said abruptly, "how about some music?"

Her daughter gurgled agreeably.

Lexi moved over to the stereo, one of the few things she'd unpacked when they'd first moved in. She couldn't stand the silence of an empty house.

Now, she grabbed an old Neil Young CD from the stack on top of the speaker and put it on.

There. That was better already.

She looked around the sunny living room, then into the adjoining dining room, through a pair of open French doors. Even crammed with boxes and mismatched furniture she'd bought secondhand, this place was far roomier than her cramped studio back in the city.

It would make a pleasant home, once she got things settled.

Funny.

She had always, while she was pregnant, pictured herself raising their child alone, as a single mom—so sure had she been that Emmett was going to walk the first time the going got tough.

She had never even considered that he might be ripped from her and their baby by a force far more powerful than Emmett's own selfish inability to grow up and commit.

Now, here she was, moving into a new apartment in the suburbs, alone with their child . . . just as she'd always imagined.

And she ached, still, for what might have been.

She would never stop wondering whether it was worse to have lost him this way, in circumstances beyond his control—or to have lost him because of his own choice.

This way, she knew he was gone forever, that there was no hope.

The other way—well, she probably always would have hoped. But for her daughter's sake, she wouldn't have been able to consider taking him back. After he'd walked out on them that first time—and he *would* have—she'd have had to consider him dead, anyway.

So maybe, as awful as it seemed, losing him to death was easier, somehow.

She reached into the box, marked "breakables," and removed something heavy that was wrapped in newspaper. As she carefully peeled away the layers of the *New York Times* sports section, she noticed an article about a basketball game and one about the Yankees at spring training camp. The date on the paper was late March.

Now here it was September already. Baseball season was almost over, and basketball season would soon begin again.

Life goes on, thought Lexi, crumpling the newspaper and tossing it into an empty box. She glanced at the large white pasta platter she'd unwrapped, trying not to remember the last time she'd used it.

She showed it to the baby, who was chewing on the strap of her seat.

"See, Em? This is a bowl Mommy uses to serve spaghetti. You'll be able to try it someday soon. You're going to love it. You'll probably call it 'pasketti' and you'll smoosh tomato sauce all over your face and have all kinds of fun with it. Daddy always loved spaghetti. He bought this platter for me."

She swallowed hard over a lump in her throat and reached back into the box, removing another newspaper-wrapped item.

"You know, Em," she said, trying to force a light note into her voice as she unwrapped a dark green

ceramic canister, "it's about time Mommy unpacked all this stuff. We've been living here since
Labor Day, and I'm really sick of eating take-out
every night and not being able to find things I need
and stepping around a maze of boxes whenever I
make a move . . ."

And being alone.

I am so damn sick of being alone.

Oh, of course she had her daughter. And her parents, who lived just a few miles from the carriage
house she'd rented on the grounds of an old Cady's
Landing estate.

But Em was just a baby. And Lexi's mother and
father, with whom she and the baby had been staying until now, had their hands full. Scott Sinclair
had been laid off from his computer sales job in
July. Meanwhile, Kathleen, who'd briefly gone into
remission around Easter, was once again fighting
for her life.

There were times lately when Lexi's world
seemed unbearably grim.

But somehow she kept going.

Not because she was some incredibly strong-
willed, brave soul who was determined to triumph
over life's trials like the heroine of a made-for-TV
movie.

But simply because she had to.

What other choice was there but to get up every
morning and do what had to be done?

A sound reached her, over Neil Young singing
Hurricane on the stereo. It was the unmistakable
noise tires made crunching over the gravel in the
drive outside.

"Somebody's here to see us, Em," she told the baby, who smiled and gurgled around the fist jammed into her mouth.

Lexi hurried over to the window that looked out to the front of the house. An unfamiliar, expensive-looking shiny black car was parked by the door.

For a moment, she wondered if whoever it was had come to see the Worths. They were her landlords, the wealthy Manhattanites who owned the estate and spent summers out here. But surely any of their local friends would know that they'd gone back to the city at the beginning of September.

"I'll be right back, Em," Lexi said, brushing off her faded jeans and going back through the living room and into the small entry hall. She opened the screen door and stepped out onto the tiny porch, finger-combing her wayward curls back from her face.

The car door was opening and someone was getting out.

The dazzling September sun shone directly into Lexi's eyes, and for a moment she could see nothing but the silhouette of a man.

Then she cupped her hand over her brows . . .

And gasped.

"Emmett," she murmured, weakly clutching the railing and gaping at the familiar face.

Then she blinked and reality set in, the way it always did.

She narrowed her gaze at the man who strode toward her and steeled herself to face him again for the first time in years.

"Hello, Lexi."

"Yale," she said simply.

He stopped a few feet from the porch and stood there, looking up at her.

Yale Bradigan.

Emmett's identical twin brother.

He wore an expensively cut caramel-colored suit with a creamy shirt and boldly patterned tie. His trousers bagged fashionably at the ankles, brushing the tops of his polished wing-tips.

She forced her eyes up, away from his clothes, to the face of the man she had grown to loathe.

But it was also the face of the man she'd loved, because Yale Bradigan had Emmett's sharply sculpted features, his full lips, his high cheekbones, and, hidden behind those designer sunglasses he wore, his wide-set light green eyes. Eyes that were just like her daughter's.

And Yale, like Emmett, had thick hair in a streaked golden shade that had always reminded Lexi of summer—of sand and sunshine.

But where Emmett's hair had been long and unruly, Yale's was impeccably, conservatively cut in a style that matched his suit and his businesslike demeanor.

His hands were jammed into his pockets, but Lexi knew that on his right hand there was a shiny gold ring. Emmett had always worn one just like it. The rings bore the Bradigan family crest and had been given to the twins by their grandfather on the day they'd graduated from high school. The old man had been the only stable parent figure the boys had ever really had.

Their parents had divorced when they were toddlers. Trevor Bradigan had subsequently died in an avalanche while skiing in Europe the Christmas his sons were eight. And Blythe Bradigan, a hopeless alcoholic, had barely been able to raise them. It was Trevor's father, Geoff, who had taken his grandsons under his wing.

Lexi would never forget how devastated both Emmett and Yale had been when their beloved grandfather had had a heart attack and died a few months before their nineteenth birthday. As far as Lexi knew, both brothers had always worn their rings in the years since.

Now, she saw a glint of gold as Yale removed his right hand from his pocket and ran it nervously through his hair.

Lexi watched him, waiting.

But he continued to stand there, his expression an enigma behind those dark glasses.

"I got your letter," he said finally.

Even the voice was Emmett's.

"It must have sat around for weeks before I got it," he continued. "I close the gallery in August, and I was in Europe until Labor Day. I didn't get the letter till I got back."

"Why don't you come in?" Lexi said, collecting herself and motioning at the door.

"Where's . . . is the baby here?"

"Yes," Lexi said simply, biting back a sarcastic reply. Where else would she be? she wanted to ask. Did he think she had the luxury of hiring a nanny or sending her daughter out to some expensive day-care program?

Of course he doesn't think that, she reminded herself, holding the door open and stepping back as Yale walked into the house.

She could hear cheerful, high-pitched babbling coming from the living room, as though the baby were singing along with Neil Young. Just the way her daddy always did.

"Can I see her?" Yale asked.

"Sure. She's in there, obviously," Lexi told Yale, and led the way. "Excuse the mess. We're still un-packing."

He said nothing, but just followed her.

"Hi, sweetie," she said, crouching and unbuck-ling her daughter from her bouncy seat, then scoop-ing her into her arms. She was rewarded with a happy laugh and a stream of drool on her cheek. "This is your uncle. His name is Yale."

Yale, still wearing his dark glasses, stood staring at the baby for a long time. The little girl, clutching a handful of Lexi's hair, smiled at him and babbled.

"She's gotten big," he said at last.

Lexi nodded.

She knew Yale had visited the baby in the hospital nursery a few times in the days after his brother's death. The nurses had told her about the handsome man who'd spent a lot of time staring through the glass at his newborn niece.

He hadn't attempted to see Lexi, though.

Not that he'd have been welcome, she thought stubbornly. Even if he and Emmett hadn't been es-tranged for a decade, she wouldn't have wanted to see Yale. Not after what he'd done to *her* all those years ago.

Still, he'd called her when she'd finally been sent

home to her parents' house after a week. Their conversation had been stilted.

"How are you feeling?" he'd asked, after inquiring about the baby and having been told she was fine.

"I'm better," Lexi had lied.

What else could she do? Tell him that her mind was numb, her heart shattered, and her body a useless wreck?

The doctor had said her recovery setback had been brought on by intense grief and shock. She had been so traumatized by Emmett's death that for days she'd been unable to do anything but stare at the ceiling and cry.

She hadn't even been able to nurse her poor baby, who, luckily, had thrived being bottle-fed by her mother and the nurses.

"How was the funeral?" she'd managed to ask Yale over the phone the day he'd called her.

"It was . . . Emmett would have liked it."

Such an odd thing to say, she had thought then. Yet she knew it was true. Emmett *would* have liked the funeral his brother had arranged for him. According to her parents, who'd attended, it had been a simple ceremony on the shore of Long Island Sound in Cady's Landing. Emmett's friend Renee had played *Forever Young* on her guitar, and a minister had said a few words about how Emmett had always been a free spirit, and how now he would live on in the air and the water and the land.

Then Yale had silently tossed his brother's ashes into the foaming water that lapped against the rocky beach. Her parents had reported that he hadn't cried or spoken through the entire ceremony, but that he had seemed subdued and, perhaps, in shock.

They'd also said he'd been accompanied by a stunning brunette.

"Thank you for handling everything for me," Lexi had told him, clutching the phone hard against her ear and trying not to cry.

"You're welcome. If you ever need anything," Yale had said before banging up, "please let me know."

Well, she *did* need something, and she *had* let him know.

And now, here he was, standing in the living room of the little rented house, which suddenly looked shabby and forlorn.

"Thanks for coming over," Lexi said.

"I tried to call first, but you don't have a phone."

"We will, but I haven't had a chance to get it hooked up yet."

"You've got your hands full with the baby and the move and everything," Yale said, nodding.

She nodded, too.

But it wasn't the truth. There had been plenty of time, if she'd wanted to unpack and settle into the new place. It had been weeks since she'd signed the new lease and moved her stuff from the storage bin where her father had put it after he'd emptied her Manhattan apartment.

And the baby wasn't *that* much work, Lexi had been surprised to discover. She'd spent months reading motherhood magazines when she was pregnant, and they all seemed filled with advice columns and articles talking about how exhausting it was to be a new mom, how you didn't get a moment to yourself, a moment to even *think* straight.

Actually, if Lexi hadn't had a moment to think straight, she'd have been grateful.

But changing diapers and holding bottles and laundering tiny clothes didn't take up all that much time, really, and while she was doing those mindless chores, she could do nothing *but* think.

Think about Emmett, and what had happened.

About what might have been . . .

Even though she knew it was only a fantasy.

She went over and over it in her head all day, always drawing the same conclusion: if Emmett were alive, he'd be gone by now anyway.

"Do you . . . can I hold her?" Yale asked, taking off his sunglasses and carefully putting them into his pocket.

"Of course," Lexi said, surprised. Yale Bradigan wasn't the kind of man you'd picture holding a baby.

And it struck her that if Emmett had lived, it was unlikely Yale would've had any contact with the child at all.

The Bradigan brothers hadn't spoken in years, for a reason only they knew. Their falling out had occurred after Yale and Lexi had broken up, but before she'd become involved with Emmett, who had steadfastly refused to discuss his brother with her or anyone else.

"Here you go." She placed her daughter into Yale's inept arms.

He took her clumsily and the baby gurgled as he tried to adjust her position.

Lexi was about to warn him to grab the cloth diaper off the couch because the baby might spit up or drool on his suit, but then decided against it. The idea of her child spewing something on Yale Bradigan's thousand-dollar jacket filled her with a perverse kind of pleasure.

"I'll get us something to drink," she said, stepping around the open carton on the floor and heading toward the kitchen. "Do you want iced tea, or hot?"

"Iced is fine."

She was nearly in the kitchen when she heard him say, in an awkward attempt at baby talk, "Hello there, Emily Victoria. That's a pretty big name for such a tiny girl."

Lexi turned back to him. "That's not her name."

"But at the hospital, the card I saw through the window, you know, on her bed in the nursery, said—"

"I know," Lexi cut him off. "I changed it."

Instead of the *why* she expected, he asked, "When?"

"After . . ."

After I found out that her daddy hadn't simply neglected to be there when she was born. After I found out he was . . .

Dead.

There it was, that horrible word again.

"I just changed my mind," she finished with a shrug.

"What's her name now?" he asked, absently stroking his niece's fine dark hair.

Lexi noticed that he was holding her awkwardly,

that the baby was trying to free her arm, which was trapped against Yale's broad chest. But she didn't say anything to him. Someplace deep inside, she was touched by the sight of this man holding her child, by the fact that he seemed oblivious to the dark, wet spot she'd already left on his lapel.

"Lexi?"

"Hmm?"

"What's her name?"

"Oh. It's Emma Rose."

"Emma Rose," he echoed, then tried it on the baby. "Hi, Emma Rose. Hi, there. Is that who you are?"

The baby cooed in delight at the face he made at her, and she grabbed his nose in her tiny fist and held on. He looked surprised, then laughed, which made Emma Rose giggle and latch on more tightly. Lexi had to smile at the comical sight.

"Hey, are you trying to tell me something?" Yale asked the baby. "I always knew my nose was big, but you don't have to make such a scene to prove the point."

"Gaaa," Emma Rose replied sweetly, and let go.

Lexi couldn't bear to watch her daughter smiling up at the man she'd grown to despise.

She went into the kitchen and poured two glasses of iced tea.

Her hands were trembling as she put the plastic pitcher back into the fridge.

It was nearly impossible to believe Yale Bradigan was standing in her living room.

Thanks to the CD that was playing, she couldn't hear what was going on. She was certain that if

Emma Rose was unhappy, she'd be screaming. She'd heard that persistent sound often enough to know it'd undoubtedly drown out a mere stereo.

Lexi's daughter had inherited her daddy's disposition—easygoing, for the most part. But if somebody crossed her . . . look out.

Emmett would have gotten a kick out of Emma Rose's temper.

Lexi picked up the glasses of iced tea, but her right hand somehow tilted and she spilled some on the floor.

What is with you? she scolded herself as she bent to wipe it up. *Why are you such a jittery mess?*

As if she didn't know.

Yale Bradigan was in her living room.

Emmett's brother.

Yale, who'd once been the golden boy of Cadv's Landing.

Yale, who'd once been Lexi's . . .

What?

Lover.

That was certainly the truth. That long-ago summer after his sophomore year at Rhode Island School of Design, when she was fresh out of high school and lifeguarding at the beach club, they'd been lovers. She clearly remembered the June day when it had begun, the affair between good-looking, sought-after Yale Bradigan and willful, rebellious, community college-bound Alexandra Sinclair.

A heavy gray sky had hung over Long Island Sound that morning, and the pebbly beach had been deserted. Lexi, shivering even in the oversized sweatshirt and denim shorts she'd thrown over her bathing suit, had been huddled on her weathered green lifeguard tower. Her long hair was pulled back into an unruly braid, a futile attempt at keeping her curls from becoming a tangled mess in the damp wind.

As soon as she'd spotted the two boys strolling on the beach, she'd known who they were.

Everyone in Cady's Landing knew the Bradigan twins.

Unlike Lexi, who had gone through the local public schools, they had attended the exclusive Pendergast Academy near Poughkeepsie—courtesy of their wealthy grandfather, according to local gossip. There wasn't a soul in town who didn't know that the twins' mother, Blythe, was a hopeless drunk, and that if it hadn't been for the old man's money, the boys and their mother would have been out on the street.

Once, just after the twins' father had been killed, Lexi had heard her mother's friend Ivy remark that it was a wonder Yale was such a promising, well-behaved child—and that it was no surprise Emmett wasn't.

Even then, Emmett, with his lazy grin and roguish swagger, had been branded a troublemaker.

That June day on the beach, as the two had approached her, Lexi had marveled at how identical brothers could possibly have such different looks.

Emmett's tawny hair was wind-tousled and hung well past the collar of his faded denim jacket. He had on worn, ragged-bottomed jeans, sneakers that had probably once been white, and black Wayfarer sunglasses despite the overcast day. As they walked, he kept bending to grab a handful of pebbles, then skipped them, one by one, across the choppy water. He clearly had *attitude*—a cocky restlessness that was distinct even from a distance.

Yale, on the other hand, strolled calmly along with his hands in his pockets, carefully stepping aside whenever the water lapped too close to his leather deck shoes. He wore khaki shorts and a navy fisherman's knit sweater, and his short blond hair was hidden beneath a plain white baseball cap. He was as dignified and conservative as his grand-mother's New England family—distant relatives of Elihu Yale.

It was Emmett to whom Lexi had found herself drawn that first day, identifying with his fiery de-meanor. She was an only child, raised by doting, overprotective parents who'd nearly smothered her with rules by the time she was in high school. She was ripe for a walk on the wild side, and would have sensed—even if she hadn't heard the local gossip—that Emmett Bradigan was undeniably wild.

But it had been Yale who'd noticed her, who'd struck up a flirtation while Emmett stood moodily smoking a cigarette at the water's edge.

And what girl in Cady's Landing wouldn't have been flattered to have the attention of a guy like Yale? Even before he'd asked her out for that night, Lexi had been mentally planning on calling her best friend, Kerry, as soon as she got home to tell her that she'd actually hung out with Yale Bradigan.

She'd ended up doing far more than just hanging

out with him that summer—until he'd broken her fragile eighteen-year-old heart and sailed off without so much as a backward glance.

Lexi sighed and returned to the present—to some spilled iced tea and the knowledge that her former first love was now waiting for her in her living room.

She refilled the glass, then made her way out of the kitchen.

"Shhh," Yale said softly, as soon as she came around the corner.

For a moment, Lexi could only stare at her daughter, whose chubby face was snuggled into Yale's shoulder as she slept.

"She conked out. Where should I put her?" he whispered.

"Um . . . in her crib . . . upstairs. I'll show you." She set the two glasses down on the cluttered coffee table, then led him up the steep flight into Emma Rose's nursery.

It was the one room in the house that Lexi had finished, and she'd stayed up several nights in a row to get it done.

It was a tiny space, really, tucked beneath the gabled roof of the carriage house, but she'd painted the sloping plank walls and ceiling a creamy white that made the room seem larger.

She had coveted a quartet of framed pastel nursery-rhyme prints in the window of a small art gallery in town, but knew there was no way she'd ever be able to afford them. Instead, she'd stenciled a pale border of roses on the walls and on the changing table and bookshelf—which she'd found at a yard sale and spray-painted white.

The two windows were covered in filmy lace curtains, topped with swags of light pink Laura Ashley-type floral-print cotton Lexi had found at the discount fabric store. The white Jenny Lind crib, a gift from her parents, was trimmed with her one splurge: a matching set of rose-covered bumpers, sheets, and dust ruffle.

Lexi had refinished the room's honey-colored wooden floor, endlessly sanding the uneven floorboards in an effort to ensure that her daughter's soft baby feet would never pick up a splinter. She had bought some inexpensive white cotton rag rugs to cover the few spots that still seemed a little too rough.

A large white wicker basket beneath one window held Emma Rose's few toys and dolls, and the bookshelves were bare except for tattered copies of *Goodnight, Moon, Green Eggs and Ham,* and the *Peter Rabbit* that had once belonged to Lexi.

"You can put her in the crib," she whispered, turning to see Yale standing in the doorway, looking around.

She wondered what he was thinking. Probably that it was a shame his niece lived in what had once been an attic storage room.

She saw him glance at the dressing table and bookshelf.

Suddenly, the pieces she'd been so proud to have refinished now seemed like used furniture plucked from among someone's cast-offs.

"Put her in the crib," she repeated, irritated not

just with Yale, who seemed to be examining every inch of the room and wore an inscrutable expression, but with herself, for having brought him up to the nursery.

He didn't even fit here, she thought, noting the way his broad shoulders filled the narrow doorway and he had to stoop because of the sloping ceiling.

With gentle—surprisingly gentle—hands, Yale lay her sleeping daughter in bed. He turned to Lexi and asked in a hushed voice, "Does she have a blanket?"

"Of course," she snapped, and Emma Rose stirred. Lexi lowered her voice and added tersely, "She has a *lot* of blankets." Which was an exaggeration. She had two, a lightweight one for summer, and a quilt for winter.

Yale looked around. "Where—"

"It's way too hot up here to cover her."

Instantly, she regretted her choice of words. Why had she called his attention to the fact that the room was stuffy, that the open windows were too small to allow much of a breeze?

But all Yale did was shrug and glance down at Emma Rose. He seemed about to say something, but didn't.

Lexi led the way back downstairs, conscious that the walls needed painting and the floors needed cleaning and that there were cobwebs in all the corners. Part of her wished she'd been more conscientious about redoing the rest of the house the way she'd slaved to get the nursery done. But another part of her didn't care what Yale thought. Let him feel sorry for them. Let him be fully aware that when his brother had died, she and Emma Rose had been left destitute.

"There's your iced tea," she said, gesturing at the glasses on the table. "It's unsweetened."

"That's fine." He perched on the couch and took a sip. "It's good."

"I remember that you like it better with sugar. And lemon. Unfortunately, we don't have any in the house." She hated herself. Why was she doing this?

He shrugged. "Emma Rose," he said. "That's a nice name."

"Thanks," she said, trying to sound civil.

"It's unusual. Where did it come from?"

"The Emma is after her father." Lexi hesitated. "I just thought Rose sounded nice with it."

She would never tell him the real reason she had chosen Rose as part of her daughter's name and roses as the motif in her room. Only Emmett would have known their significance, would have realized that it was a tribute.

Yale nodded and cleared his throat. "Aren't you going to sit and have your tea?"

"Actually, I have a lot to do, and I need to get it done while she's napping," she said, kneeling in front of the box she'd been unpacking earlier. It was partly true, she supposed—it *would* be a good idea to get this breakable stuff put away. But mostly, she just needed to be busy; and to be here, across the room from Yale, instead of sitting next to him on the couch.

Close to him, she might notice things she shouldn't notice.

Like how full his lips were, and how broad his shoulders were, and how a few strands of his golden hair were out of place and just begged for someone to smooth them down.

Well, it wasn't going to be *her*.

Not this time.

"Do you need any help?"

Startled, she looked up at him. He was watching her, wearing a guarded expression.

"No, thanks," she said after a moment. "I'm fine."

He shrugged and took on a businesslike tone. "As I said outside, I got your letter."

"And . . . ?"

"And before I agree to anything, I'd like to know a little more about what you've proposed."

She clenched her jaw and pulled a newspaper-wrapped platter out of the box. "It's actually very simple, Yale. I'm broke, and I have to find a way to provide for your niece. My parents can't help me because . . ." She shook her head, not about to go into the Sinclairs' recent run of tragedies. "They've done enough already, taking me and Emma Rose in for the past five months, and helping me move out of the city apartment and into this place."

"I'm sure they've been a big help."

She nodded. "And as far as my own financial status goes—well, before the baby was born, I was working as a word-processing temp." She waited, almost expecting some kind of snide remark from him over her lack of a tangible career. Emmett had once said that his brother had only contempt for people who did what he and Lexi did—flitted from one vocation to another in a free-spirited attempt to keep a roof over their heads and food on the table.

Now, with no medical insurance and a mountain of past-due hospital bills, Lexi had come to realize Yale's disdain was pretty close to the mark. It *was* irresponsible for her and Emmett to have sailed blithely through life with little regard for such mundane things as insurance, or savings accounts, or even good credit.

Emmett, who had been chasing his dream of writing the great American novel, had, of course, died penniless.

And as a result, Lexi and Emma Rose were in trouble . . . trouble so overwhelming that Lexi had been forced to swallow her pride and turn to the one man she'd sworn she'd never speak to again, much less ask for an enormous favor.

With shaking hands, she peeled away the last layer of newsprint and set the cobalt fruit platter on the floor.

"What I want to do," she told Yale, "is borrow enough money from you to pay the medical bills we've accumulated, and then start my own business. I tried to get a loan, but every bank I went to turned me down."

"So you wrote in the letter. What kind of business?"

She paused, knowing it was the kind of thing a man like Yale might find amusing.

"Baskets," she said finally, looking him in the eye.

"Basket weaving?"

"Of course not basket *weaving*," she said, as though it was the most ridiculous thing she'd ever heard of. "I plan to sell gift baskets—you know, theme baskets."

He nodded, apparently waiting for her to elaborate.

"Some of them," she said, clearing her throat, "would be filled with stuff like, you know, teas and fruit and tins of cookies, that kind of thing. Some would be geared toward specific holidays—Christmas and Valentine's Day and, obviously, Easter."

He didn't comment, so she went on, "And I, um, could do baskets of toys for kids—different kinds of things for different ages. Like, for a baby I'd do rattles and squeaky toys and cloth books, but for a ten-year-old I'd do jacks and yo-yos and board games. Or, for people who are in the hospital, I could do stationery and books and puzzles and—oh, I don't know, maybe a teddy bear or something."

Running out of steam, she chewed her lower lip and waited for him to comment.

It took a while.

Finally, he laced his fingers together and propped them behind his head. "Sounds like an interesting idea."

"The teddy bear?"

"The whole thing. But," he added, and she deflated again, "you need a lot more than a good idea if you're going to make it in business. Lexi, do you know how many people try to do things like this every day?"

She lifted her chin. "I'm ready to knock myself

out to make this work, Yale. I'm not going to goof around. I'm totally serious about this."

"Where would you get your inventory?"

"I've already checked into that. There's a supplier I could use for most of it, and I could make some of the stuff myself. Like cookies, and some of the craft things. I've always been artistic."

"I know."

To her surprise, he didn't say it sarcastically.

There had been a time, years ago, when she'd told him she was going to become a famous painter, and he'd laughed in her face. He was an expert on the subject back then, studying art at RISD—and he still was, as the manager of one of SoHo's most successful galleries.

"I have no doubt that you have the creative flair for something like this, Lexi. But you have to admit that your track record as a responsible, employed adult is less than admirable."

"Look," she said, starting to get up, "if you don't want to help me—"

He held up a hand like a traffic cop, interrupting her. "Sit down, okay? Of course I want to help you. Emma Rose is my own flesh and blood."

She stared at him, wondered at the slightly hoarse tone in his voice when he'd uttered her daughter's name. Could it be that Yale Bradigan—who had always had a steely core to match his emotionless facade—finally cared about someone other than himself? Had Emmett's death accomplished what even the loss of their father and grandfather hadn't done?

Had it made Yale Bradigan human?

"When you say you want to help me," Lexi said, looking at him through narrowed eyes, "you mean financially, right?"

"Of course."

"I just wanted that to be clear. I need your money, Yale. And that's *all* I need." She said it coldly, bluntly. And it was the truth.

No . . . she *wanted* it to be the truth.

She didn't want to need him in any other way. Didn't want his input on her business; or his friendship, even if he was offering it; or, above all, his interference in Emma Rose's life.

And she didn't want to need his arms around her the way she once had . . .

Didn't want to need his lips on hers, warm and probing . . .

Didn't want to need the feel of his body, hard and insistent, against hers . . .

"Lexi?"

She blinked. "What?"

"I asked you what you need."

"Need . . . ?" She felt her cheeks growing hot.

"Money. How much do you need?"

"Oh . . ." She struggled to focus on the question. "Just like that?" she asked. "I tell you an amount and you write out a check?"

"Not exactly. I can give you some today, if you need it. Payment of the rest will have to be worked out in a contract I'll draw up."

"Don't worry, Yale," she said icily. "I'll pay back every penny, with interest."

"I know you will. But I'm sure you understand that my financial matters are complex, and I can't just hand over thousands of dollars at the drop of a hat."

She nodded humbly, hating this whole thing.

Maybe it would have been better if he'd just said no, that he couldn't help her and that for all he cared, she and his niece could simply starve.

No, she told herself, *that wouldn't have been better. You need him.*

Correction . . . she needed his money.

She would never, as long as she lived, need Yale Bradigan in any other way . . .

Never again.

At this hour of a Tuesday afternoon, there wasn't much traffic on the Hutchinson Parkway through Westchester County. Yale mindlessly maneuvered his sleek black Lexus along the winding road, thinking about things.

He had left after setting up an appointment to meet Lexi for lunch on Friday in the city. Just her, of course . . . not Emma Rose.

He swallowed, remembering the child's sweet baby smell and silky baby hair and the way she'd nuzzled her soft baby skin against his neck. She'd fallen asleep in his arms, the way her mother used to . . .

Lexi.

Oh, God.

Lexi.

Seeing her again had been like being broadsided by a steel beam. When she'd stepped out onto that porch—wearing that too-big flannel shirt and baggy jeans that hung on her tiny five-foot-two frame, the sunlight glinting on her mass of long black curls—he'd felt as though he couldn't breathe, as though his knees were going to buckle and allow him to crumple to the ground.

What he wanted to do was run up onto the porch and scoop her into his arms, to stroke her head and tell her not to worry about anything ever again. He was going to take care of her and the baby, and he was going to take away all the hurt that was etched across her beautiful face.

What he had done instead was take care of business in true Yale Bradigan style.

And in the process he had realized two things.

The first was that he wanted—*needed*—to be a part of that baby's life.

The second was that he wanted—*needed*—to be a part of Lexi's.

Neither was likely to happen, given the cold reception Lexi had given him.

He recalled the way her chin had lifted stubbornly every time she'd looked at him, the way her brown eyes had studied him shrewdly and carefully, but never with warmth or any kind of affection.

Well, what did he expect?

Lexi didn't forgive easily, and she never forgot.

Yale sighed and looked at the clock on the dashboard.

It was nearly twelve-thirty. He was supposed to meet Justine for lunch at the Plaza at one.

He stepped on the gas and checked the rearview mirror for cops. A speeding ticket would make him even later, and Justine would be furious.

God, he was sick of her.

Sick of her petulant voice, with its trace of a Brooklyn accent; sick of the way she clung to his arm in public every chance she got; sick even of her Miss America-brand of dyed blond beauty, with the designer clothes and dazzling jewelry, the elaborate hairstyle and makeup.

Justine Di Pierro was as far from Lexi Sinclair as a woman could be.

And Yale was going to marry her on Valentine's Day.

Two

"Hi, Dad."

"Lexi!" Scott Sinclair looked up from the peppers he'd been dicing on the kitchen counter and hurried over to open the screen door for her.

She stepped into the familiar house and was comforted, as always, by the worn but homey atmosphere. The kitchen was her favorite room in the house, with starched eyelet curtains at the paned windows, a row of blue-and-yellow canisters on the counter, and a navy-and-white-checkered tablecloth on the booth in the sunny nook.

Her father was obviously in the middle of making brunch. Now that he had so much time on his hands, he was quite a cook. His specialty was a Mexican omelet, and judging by the ingredients laid out on the counter, one was currently under way.

"Hello, there, Emma Rose," he greeted his granddaughter, who was dressed in a tiny pair of jeans and a baseball cap. "What have you got on? Lex, why is she dressed like a boy?"

"Dad, all girls wear jeans and baseball caps," Lexi said, shaking her head and depositing the baby in her father's arms. She swung the diaper bag off her shoulder and dumped it on a chair.

"But she still doesn't have much hair. People will think she's a boy," he persisted. "She looks like a Dead End Kid."

Lexi rolled her eyes.

She thought Emma Rose looked adorable in her outfit.

And besides, she wasn't about to tell her father where it had come from.

She'd found it, wrapped in reindeer-and-Santa print paper, under the tree in her apartment on Christmas morning months before Emma Rose had been born. She'd raised an eyebrow at Emmett, who was lounging in sweatpants on the couch.

"It's for the kid," he'd said with a shrug. "From his old man. You know, it's Christmas and everything. I thought he should have a present—and if he's not a he . . . well, it would be okay for a girl, too, I guess."

She had thrown her arms around him, tears running down her face.

Back then, of course, she had cried at the drop of a hat.

But pregnancy hormones aside, Lexi had been genuinely touched at what he'd done. She had thought it was a sign that maybe Emmett was changing—that maybe, once the baby was born, he would decide he wanted to marry her and become part of a family after all.

"Alexandra, you look very nice."

She glanced up to see her mother standing in the doorway.

"Kathleen, what are you doing out of bed?" Scott scolded.

"I wanted to say hello to my daughter and grand-daughter." She pulled her terry robe closer around her painfully thin frame.

Lexi went over and planted a kiss on her mother's pale cheek. "How are you feeling, Mom?" she asked, trying not to notice that her mother's ever-present head scarf was askew, revealing a patch of her nearly bald scalp. Kathleen's eyes were gaunt and weary, and the skin on her face was sunken.

"I feel better than I look, thank God," she said, obviously aware that Lexi was staring. She reached up and straightened her scarf, then shrugged. "You know how it is the day after my chemo. I'm queasy and exhausted. But it'll get better. Every day it gets a little better."

"And you should stay in bed until you're back to normal," Scott said sternly, shaking his head at his wife.

"I'll go back in a minute. Lexi, how does that dress fit?"

"Great." She smoothed the black crepe skirt and studied her mother warily, looking for a sign that Kathleen was upset to see it on her.

After all, this was the dress her mother had bought just before she'd become ill. Lexi had been with her when she'd bought it at Neiman-Marcus after hemming and hawing for over an hour. It was expensive, and Kathleen had felt guilty about spending so much money on herself.

But Lexi had talked her into getting it, and she still remembered how thrilled her mother had been as she'd taken the tissue-wrapped package from the clerk. She'd tried it on the second they'd returned home, examining herself in the mirror and deciding it was a worthwhile splurge.

A week later, she had found the first lump under her arm.

A month later, after a radical mastectomy, she had given the dress to Lexi. "It doesn't fit me right anymore," she had said simply. "But you're built like I used to be. It'll be perfect on you."

Lexi had accepted the dress, of course, knowing her mother really wanted her to have it.

Neither of them had realized that Lexi was a month pregnant at the time.

She hadn't been able to wear the dress, either . . . until now.

It was the only thing in her closet that was fit for lunch in Manhattan with Yale Bradigan.

"What time is your train?" asked Kathleen, glancing at the clock over the sink.

"I have twenty minutes, but I'd better go now. I've got to buy a ticket, and I want to get the paper to read on the way in."

That way, she'd at least know what was going on in the world and could discuss something with Yale other than the money he was lending her. She had a feeling he wouldn't be interested in a debate about cloth diapers versus disposable or powdered formula versus ready-to-feed—which was the sorry extent of her conversational repertoire these days.

"Good luck, Lex," said her father, carrying Emma Rose over to the high chair that stood waiting beside the table. It was the one they'd used for Lexi as a baby. Her father had found it in the attic, cleaned it up, and had it waiting when she and Emma Rose had been released from the hospital.

They had come straight home to Cady's Landing that rainy March day. It had been another two weeks before Lexi had been able to bring herself to set foot in her Manhattan apartment. There were too many memories there.

She had been back to the city only once, in fact, since she'd left the hospital. She'd forced herself to go back to the apartment, thinking she could pack things up to move. She'd crumbled after five minutes, clutching a sweatshirt Emmett had left draped over a chair in her bedroom, her face buried in the soft fleece that still smelled like him.

So it had been her father who'd taken over for her. Scott had gone down to Manhattan and cleaned out the place, putting almost everything into a rented storage bin at Cady's Landing until Lexi and Emma Rose moved into their new home.

"Goodbye, sweetheart," Lexi said, bending over to plant a kiss on Emma Rose's head. Her daughter didn't look up. She was intent on banging a set of plastic keys against the high chair tray.

"Don't worry about her," Scott said, turning on the burner beneath the omelet pan on the stove. "She'll be fine."

"I know she will. Remember, Dad, she can't eat table food yet. There's a jar of strained pears in the diaper bag for her."

"Okay, okay . . ."

"Dad," Lexi said in a warning voice. "Don't give her any Mexican omelet."

The last time she'd left Emma Rose in her father's

care for the afternoon, she'd come home to find her munching on a piece of bagel. Alarmed, Lexi had called the pediatrician's office and been told that a five-month-old who didn't have any teeth shouldn't be eating anything but baby food and rice cereal until at least six months.

Scott Sinclair had shrugged it off, saying, "When you were little, we used to give you everything we ate."

And Lexi, exasperated, had found herself embroiled in a huge discussion about whether doctors knew better then or now. Finally, she'd burst into tears, telling her father, "I'm just trying to be a good mother."

He'd backed off swiftly, patting her on the back and saying, "I know you are, and I'm proud of you."

And Lexi had wept for a long time, feeling overwhelmed by the burden of being Emma Rose's only parent. How could she, a person who didn't even have a credit card and had never held a job for more than several months in her life, be someone's mommy?

How could Emmett have gone off and gotten himself killed?

Not that he would have been a responsible parent.

But then, you never knew.

Look at me, Lexi thought. *I've grown up. Maybe he would have, too.*

"Dad, if I come back and she's got chili peppers on her breath, I swear, you'll never babysit her again," Lexi warned, slinging her black purse over her shoulder.

"I'll take good care of her," Scott promised.

"Don't worry, Alexandra," Kathleen said, "I'll check in on them."

"You'll stay in bed, where you belong," her husband warned. "Emma Rose and I will be fine without either of you. Lexi, go. You'll be late. And don't let that jerk give you a hard time."

"I won't," she said, and left.

As she got into the car—her mother's fifteen-year-old Chevy, which she'd lent Lexi until she could afford one of her own—she found herself irritated with her father for calling Yale Bradigan a jerk.

Not that Lexi herself hadn't called him that, and worse, over the years.

But now she found herself wanting to defend him. After all, no matter what he'd done to her in the past, and no matter what had happened between him and Emmett, he had agreed to help her and Emma Rose now. She was indebted to him.

But nothing more, she reminded herself, as she drove through the shady, quiet streets of Cady's Landing toward the Metro North station.

Still, after she had parked at a meter in the commuter lot, she pulled out a compact and reapplied her lipstick, then brushed her hair one last time and squirted on a hint of perfume.

As she ran for the train, she told herself that it wasn't for Yale's benefit.

She simply wanted to look and feel good after so many months of being shut away from the world.

That's all it is, she told herself firmly. *Yale has*

nothing to do with it. And after today, I'll never have to see him again.

What if I never see her again after today? Yale wondered, watching Lexi being led to his table by the maître d'.

He couldn't bear the thought of never again looking into those willful brown eyes, never seeing her stubbornly toss her curls, never hearing that voice of hers, with its slightly husky quality that had always aroused him.

But that part of their relationship was over, he reminded himself. Now she was the mother of his niece. They weren't even related as in-laws.

Oh, Emmett, why the hell didn't you marry her? he wondered. *She's not even your widow. The kid doesn't even have your name.*

Lexi had told him, firmly, before he'd left her house on Tuesday, that the baby was Emma Rose Sinclair.

"Why not Bradigan?" he'd asked her, feeling a pang in his gut.

"Because I'm her mother, and your brother wasn't my husband. He chose not to marry me— even after he knew the baby was on her way. He said a piece of paper didn't matter."

The stark pain on her face had twisted Yale's insides, had made him want to say, "Marry me, Lexi. Marry me and give the baby my name. She has Bradigan blood. She should have my name."

But of course, he hadn't said that. He hadn't said anything.

He couldn't.

He was getting married—but to Justine Di Pierro.

He was actually going to wed a woman he didn't love.

Not that he loved Lexi. He couldn't possibly love her. If he did, he'd never have been able to hurt her the way he had.

"Hello, Yale," she said, arriving at his table.

He stood and clasped her hand. It was small—she was tiny all over—but there was nothing fragile about it. Lexi Sinclair's handshake was firm and no-nonsense.

And yet her fingers seemed to linger in his a moment longer than was strictly necessary. And Yale wasn't quite sure who was responsible—him, or Lexi.

Then her fingers were slipping out of his and she was sitting in the chair the maître d' had pulled out for her before discreetly making his exit.

"Nice place," Lexi commented, looking around the room.

"It is," he agreed. He'd chosen the elegant café off Lexington because it was relatively small and quiet, and close to Grand Central. He knew Lexi wouldn't have money for a taxi, and the thought of her on the subway made him nervous.

People got mugged there, and once in a while some psycho pushed someone in front of a train. And then there were the accidents—all you needed was for a motorman to ignore one red signal, and—

You're being ridiculous, Yale thought to himself.

Lexi had, of course, ridden the subway daily when she'd lived in the city, pregnant and at all hours of the night. And she wasn't the type to complain or worry about something so mundane.

But now things were different. Now she had a child to go home to, a child who had already lost one parent.

If Yale was feeling overprotective, there was a good reason.

The waiter appeared, handed them menus and asked for their drink orders.

"Lexi?" Yale glanced at her.

"I'd like a . . . a glass of chardonnay, please."

He'd never known her to drink wine. She had always preferred beer; she was the kind of woman who looked and felt comfortable drinking from a bottle of Molson. He had always admired that about her. It was sexy, the way she was sexy in jeans and flannel, with her hair pulled back in a messy braid.

He ordered chardonnay, too. When the waiter had left, Yale looked across the table at Lexi. She was glancing at the menu. The white votive candle that flickered in the small floral centerpiece cast her face in a glow, softening her features and her expression.

"How's the food here?" she asked, fiddling with the collar of her black dress—a dress made of some soft fabric that clung to her curves.

He had never, he realized, seen her dressed up.

"The food is excellent," he said, forcing his eyes away from the swell of her breasts. He cleared his throat. "Um, the swordfish is wonderful. And the quiche . . . the quiche is also . . . wonderful."

And you, Lexi, are wonderful.

But he would never tell her.

He never had, when he'd had the chance, and he couldn't now.

"I'll have the swordfish," she said, setting the menu aside.

"So will I."

The waiter brought their drinks and took their orders. When he had left, Yale lifted his glass.

"We should drink a toast," he suggested impulsively.

She looked startled. "Why?"

That was pure Lexi, that single, straightforward word. So was the narrowed look she was directing at him.

"Because," he told her, "it's been a long time since you and I sat across a table together, and I thought it would be nice if we—"

"Yale," she interrupted, "don't even pretend that this is a pleasant social occasion. I'm here because I need money and you're going to lend it to me. We both know that. And if you do happen to recall the last time we sat across a table together, you know that it was the night you dumped me."

"Was it?" He forced himself to say it mildly, then sipped his wine and set the glass down. "It was so long ago, I guess I forgot."

Her eyes flared. "I'm not surprised to hear that. I guess you've forgotten a lot of things that happened back then."

"Not everything, Lexi."

He studied her face for a long moment, his gaze lingering on her full lips. There was a tiny smudge of red just below her mouth, as though she'd hastily applied her lipstick with an unsteady hand. He fought the urge to reach out and rub it off with his fingertip.

She raised her glass to her lips, taking a long swallow of her wine and obliterating his view of the lipstick smear.

"You know what, Lexi?" he asked with a shrug. "You're right. We're here to talk about money, not about what happened between us. That's history. And I've never been very interested in the past. So let's move on, shall we?"

She nodded and watched as he reached beneath the table for his briefcase. He drew out the two-page document his lawyer had drawn up the day before and handed it across the table.

"What's this?" she asked, glancing at it.

"A simple contract," he told her, handing her his gold fountain pen. "It states the amount I'm lending you, to be paid in installments over the next few months, and that you have every intention of paying it back—"

"By the year 2045?" she asked, scanning the second page. "That's almost fifty years from now, Yale. I'm not going to take that long to—"

"Take as long as you need, Lexi," he said quietly. "I told you, I want to help you."

"But—" She turned back to the first page, shaking her head. "I don't need this much money, Yale. I don't even need *half* this for—"

"Take it, Lexi. If you don't use it, put it in the bank and accumulate interest, then pay it back when you're ready. That way, it'll be there if you ever need it."

"I won't. Once my business is up and running, I'll be fine."

"I'm sure you will. But we're talking about my niece here. My flesh and blood. I want to make sure she doesn't need anything you can't afford to give her."

As soon as the words were out of his mouth, he knew he'd made a mistake.

Fire shot through Lexi—it was evident in her barely maintained composure, in her eyes when she looked at him. If they hadn't been in this restaurant, with its soft classical music and clinking silverware and hushed voices, she'd be shouting at him.

As it was, she was obviously struggling to maintain control when she said, in a strained voice, "Don't you *ever* think that my daughter will want for anything. I'm her mother, and I'll make sure she has everything she needs, Yale. God, I wish I'd never asked you for this money."

She lifted the contract and held it in her trembling hands as if poised on the verge of tearing it in two.

"Don't do that, Lexi."

"I feel like I'm selling my soul to the devil. If you think you're going to play any role in her life, just because you've handed over a few checks God knows you can afford, you can think again."

"I'm sorry, Lexi, I didn't mean—"

"I know what you meant when you said that, Yale. You meant that thanks to Lexi the Loser, who's never held a real job in her life, poor little Emma Rose is going to be destitute. That she won't have a fancy private-school education, like you did. And she won't live in a mansion in Sound Heights, like you—"

"My grandfather paid the mortgage on that house, Lexi," he cut in. "If it weren't for him, my brother and I would have been living on the streets. God knows my mother never earned a cent or paid a bill in her life."

"How dare you compare me to your mother?"

"Of course I'm not doing that," he protested, noticing that both her fists were clenching the white tablecloth. He had a sudden vision of Lexi giving it a violent tug, sending the crystal and flowers crashing to the floor. She'd been known to do that sort of thing.

"Listen," he said gently, wanting to reach out and touch her hand, but knowing she would only pull it away. "All I mean to say is that if you need anything for Emma Rose, I can help you. I love her, Lexi."

That had slipped out.

Lexi looked up in surprise.

He hesitated, then took a deep breath and decided to tell her the truth. "When I saw that baby for the first time in the nursery, Lexi, she touched some part of me that I never even knew existed. I'm not the kind of man who's always been crazy about kids. I never even wanted to have one. But that little girl . . . I don't know, Lex. I guess I realized she's a part of me in a way that I can't just ignore. She might not have my name, but she has Bradigan blood, and she even looks like me—like Emmett, of course," he added hastily. "But you know what I'm saying."

To his amazement, she nodded. "I know. She *does* look like Emmett."

"And you. She has your coloring."

Lexi nodded, wearing a tiny smile for the first time since she'd arrived.

"Let's not do this, Lexi," he said quietly, after a moment. "Let's not tear away at each other like this. The past is over. Emma Rose is your future. And that's what I'm concerned about. I want to help both of you."

She sipped her wine, and Yale had the distinct impression she was swallowing her pride along with it. She put the glass down and said, "You're right. I need your help. I asked for your help. It's no use for me to go crazy on you."

"Why don't you sign the contract? Unless, of course, you want to have a lawyer take a look at it."

"What, are you nuts? I can't afford a lawyer." She grinned suddenly, then picked up the pen and scrawled her signature on the second page. "There. Signed, sealed, and delivered."

"Thank you." He accepted it, then reached into his pocket and pulled out a check. "Here's the first payment. I can send the rest through the mail."

She accepted it with a nod. "That would be fine."

He wanted to add, *unless you wouldn't mind if I brought them in person.*

But why would he do that?

To see the baby, he told himself. *Only to see the baby, of course.*

But Lexi had just warned him that he wouldn't be a part of Emma Rose's life.

Maybe she'll come around, he thought. But then again, knowing how muleheaded Lexi Sinclair could be, he realized he'd be lucky if he ever saw her or Emma Rose again.

"Yale?" she asked abruptly, after stashing the check in her purse.

"Yes?"

"What happened between you and Emmett?"

He frowned. "I don't want to talk about that."

"I figured." She fiddled with the stem of her wineglass. "You know, after the way you two didn't speak to each other for all those years, I find it surprising that you even went to the funeral, let alone planned it."

He was silent for a long time, thinking of that gray day when he had scattered his brother's ashes over the icy waters of the sound.

When he met Lexi's gaze again, he hoped the raw emotion he felt wasn't there for her to probe. He shrugged. "I could hardly rely on my mother to do it." Lexi knew, of course, that Blythe Bradigan was in a mental health facility upstate, and had been for years. "Besides, Emmett was my brother. No matter what happened between us, he was my brother."

My twin. My other half.

He swallowed hard over the lump in his throat.

"I miss him so much," Lexi said, and he looked up to see tears glistening beneath her thick black eyelashes. "There were times, you know, when I didn't see him for a while. He would take off, for days or even months at a time, and never tell me

where he'd been. Emmett always needed his space,
you know?" She gave a short, bitter laugh.

"Didn't that bother you?"

"Not at first. I liked my space, too, in the beginning. That was why we were so perfect together.
We were both—free spirits seems like such a label,
but it's pretty accurate. But then I grew up. I wanted
to settle down—way before the baby came along.
I wanted to get married."

"And Emmett didn't."

"Nope." She shook her head. "We broke up over
it. But then we got together again, of course. That
was the night we made Emma Rose."

There was a haunted, faraway expression in her
eyes.

The waiter appeared just as Yale was about to
draw her back from wherever she was. He set their
entrees on the table, ground fresh pepper over their
plates, refilled their water glasses.

By the time he left, Lexi had snapped out of it.

"I'm starving," she said, glancing at the elegant
arrangement of swordfish and grilled vegetables in
front of her.

"Go ahead."

As they ate, their conversation revolved around
local politics, movies, and books. Yale had never
known Lexi to pay much attention to anything that
was going on in the city. She had always been
wrapped up in her own world. And now, with a new
baby and a whole new lifestyle, he would have expected her to be more self-absorbed than ever.

"I'm really surprised you know about that," he
said, when she asked him what he thought about

the most recent tabloid scandal, which involved a Manhattan socialite and her supposed affair with a married Hollywood director.

"Why wouldn't I know about it?"

"Because you never paid attention to that sort of thing."

Was she blushing?

"Actually," she said candidly, "I still don't. I read the *New York Post* on the train on the way in today so I'd have something interesting to talk about."

He laughed, and so did she.

Then he said, "You were worried about talking to me?"

"In a way." She shrugged. "It's not as though you and I have been on the best of terms. And . . . well, we have absolutely nothing in common."

"We have Emmett."

"Yeah? And what do you know about him?" she asked, her tone suddenly sharp. She set down her fork. "You didn't care about him the last ten years he was alive."

"You don't know that."

"If you cared, you'd have tried to rebuild your relationship."

He tried to remain casual. "How do you know I didn't?"

"Are you saying it was his fault, whatever happened between you?"

"I'm not saying anything about that. I told you, I don't want to discuss it."

"No, but you want to sit here and act like you're all grief-stricken because your brother died in a fire, and—"

"My brother," he cut in abruptly, "didn't 'die' in that fire, Lexi. He was murdered."

Lexi gasped.

For a moment, she could only stare into Yale Bradigan's stark green eyes, his blunt, shocking words echoing wildly in her head.

Murdered.

"Why?" she finally managed, bewildered. Her stomach was lurching crazily, and so was the room. She closed her eyes briefly and reached for her water glass.

"I have no idea." He folded his arms and watched as she took a sip of water.

She swallowed it, feeling it sloshing its way toward her queasy stomach, and took a deep breath. "Who would want to kill Emmett?"

"I thought you might know. But obviously, you didn't even suspect that his death wasn't an accident."

"Of course I didn't." She shook her head. "What makes you think it wasn't?"

"Just a feeling," he said, and raised a hand to summon the waiter as he passed.

"A 'feeling'?" She wanted to laugh and would have if his announcement hadn't rattled her so. "That's not exactly a good basis for suspecting murder, Yale."

"Sir?" The waiter hovered at his elbow.

"I'd like a cup of coffee," he said, and motioned at Lexi. "You, too?"

"All right," she said absently.

"Two coffees," Yale told the waiter.

He turned back to Lexi, whose mind was spinning. "Are you still eating?"

"Of course not." She had all but forgotten the food that sat cold on the plate in front of her.

"I didn't think so." He pushed his own plate of half-eaten food away. "How much do you know about Emmett's death?"

She shook her head. It wasn't something she'd ever discussed before now—not in detail. She'd been too consumed by shock and grief, along with the overwhelming emotional responsibilities of new motherhood.

"How much do you know?" Yale persisted.

"I know that there was a fire in his apartment. And there wasn't much . . . left when they got to him." She closed her eyes to blot out the image of the charred body of the man she had loved.

"No, there wasn't," Yale said quietly. "He was burned pretty badly."

"Are you saying someone set the fire deliberately?" Lexi asked, trying to detach herself emotionally and not quite succeeding. "Because if you are, you're probably wrong. That apartment of his was a firetrap. There were exposed wires all over the place."

She closed her eyes again, remembering the wooden rowhouse where Emmett rented a second-floor apartment. The owners, an elderly couple, lived on the first floor, which had been empty when the house burned down. They spent the winter months in Miami, and hadn't been due to return until April.

"Knowing my brother, I'd say he wasn't overly concerned with fire codes," Yale said tightly. "But yes, I am saying that someone may have set the fire deliberately."

"Hoping to kill Emmett?"

"Maybe."

"What do you mean?"

"He may already have been dead. The fire may have been set to destroy the evidence."

Lexi contemplated that. "The fire investigators told my parents that Emmett had fallen asleep smoking."

"That's right. I checked into the report myself—I am his official next of kin, after all," Yale added, when she shot him a look. "The report also stated that several empty liquor bottles were found near the body. It appeared he'd been drinking heavily and had passed out with a cigarette in his mouth."

She nodded.

"What are you thinking, Lexi?" Yale asked, studying her face.

"Nothing . . ."

"Yes, you are," he said, leaning forward and resting his chin on his hand. "I can tell by the look on your face."

"It's just . . ." She paused, not wanting to say it aloud.

"What?"

"It's just that he had quit smoking," she said. "I quit when I found out I was carrying the baby, and he did, too. He did it for me. Because the smell of cigarettes made me really sick when I was pregnant."

"Maybe he didn't really quit. Maybe he lied to you."

"That's what I figured, when my parents told me about the cigarettes being involved in the fire. But the liquor bottles . . ."

"What about them?"

"Emmett gave up drinking a few years ago." She contemplated telling him why—that after visiting his mother in the hospital and seeing what booze had done to her, Emmett swore he'd never end up the same way. But she didn't want to get into that with Yale. Not now.

"He didn't drink at all, as far as you know?"

"Not really. Maybe he'd occasionally have a bottle of wine, or a beer, but not—"

"Bourbon?"

"No. Never."

"That's what they found near his body."

"So I guess he lied about that, too," Lexi said, looking Yale in the eye.

"Maybe. But as far as I know, my brother never lied."

And Lexi remembered what Emmett had told her so long ago.

He didn't make promises.

He didn't tell lies.

But then, he *had* made a promise to her, about being there when the baby was born.

Maybe he'd started lying, too.

"Lexi," Yale said, "I may not know much about my brother's life—at least, not the way it was recently. But believe me . . . I *know* Emmett was murdered. In my gut, I know it. I just don't know why."

The waiter reappeared with two oversized cups of steaming coffee. Yale promptly dumped three sugars into his.

"That's how your brother always drank his," Lexi commented, watching him. "He liked it hot and black and sweet."

"So do I."

There was a moment of silence as they both stirred their coffee.

"He was always involved with shady characters," she told Yale slowly, staring off into space. "I know he hung out at these seedy bars in the Village—once in a while, when we were out together, we'd bump into someone he knew. Sometimes, they were people I wouldn't want to see on a dark street alone. He never told me how he knew any of them. There were a lot of things he didn't tell me."

And there were things she wasn't about to tell Yale. One thing in particular. She blocked it out of her mind.

"He was always that way," Yale told her. "When we were kids, he was always befriending lowlifes, people I wouldn't give the time of day to."

"Emmett was a good person. Compassionate," Lexi said levelly, leaving the rest of it—*unlike you*—unsaid.

"He was good," Yale agreed, looking unfazed by her implication. "But that doesn't mean he didn't get tangled up in something by accident. Something that was way over his head. It happens, you know."

"I know." She sighed, wrapping her hands around

the cup in front of her, as though she could absorb
its warmth and melt the chilling awareness that was
beginning to seep into her. Again she tried to forget
the memory that was trying to edge its way into
her mind, and into the conversation. She could tell
Yale about that.

She wouldn't.

"I just don't want to believe that Emmett's death
was anything other than an accident," she said instead. "Because if someone deliberately stole my
daughter's father from her . . ."

"Lexi," Yale said, in a surprisingly gentle tone,
"if Emmett hadn't been—if he hadn't died, do you
honestly believe he'd be there for Emma Rose?"

She wanted, more than anything, to say yes.

Yes, she thought he'd have changed.

That he'd have been there for her daughter, and
for her.

But that would have been a lie, and she suspected
Yale would have seen through it anyway.

So she shrugged. "No. No, he probably wouldn't
have been there. What is she, five months old?"
Her tone was both caustic and resigned. "Let's see,
by now, he probably would have taken off for good.
Or I would have kicked him out, to spare my daughter the inevitable."

Yale nodded. "That's pretty much what I thought."

"But it doesn't mean I didn't love him, Yale."
Lexi's voice was ragged, a near-whisper. "It doesn't
mean I'd rather have him dead . . . although there
was a time, not long ago, when I thought it was
easier this way. It isn't. Because even though I'm
ninety-nine percent sure that Emmett would have

left me and Emma Rose anyway, a minuscule one percent of me thinks, what if he hadn't? What if fatherhood had somehow transformed him into a grown-up?"

Oh, Lord, she was crying.

She wiped at the tear that slipped from her right eye, and then at the one that trickled down her left cheek.

"Aw, Lex . . ." Yale reached across the table, caught her hand. "It'll be okay. I didn't mean to get you all worked up."

"I'm not worked up," she said stiffly, sniffling and struggling to regain her composure. "I just . . . I have to go now, okay?"

"Now?"

She pushed her chair back. "Emma Rose is with my parents, and I—I don't like to leave her. I never have for this long, and—"

"Wait, Lexi, let me drop you at—"

"I can walk to Grand Central," she said, standing and grabbing her bag from the back of her chair. "Thank you for lunch, Yale. And for . . . the check. I'll see you."

With that, she fled out onto the sunny sidewalk, teeming with a familiar midtown throng of office workers and bums and tourists and well-heeled neighborhood residents.

Had it really been only a few months ago that she'd belonged here? Lexi wondered as she shoved her way down the crowded avenue.

She stopped to wait for a light and caught sight of a couple on the opposite corner. The man had a baby strapped to his back in an infant carrier, and the woman was wiping something off the little boy's chin. They were all laughing—the father, the mother, and the child; laughing together, carefree in the bright September sunshine.

Lexi fumbled in her bag for her black sunglasses and hurriedly put them on.

As she passed the little family on her way across the street, none of them looked in her direction, of course. They were caught up in their own happy world.

But even if they had noticed her, the sunglasses hid her envious, wistful stare, and the tears that once again welled in her eyes.

"Do you have any bags, ma'am?"

Meredith MacFee looked up at the clerk behind the hotel desk. "Just this." She held up her small black Chanel pocketbook and grinned saucily at him. He was a meek little man, the type who had probably been a virgin until his wedding day in the fifties, and who'd probably slept only with his wife ever since.

"Very well, then," he said, turning slightly red and pushing his glasses further up on his nose. "Here's your key. Room 11J."

"Thank you." She accepted it and headed for the elevator.

The lobby, which once must have been elegant but now seemed slightly worn, was deserted except for a few traveling executives and the occasional foreign tourist. She'd chosen this place because it was clean and conveniently located, yet its meeting facilities and restaurant weren't of the caliber that drew New Yorkers. The chances of her running into anyone she knew here, particularly on a Friday afternoon, were slim.

A group of Japanese businessmen waited in front of the elevator bank. They stopped talking when she approached, and all four eyed the cleavage that spilled from the low-cut neckline beneath her khaki Burberry.

Meredith smiled to herself and stepped onto the elevator when the doors opened in front of her. The men followed, having resumed their conversation in Japanese. It was now punctuated with winks and knowing glances, and she suspected they were talking about her.

Amused, she stared at the doors and deliberately twirled a strand of her long, straight blond hair around her finger in a seductive manner. She was careful not to tug too hard, lest she pull the wig askew.

At the eleventh floor, she stepped off, unable to resist tossing a casual, "Later, boys," over her shoulder.

In your dreams, she added to herself, sashaying down the carpeted hallway on her impossibly high heels.

In real life—the life where she was an oh, so upstanding socialite married to one of the wealthiest real estate developers in Manhattan—she would never have worn shoes this tacky. Not to mention the dress! She had ordered it a size too small, from a Victoria's Secret catalogue her maid had left behind one day.

She stepped into room 11J. It was small and functional, and smelled vaguely of roach repellent. But it had a bed, which was what counted.

She glanced around, spotted a telephone on the desk in front of the window, and crossed to it.

Slipping out of her coat, she tossed it over a chair with one hand while she dialed with the other.

There were four rings, and then she got the voice mail.

At the tone, Meredith purred, "Hi, it's me. I'm here waiting for you, in room 11J. Hope your lunch meeting doesn't last all afternoon, because I was counting on you to do that with me."

She hung up, smiling to herself. Her body quivered and her nipples tightened at the mere thought of what lay ahead. The man was the consummate lover, a connoisseur of pure pleasure.

Yet lately, he'd become elusive. The fewer and more fleeting their encounters became, the more insatiable Meredith's appetite. She was becoming obsessed—an addict desperate to possess him.

You've always wanted what you couldn't have, my dear, she reminded herself, and sighed.

For a few hours today, she could have him. He had promised.

She stripped down to the black g-string and see-through lace bra that flattered her still-firm forty-year-old body and stretched out on the bed to await Yale Bradigan's arrival.

Three

Lexi spent Saturday morning waiting for her Chevy to be fixed.

Yesterday, she'd returned to the commuter parking lot to find that the car wouldn't start. She'd had it towed to a local service station where the owner had said he wouldn't have a chance to so much as look at it until today.

By the time her father had dropped her and Emma Rose off at home last night, after taking them out to eat at a local diner, she'd been physically and emotionally drained. She'd crawled into bed and fallen immediately into a dreamless sleep.

Now, sitting in the dingy service station waiting room, holding a snoozing Emma Rose on her lap, she had plenty of time to think about the thing she had successfully managed to avoid until now.

By the time Ned, the mechanic, presented her with a repair bill for $483.57, she was distracted enough to just write a check for the full amount.

She had reached a decision while waiting, and having done so, she was eager to get home.

Her mind was fixed on several cartons, sealed with packing tape, that sat in her bedroom closet. They were Emmett's belongings.

She had snooped through them one night in March, slitting the tape with a razor blade and then retaping the boxes when she was through. She wasn't sure what she was looking for—maybe evidence that he had a secret life of some sort. Or that he was up to something illegal or immoral.

Or maybe, just a clue to who he really was.

What she'd found was a pile of clothing, and stacks of books, and half-written short stories and fragments of novels, and a few CDs and tapes . . .

And a locked metal box.

There was no way to open it without breaking the lock.

Perplexed, she'd tried to figure out what could be inside.

It wasn't heavy; not really.

She shook it and heard a muffled sliding, thumping sound, as though it contained papers or maybe a book.

She'd put it back into the carton where she'd found it because there was nothing else she could do. She'd resealed it, and she'd forgotten about it . . .

Almost.

Yesterday, as she was sitting in the restaurant with Yale, the thought of that locked metal box had come zinging back to her. She had tried to dismiss the wave of curiosity that came with it, tried to tell herself that the box probably contained nothing important, nothing that might reveal whether Emmett had any enemies . . .

Enemies who might hate him enough to kill him.

Now all she wanted was to get home and retrieve

the box. She would get it open any way she could; she'd break the lock with a sledgehammer if she had to.

After strapping the still-sleeping baby into her carseat in back, Lexi pulled the newly fixed Chevy out onto Main Street and drove impatiently along in the slow-moving Saturday morning traffic.

There was a time, when she was growing up, when she could have made it from the heart of town out to the carriage house on Cobble Road in less than five minutes.

Today, it took her that long to go a single block, crawling past the newly refurbished brick post office building and a row of awning-fronted shops and cafés.

Back when her parents bought their house, Cady's Landing was a middle-class Westchester County suburb. But over the past two decades, thanks to an influx of wealthy Manhattanites, the town had exploded into a crowded, upscale wonderland.

Now the quaint downtown district was filled with exclusive stores and pricy gourmet markets. The diagonal parking spaces that lined Main Street were always jammed, invariably with Mercedeses and BMWs and Lexuses. Local real estate prices had skyrocketed, and most of the once dilapidated Victorian houses on the shady streets of Cady's Landing had been restored to their former glory. The woods that had fringed much of the shoreline had been replaced with new townhouse developments.

As Lexi turned from Main onto Water Street, she glimpsed the white-pillared bank building and realized that she had forgotten to deposit Yale's payment into her bank account. It could have waited until Monday . . . if she hadn't just written a check for almost five hundred dollars. And the bank was open only until noon on Saturdays.

There was nothing to do but pull into the crowded lot.

Another half hour had passed by the time Lexi had hunted for a parking space, waited—while holding a squirmy, heavy Emma Rose—in a line that stretched out the door, and made her deposit. It took another twenty minutes to get out of town.

By then, Emma Rose was crying angrily from the back seat, beyond hungry.

Finally, Lexi pulled into the driveway of the carriage house. Frustrated, she thought of the cartons that waited up in her bedroom closet. She wanted nothing more than to dash up there and find the mysterious metal box.

But she couldn't, not with Emma Rose long overdue for her lunch and protesting angrily in great gasping sobs.

Lexi hurried the baby into the house and grabbed a bottle from the refrigerator. She sat on the couch for the next half hour, feeding her daughter while thinking the whole time of the box.

What could possibly be in it?

It might be nothing of importance.

Maybe it was the manuscript of the novel Emmett had been working on recently, the one he'd said he was going to actually finish.

Or maybe it was a stack of unpaid bills, or letters from old girlfriends, or . . .

God, what can it be?

At last, Emma Rose lay gurgling in Lexi's arms, her belly full and her expression downright jolly.

"Mommy has something to do upstairs," Lexi told her. "Come on, let's go up. Can you be a good girl while Mommy looks through some things?"

"Ah goo," Emma Rose promised.

Lexi carried the baby up and set her in the middle of her bed.

The master bedroom across the narrow landing from the nursery was a decent-sized room with windows on two sides, which at least allowed for a cross-breeze. The walls were sloped here, too, but Lexi, who was five-two, never had to stoop.

She had yet to decorate the room, but at least there were no boxes, aside from Emmett's three in the closet. Lexi's clothes were all hanging up or folded in the slightly-battered bureau that had been in her city apartment. Her few framed photographs, including one of her with Emmett, sat on the dresser top, along with some toiletries and the old-fashioned comb-and-brush set that had once belonged to her grandmother.

The antique white iron bed had also belonged to Grandma Nealon. It was the bed Lexi had shared with Emmett, the bed where they had created their daughter that rainy June night . . .

It was too painful to remember.

She sprawled out next to Emma Rose, who kicked her chubby legs in the air and tried to roll over.

"Pretty soon Mommy's not going to be able to

leave you on the bed, right, Em? Because you're going to be rolling and crawling all over the place."

As if to prove her point, Emma Rose threw herself to one side, flipping spontaneously onto her stomach.

"Oh, Em!" Lexi scooped her startled daughter into her arms and held her close. "You did it! You rolled over!"

Emma Rose scowled, apparently not at all pleased to have been plucked from the position she had worked so hard to reach.

Lexi hastily put her down on her back once more.

"Go ahead," she told her daughter. "Try again."

Emma Rose went back to work, grunting in frustration as she hoisted her legs into the air.

Lexi stood and watched for a moment, wishing there were someone else around, someone with whom she could share Emma Rose's achievement. She could call her parents. But her mother still wasn't feeling well, and her father, she remembered, was going to spend the day fishing.

He did that a lot, now that he was out of work. Lexi suspected that it was therapeutic, the time he spent alone in a sun-dappled inlet at the edge of the sound. He had unexpectedly lost the job he had worked at for as long as Lexi could remember, and now he faced the prospect of losing his wife, too.

Lexi knew her father was fully aware that Kathleen was dying, yet he never spoke of it. The way he talked—making plans for next summer and even further down the road, much further—his wife was going to be around forever. She wanted to chide him for having false hope whenever he said something like, "When Emma Rose goes to kindergarten, she'll have the lead in the Christmas pageant, and her grandma and I will be watching from the front row."

A few times, she'd heard her mother murmur a feeble protest when Scott had spoken of the future as though Kathleen was going to be a part of it. But lately, as her prognosis had grown exceedingly grim, Kathleen had seemed almost unable to face the truth herself.

Lexi sighed and turned toward the closet.

It was time she herself faced the truth, whatever that was, about Emmett.

"Bunny, what are you thinking about?"

Yale clenched his jaw, hating the way Justine insisted on calling him Bunny. She did it only when she was in a cutesy-poo, playful mood.

She lounged on the overstuffed couch in the living area of his loft, twirling a strand of dyed, hairspray-stiff blond hair around her finger and waving her long legs, clad in black Spandex, in the air.

"Nothing," he told her. "I'm not thinking about anything."

"Obviously, you are," she said petulantly. "I asked you the same question twice, and I swear you didn't even hear me."

"What question?"

She pouted. "See? You were ignoring me."

"I wasn't ignoring you. I was busy thinking . . . about work," he lied. "There's a huge problem with some documents at the office."

"Oh." She perked up, apparently pleased to hear that.

He wondered if she had, for a moment, suspected the truth . . . that his mind had been on another woman.

"Anyway," she went on, inspecting her reflection in a sterling silver coaster she'd picked up from the coffee table, "I was asking you if you mind that I'm busy tonight."

"What?" He looked at her blankly.

"With my cousin Angela's bachelorette party, remember?"

"Oh, that. Of course I don't mind, Justine. You go ahead and have a good time. Don't worry about me."

"I won't worry about you." She leaned toward the chair where he sat and trailed a long, tomato-red fingernail along his jaw. "I was just thinking that you might miss having me all cozy in bed with you tonight."

"Of course I will." Despite his irritation with her, he felt himself stirring, found himself aroused.

"And I was thinking," she moved the fingertip down, slipping it beneath the collar of the white cotton knit shirt he wore, "that I could do my best to make sure you have a good time with me now, before I leave for the party."

He shrugged, feeling her lips on the skin of his neck. She nibbled expertly at the sensitive hollow below his ear, and though his body reacted predictably, his mind was somewhere else.

He didn't want it to be Justine offering herself

to him wantonly, ready to pleasure him, to cater to his every whim.

He wanted someone else.

Someone he could never have.

The phone rang then, and Justine moaned a little protest. "Let the machine get it, Bunny."

"I can't. It might be your father."

"That's true."

At the mention of Franco Di Pierro, Justine quickly sat back and reached for a magazine she'd been reading earlier. When it came down to it, Daddy's girl knew business came first. It had in the household she'd been raised in, and it should for the man she was going to marry.

Yale grabbed for the telephone, hoping it wasn't Franco. He wasn't in the mood to talk business right now, not with his mind elsewhere.

"Hello, Yale?"

He caught his breath. The voice belonged not to his gallery associate, but to the woman who had filled his thoughts ever since she'd left him yesterday.

"Hi," he said cautiously, noticing that Justine had glanced up at him. He shook his head at her, indicating that it wasn't her father. She went back to her magazine, but he was fully aware that she was eavesdropping.

"I need to talk to you," Lexi said urgently, over the staticky sound of background noise. "It's important. But I'm on a pay phone, and I don't have enough change with me to pay for a long conversation, which is what we need to have. It's about Emmett's death."

"Excuse me?"

"You heard me. Yale, can you come up here?"

"I think it could be arranged," he said in a businesslike tone, conscious of Justine listening. "When?"

"As soon as you can get here. Preferably today. Can you come?"

"Yes. I'll leave right away. Thank you. Goodbye." He hung up, his heart racing.

"What was that all about?" Justine asked, her finger poised to turn the page.

"It was just one of my clients, wondering if I can locate a particular painting for her."

"Oh."

"I'll have to get busy on it right away," he said, already heading for the bedroom, where his car keys waited on his dresser.

"Right away? But what about—"

"Justine, you know there's nothing I'd rather do than stay here with you. But this is business. Besides, you have your party to go to, don't you?"

"I guess," she agreed, tossing the magazine on the table and standing. "Will you call me in the morning?"

"Don't I always?"

She nodded. "Can you drive me home on your way?"

He shook his head. "It's not on the way. I have to go down to SoHo," he said, and pulled a twenty and a ten out of his pocket. "Here's cabfare."

Minutes later, with Justine safely in a taxi on the way up Third Avenue to her Upper East Side apartment, Yale strode across the parking garage adjacent to his building. He wasted no time in starting his black Lexus, pulling into the crowded, honking traffic on East Twelfth Street.

He was trembling, he realized, as he turned the corner to head toward the FDR.

He wasn't sure whether it was because of what Lexi had said—that she needed to talk to him about Emmett's death—or because he was going to see her again.

In the back seat of a rickety yellow cab heading uptown, Justine Di Pierro stared moodily out the window.

Something was bothering her, something she couldn't put her finger on.

But it had to do with Yale. Lately he had been . . . different. Detached. Even before he'd left for Europe at the end of July. When he'd come back, he'd been positively preoccupied.

Not that Yale had ever been the type who went around spewing his emotions. He was so different from the people who inhabited Justine's world.

Growing up the only daughter in a large Italian family, she had been surrounded by people with enormous hearts and volatile tempers.

Her mother, Carmella, managed to be sleek and fashionable and charming, and yet always an affectionate, traditional Old World wife who made a pot of sauce every Sunday and never complained about catering to a houseful of domineering men.

And Franco Di Pierro was nothing if not domineering. Yet Justine adored him. Her father was the kind of man who wasn't ashamed to cry, who worshipped his mother, and who never missed Mass on Sundays and on Holy Days of Obligation. He was a capricious man who might hug one of his sons one moment and slap him across the face the next. But he would never, ever lay a hand on the daughter he had nicknamed "Teeny," and she knew it.

As far as her father was concerned, anything his baby wanted should be hers. He'd bought her a fur for her thirteenth birthday and a Range Rover for her sixteenth. But when a rash of carjackings had struck their Brooklyn neighborhood shortly afterward, he'd traded in the car and promised to have her driven wherever she needed to go.

Sure enough, anytime Justine needed a ride from that day until years later, when she moved out of the house, one of her many "uncles," all of whom seemed to drive shiny black Cadillacs, would take her.

They weren't really related to her, of course. Her father's only brother, Nino, was back in Sicily with Justine's grandmother. Justine had seen them yearly when she was growing up, though now that Nana was well into her eighties, their visits had become rare. But the men who were so eager to help her father, the men he called his *compares,* had been a part of Justine's life for as long as she could remember.

There was Uncle Giovanni, whose nickname was "Gio"—he smoked cigars and didn't say much.

And Uncle Carl, who was constantly telling jokes and flashing his prominent gold tooth.

And Uncle Santo, who always had a pocket full

of bubblegum for Justine, and who had a tattoo of a naked woman on his bicep.

As Justine's brothers, Johnny and Joey, grew older, they spent more time with Daddy and the uncles. Now that they were both married, they were a part of Franco Di Pierro's business dealings.

Growing up, she had been aware that the men seemed to spend a lot of time sitting around the dining room table in the Di Pierros' comfortable brick house, talking in low voices. Once in a while unfamiliar faces would be there with them. And a lot of times, after everyone was asleep, the phone rang in the middle of the night. Then her father would get dressed and leave, but he was always home in the morning when Justine got up.

She had a good idea what her father's business entailed—and she was proud of him. She saw the way the other men, including her brothers, respected him.

As far as she was concerned, her father was king.

And she was his princess.

Whatever she wanted, he got for her.

Including Yale Bradigan.

In the front seat, the dark-skinned cab driver turned and said something to her.

"What?" she asked, leaning forward.

He repeated it in broken English, something about traffic and the FDR.

She looked around and realized that they were sitting still at Third and Twentieth, stuck in gridlock.

"Go ahead, take the FDR," she said reluctantly, even though she'd specifically told him not to earlier. She always got nervous in taxis—the higher the speed limit, it seemed, the more recklessly drivers drove. Her father had warned her that if someone other than one of the uncles was driving her, she should tell them to avoid the expressways. Not just because traffic on city streets tended to move more slowly, but because if she got into trouble, she could always jump out and run.

"You're a beautiful girl, Teeny," Justine's father had told her. "That means you have to be careful around strange men."

Even now that she'd been living on her own for three years, her father was overprotective. He was the one who had found her the East Seventy-first Street apartment, making sure it was in an elevator doorman building, on a high floor. He had paid for the installation of an alarm system, and whenever he visited, he slipped the doorman a big tip, saying, "Be sure you keep an eye on my little girl for me."

Daddy wouldn't be very happy if he knew she was in a cab that was hurling crazily around the entrance ramp onto the FDR, Justine thought, holding on to the seat and keeping a wary eye on traffic.

She thought about what she was going to wear to Angela's party. Angie was Uncle Gio's daughter, so she wasn't technically Justine's cousin. In fact, Justine wasn't crazy about Angela. She wasn't very attractive, for one thing. She was overweight and her hair was frizzy and she had a faint dark mustache over her upper lip. Justine couldn't imagine why she didn't have electrolysis.

But then, it didn't seem to bother Angela's fiancé, Louie. He wasn't so hot-looking himself, with his pot belly and large, fleshy features. And he was coarse, too—always scratching himself or burping. He liked to talk only about sports and his job as a maintenance worker at the Meadowlands.

No, Justine and Angela had nothing in common, and Louie was certainly nothing like Yale.

Justine smiled, thinking of the man who would be her husband in a few more months.

The first time she'd seen him, as she liked to say to everyone—except, of course, her father—she'd "picked him up in a bar." He had been sitting having a drink in a trendy restaurant on lower Fifth Avenue when she'd spotted him. Justine, there with two of her friends, had announced to them that she was going home with him that night. The doubtful and amused glances they'd exchanged had made her all the more determined.

Everything about Yale said *class*—and *WASP*. He was different from the men she had dated, with his expensive clothes and impeccable grooming and articulate speech.

She'd realized he was drunk that night—only because she had watched him down one Glenlivet after another, and she could smell it on his breath when she went over and started talking to him. But he'd seemed lucid, and his eyes had lit up when he'd seen her.

Justine was used to that reaction from men. She spent a lot of time and money on her looks. Plastic surgery when she was sixteen had altered her aquiline Mediterranean nose and given her more of an all-American look, and so had the costly regular bleach job that transformed her from a brunette to a honey blonde.

She worked out constantly to keep her figure and always wore heels to conceal the fact that she was only five-four. She bought all her clothes at the finest stores in the city, thanks to her father's credit cards, and regularly visited salons for facials, manicures, massages, and a variety of other beauty ministrations. She never left her apartment without full makeup and had cultivated a trademark perfume, one that was imported from Paris, costing her father several thousand dollars a year.

Daddy never complained. He paid her bills and asked her, whenever he saw her, whether she needed anything.

The day after she'd awakened in Yale's loft in the Village after a night of the most supreme lovemaking she had ever experienced, she had told her father that yes, she did need something. Desperately.

"What is it, Teeny?"

You have no idea, Daddy, she had thought to herself, as her mind replayed, in explicit detail, her passionate encounter with Yale Bradigan.

She told Franco about the man she'd met, who owned an art gallery in SoHo that he was just trying to get off the ground. She told her father that she wanted to marry him.

Secretly, she had wondered how her father was going to win Yale for her. After all, despite the smoldering passion that had tantalized her through that night of pleasure, he'd treated her with indifference the morning after, sending her home in a cab without so much as a cup of coffee or a promise to call.

But somehow, her father had won Yale for her.

That was all that mattered to Justine. She didn't care how Franco had done it—she didn't want to know—and she didn't care that her fiancé wasn't given to affection or long-winded declarations of his love for her.

He was going to be her husband.

For the rest of her life, she would share his life and his bed—the latter the most enchanting place she'd ever had the pure pleasure of occupying.

Yale Bradigan had a sublime flair for pleasuring a woman. The things he'd done to Justine that first night had made an addict out of her, had made her feel so wanton, so naughty, that she'd felt compelled to go straight to confession afterward.

His bedroom skills had, admittedly, cooled after that. But he had a lot on his mind, what with his gallery business booming, and losing his brother in that fire back in March.

Not that Justine had even known before then that Yale had a twin. He'd told her when they'd met that he had no family; that he was an orphan.

But it turned out that his mother was still living—tucked away in a mental hospital somewhere upstate. Justine had pieced that together from what she'd overheard among the mourners at the funeral. When she'd asked Yale, later that day, why he'd lied about his family, he'd dismissed her question with characteristic disinterest.

"I don't remember telling you they were dead

when we met. You must have heard me wrong," was all he said before changing the subject.

Ever since, he'd been more emotionally removed from her than ever. And their physical relationship, which had already been cooling off before that, continued to fade. It wasn't that they didn't make love as often, because they did. But more and more, Yale seemed only to be going through the motions.

And in the back of her mind, Justine couldn't help wondering if it had to do with more than just his business and his brother's death.

If, maybe, there were another woman involved . . .

But there can't be, she told herself every time the idea flitted into her mind. Her fiancé knew how her father would react if he ever caught wind that Yale had so much as flirted with another woman.

There was no way.

And yet . . .

Justine blinked.

There, out the window of the taxi—

A familiar black Lexus was passing in the left lane.

It was speeding, as though the driver was in a mad rush to get someplace. But before it was out of sight, Justine glimpsed the New York vanity plate above the bumper.

ARTISTE.

It was Yale.

And he was heading *uptown.*

Four

The moment she saw Yale's now-familiar black car pass the carriage house and pull into the driveway, Lexi turned away from the living room window, where she'd been watching for him.

"It's about time. He's here, Em," she told her daughter, who was squirming in her arms.

Emma Rose wanted to be put down so that she could play, and had for the last half hour, but Lexi couldn't seem to let her go. She was rattled by what she'd discovered, and somehow, hanging onto her daughter, feeling Emma Rose's rhythmic heartbeat against her own, was reassuring.

Lexi shifted the baby to her other hip as she hurried to the door. She had locked it before she'd called Yale, and had gone back several times to make sure it was still secure. She'd closed all the first-floor windows, too, and been dismayed to see that several of them didn't have latches. She had never bothered to check until now. And she rarely ever bothered to lock the door since she'd moved back up to the country.

As she turned the bolt and opened the door for Yale, a warm September breeze swept in.

Emma Rose squealed in delight.

"I know, sweetie," Lexi said to her, stepping outside. "I know it's been stuffy in there. I'm sorry I had to close the door and the windows."

"It took me longer than I expected," Yale called, jumping out of his car. "The Hutch was jammed, so I crossed over to 95, which was fine for about a mile. There was an accident, and it took me an hour to get to the next exit. I took back roads the rest of the way here."

He finished his explanation as he arrived on the steps. Though he was wearing dark sunglasses, she could feel his gaze sweeping her face, probing her. Then he turned toward the baby, who was watching him intently.

"Hello, Emma Rose," he said, reaching up and offering her a finger.

Her tiny fist, glistening wet from drool, reached out and wrapped around it immediately.

"Some grip," he told the baby, then looked at Lexi. "What happened?"

"I'll tell you inside," she said, looking around at the shady driveway and yard to make sure they were empty. Not that she actually expected to see someone lurking behind a tree, watching her . . .

But suddenly she didn't feel safe here. The private property that had seemed so luxurious after crowded city living now seemed isolated, and almost . . . ominous.

She turned to open the screen door, then jumped as Yale said, "Whoa, wait!"

Startled, she turned back.

But he was grinning. "The baby won't let go," he explained, prying Emma Rose's hand from around his finger. "She almost took my arm off when you turned."

"Oh . . ." Lexi could only smile faintly.

His grin faded. He took off his sunglasses and she saw the concern in his light green eyes. "What is it, Lexi? Why are you so jumpy?"

"Come on in," was all she said, holding the door open for him.

As soon as he had stepped across the threshold, she quickly closed the storm door again and locked it.

He watched her intently, not seeming to notice that Emma Rose was gleefully babbling at him.

"Let's go into the living room," she said, hoisting the baby so that she was facing over Lexi's shoulder. Emma Rose clutched at her sweatshirt as though she were trying to claw her way toward Yale's arms.

It dawned on Lexi that the baby was drawn to him, which wasn't all that surprising, in a sense, because she had always had a sunny personality. From the time she was a month old, she was apt to smile cheerfully at strangers on the street if they so much as noticed and waved at her.

But during the past week or so, she had started to display shades of the typical six-month-old's case of stranger anxiety. And Yale wasn't the type of man Lexi would expect to charm a child—at least, not the Yale she had known.

Somehow, though, it seemed that his few stilted, playful attempts to bond with Emma Rose had resulted in the baby's being fascinated by him, for whatever reason.

It was almost as if she realized he was her uncle—her only remaining link with the father she would never know. She was studying his face intently, as though it was familiar, though Lexi knew a baby her age probably wouldn't remember someone she'd met only briefly nearly a week ago. Yet every time he spoke, Emma Rose's eyebrows rose and she smiled broadly, as though his voice had triggered a positive instinct deep inside her.

She likes him, Lexi realized with a pang. Maybe she shouldn't have been so hasty, the other day, to declare that she didn't want Yale to be a part of his niece's life.

"You've unpacked the rest of your stuff," Yale noted, standing in the middle of the living room floor and looking around.

"Yeah . . . I figured it was time we settled in. I did it Wednesday and Thursday."

"But you still don't have a phone."

"No. I haven't had time to arrange for the hookup." And until now, she hadn't had the money.

"I don't like your being here alone with the baby without a telephone, Lexi. You're in the middle of nowhere."

Tell me about it, she thought grimly, setting Emma Rose into her bouncy seat.

The baby whimpered a protest, and her smile shadowed into a scowl.

"Here, sweetie, play with your cup," Lexi said, handing her the red plastic cup that had captivated Emma Rose's attention when she'd unpacked it the other day.

Emma Rose gripped it for a moment, then tossed it moodily onto the floor.

Lexi retrieved it, gave it back to her, and turned to Yale.

He had seated himself on the couch, facing her. She noticed how muscular and tanned his arms were in that short-sleeved white Ralph Lauren shirt.

And he was wearing jeans, which surprised her. They weren't faded and worn like the ones she had on, or threadbare—even ripped—the way Emmett's had always been. Yale's jeans were still a crisp indigo, as though they were relatively new, and she could tell they weren't your everyday Levi's. Like everything else he owned, they were probably extravagant and top-of-the-line.

But at least they were jeans.

At least they put him one rung closer to the rest of civilization, instead of firmly in that unreachable "Yale netherworld" he'd always inhabited.

"Why don't you sit and tell me what's going on, Lexi?" he suggested, still watching her with those disconcerting green eyes of his.

There was nowhere for her to sit but the floor—unless she wanted to be as close to him as she'd have to be on the couch.

Which she didn't.

Yes, you do, an irritating voice whispered in her ear. *Especially now. You know damn well that you want him to put those strong arms of his around you, and you want him to hold you and tell you not to be afraid.*

Setting her chin resolutely, Lexi plunked herself down on the floor beside Emma Rose's bouncy seat.

"What happened?" he pressed. "You're obviously upset."

She nodded, took a deep breath, and began. "After we had lunch yesterday, I started thinking about Emmett." *As if he hasn't been on your mind every second since he died.* "I mean, I started thinking about what you said—that there's a chance he was . . ."

"Murdered."

"Yes." She swallowed hard. "I remembered that he had brought some of his stuff over to my apartment about two weeks before . . . the baby was born." She would rather remember that March day as a commemoration of Emma Rose's birth, and not of Emmett's death.

Yale leaned forward, his eyes narrowed. "And . . . ?"

"I know it wasn't a terrific thing to do, but I looked through the boxes," she admitted, shifting her gaze to Emma Rose, who was fussing in her seat. "They were sealed with packing tape, but I slit it, then resealed it after I was done . . ."

"Snooping?" he supplied, and she glanced up to see that he wore a piqued expression.

"Actually, yes," she admitted, setting her jaw. She wondered why on earth she had ever called Yale, why she had felt the need to tell him what had happened. "But whether or not I had any right to go through Emmett's things is beside the point, isn't it?"

He shrugged. "That's your business."

"Yes, it is. What matters is that I knew what was in those boxes. Some clothes he liked to wear, and some books, and some of his writing stuff—he was still working on that, in case you didn't know."

"What? Writing?" Yale's tone was sardonic. "I thought he gave that up years ago. I thought he was a jack-of-all-trades."

"He did what he had to to make a living," she defended, feeling a fiercely protective instinct boil up inside her. "He found work wherever he could, just as . . . just as I did."

"The two of you were a good pair, weren't you, then?"

"Yes." She wanted to shout at him that while she and Emmett might not have had high-powered careers, or even enough money to pay the bills at times, they'd had something he wouldn't know anything about: Love.

But she managed to control herself this time.

She'd learned long ago that a man like Yale Bradigan didn't respond to emotional outbursts. Whenever she'd unleashed a torrent of anger at him back in the days when they were together, his maddening reaction had always been to regard her calmly, then retreat—mentally and physically.

And right now, much as she hated to admit it, she needed Yale.

So she ignored his infuriatingly smug expression and her own resentment and went on. "Anyway, in with his things, I found a locked metal box."

"Did you open it?"

"I said it was locked."

He shrugged. The look on his face told her what he was thinking—that her conscience, not to mention the tape sealing Emmett's boxes, hadn't stopped her from prying where she didn't belong in the first place. Why had she let a lock deter her?

"Obviously, Emmett didn't want anyone to see whatever was inside," she told Yale, retrieving the red cup that had just gone clattering across the floor again, amid the baby's babbling protests.

"Obviously not."

"So I put the box back and resealed the cartons, and I forgot about the whole thing—until yesterday. Thanks to you," she added, in a tone that told him she'd have been better off if he'd never raised her suspicions.

"And now . . . ?"

"And now, I decided I should find the metal box again," she told him. "Because if you're right, and if someone really did kill Emmett, then maybe there's a clue about who did it in that box."

He nodded, watching her.

"So I went upstairs—I had his things stored in my closet, and I hadn't touched them since we moved in—and I opened the tape that sealed the cartons . . ."

"And . . . ?"

"And the metal box was gone."

For a moment, he showed absolutely no reaction. Then his eyes widened, and he echoed, "Gone?"

"It was nowhere to be found. I looked through every one of those boxes, over and over, and there was no sign of it."

"Maybe . . ." He hesitated as though he didn't want to say whatever had come into his mind.

"Maybe what?"

"Maybe you imagined that it was there in the first place."

Her jaw dropped. "Are you out of your mind? How could I imagine something like that?"

"You were pregnant at the time—don't pregnant women go through all sorts of mental . . . things?"

She got to her feet, shaking with fury. "Get out of here, Yale," she ordered, pointing at the door. "Now."

As if on cue, Emma Rose opened her mouth and began to wail.

"Hold on a minute, Lexi—"

"No! I'm telling you that someone stole that box, and you're telling me that I'm imagining things? After you're the one who planted this whole thing in my head, that someone killed Emmett?"

The baby cried harder, and Yale looked down at the bouncy seat, then at Lexi, with a pointed expression.

She bent and picked up Emma Rose, cuddling her and stroking her little head. "Shhh, Em, it's all right. Don't cry, sweetheart. Don't cry . . ."

"She's upset because you're hollering," Yale said.

"She is not! She's upset because she's—she's been fussy ever since I put her in the seat. Don't tell me about my daughter. You have nothing to do with her."

"I know; you keep reminding of that, don't you?" he asked. Now he was standing, too. "Lexi, she's my niece, remember? I care about her. And . . . never mind."

"What?" She rocked the baby, who had quieted, and looked at Yale.

"I want to be a part of her life," he said, and held up a hand to stop the protest that immediately sprang to her lips. She sensed, when he continued, that he was forcing each word from his lips with unaccustomed candor. "I know that in the past, you and I haven't exactly had a smooth relationship. I'm sorry for that—more sorry than you'll ever know. And I realize that Emmett and I weren't getting along, either—"

"You hadn't spoken to each other in ten years. Yeah, I guess I'd call that not getting along." She hated herself for interrupting with the sarcastic comment, for the way she was making this man—who had never before spoken from his heart—spill himself to her this way.

Her instincts told her to go to him, to put a gentle hand on his shoulder and tell him it was okay—that she'd listen, that she'd consider what he was asking.

But some bitter, stubborn streak—formed in the years since he had blithely broken her heart and turned his back on her—kept her from softening. Her jaw hurt from keeping it stiff and held high; her mouth ached with the effort of restraining words she wouldn't let herself say.

He stared at her for a moment, his gaze impenetrable.

"Forget it," he said abruptly, and started for the door.

She waited until he'd put his hand on the bolt.

Then she opened her mouth and spoke.

It was an impulsive, impassioned plea, one that took her by surprise, as though it had come from someone else.

"Yale?" she called, turning toward him. "Please don't go."

He froze, one hand on the lock, the other on the knob.

For a moment, he was too shocked to respond.

Lexi—obstinate, tenacious, prickly Lexi—would never retract a command. Especially where he was concerned.

He knew her very well, even after all this time apart. When she said something, she followed through. She wasn't a woman who apologized—especially not to the likes of Yale Bradigan, a man who had done his best, several years ago, to shatter her fragile teenaged heart into so many pieces it was a miracle it had ever become whole enough to love again.

But it's Emmett she loves, he reminded himself, *not you.*

"Yale?" she said again, this time softly, almost . . . timidly.

She might have loved Emmett—but it was Yale who was here with her.

Yale was the one she needed now.

He turned toward her, slowly.

She looked vulnerable standing in the archway, wearing that enormous gray sweatshirt and the jeans that bagged on her narrow hips, that tangle of dark hair tumbling over her shoulder. And the way she was holding her daughter—clutching her to her breast, as if to protect both Emma Rose and herself from any more hurt . . .

Yale swallowed and walked to her.

She looked relieved. "Um . . . I don't want to get into what happened between you and me, or between you and Emmett—not that I think you have any intention of telling me," she added somewhat sharply, and he thought, ruefully, that Lexi would always be Lexi.

She might be more mature, and she might have learned not to let her sharp tongue dig her into emotional ditches; she might have even learned to give an inch . . . but she would never forget. Or forgive.

That, Yale knew beyond a doubt.

"What I want to do is . . . figure out who killed Emmett. I think I can help."

His heart beat a little faster. "You have an idea what happened to him?"

"No. I wish I did, but . . . all I know—and you can choose to believe me or you can decide I'm hallucinating or lying, but if so, please keep that to yourself—all I know," she went on breathlessly, "is that the locked box Emmett stored at my apartment is gone. Someone took it."

"Maybe *he* did."

"Why would he? He gave it to me for a reason. I thought it was kind of odd that he'd bring all that stuff over to my house in the first place. He used to keep a few things there—some clothes, and, you know, a toothbrush, a hairbrush . . . but he kept most of his stuff in his apartment."

"Why do you suppose he did that?"

Lexi smiled somewhat regretfully. "Because he wanted to keep his distance. Sure, he'd eat at my place, and sleep there, and a lot of times he just hung out, even if I wasn't home. But he made sure he always had to go home after a day or two—to get things he needed. That way, he had space."

Yale nodded, surprised—yet not, when he really thought about it—at her understanding, even acceptance, of the emotional limits set by the man she had loved.

"So if he didn't want to keep his belongings at your place, why do you think he suddenly changed his mind?" he asked, watching her face carefully.

She gave a short, somewhat bitter laugh. "It sure wasn't because he'd suddenly decided he might want to move in, after all."

"Is that what you thought at the time?"

"I thought . . ." Emma Rose tugged on Lexi's hair, and he sensed that she used it as an excuse to look away so that she wouldn't have to meet his gaze. "I thought maybe with the baby coming, and everything, he might have decided he wanted to be around more. That's what he said, anyway . . . and I guess I believed him. Like an idiot."

"You weren't an idiot, Lexi." He wanted to reach out and touch her, wanted to tell her not to regret taking the man she'd loved at his word. He wanted to tell her not to lose her ability to love, to trust . . .

But how could he?

How would she react to a reassuring touch, to encouraging words, coming from *him,* of all people?

Yale Bradigan was undoubtedly the last man on earth she would ever love or trust again.

So he beat down his instincts and kept his distance, telling himself that she would, after all, expect nothing more from him.

"I believed him because *I* wanted to," she said. "Maybe I needed to. I was carrying his child, and I wanted to think that maybe instead of being just her father, he'd be her *daddy*."

He knew, without asking, exactly what she meant.

A *father* was someone who made a biological contribution, and nothing more, beyond maybe a perfunctory visit now and then.

A *daddy* was—well, he was *there*. A daddy was someone who tucked you in at night and checked the closet for monsters; someone who carried you on his shoulders at parades and bought you cotton candy, who made you take out the trash and make your bed and taught you how to hit a baseball and tie a tie.

A daddy.

Yale had always wanted a daddy.

Trevor Bradigan had been his *father*. And he'd died before his sons had ever had the chance to really understand what they'd been missing even while he was alive.

Just as Emma Rose had lost Emmett—who'd never had the chance to prove himself—or fail at fatherhood the way he'd failed everything else in his life.

At least, as far as Yale was concerned.

"Anyway," Lexi went on, her shoulders rising, then sinking in a weary shrug, "I guess the reason Emmett left those boxes with me was because they contained something he didn't want anyone else to find."

"And now, you think someone did."

"Obviously. Someone must have broken into my apartment while I was in the hospital and stolen the box. If not then, it had to be after we moved in here. Emmett's boxes were in a padlocked storage bin during the months I was living with my parents." She looked around the living room, her gaze falling on the closed windows, which revealed the long shadows of late afternoon.

"And you're afraid," Yale said, watching her.

"Of course I am. I live here alone, with my baby. I don't want to think about some slimy stranger creeping around when I'm not here, or . . . or when I am."

He walked to the double window over the couch and inspected it. "The latch is broken," he observed, touching it.

"No kidding. Most of the window locks are missing altogether."

"How about the back door? There is one, isn't there?"

"In the kitchen. I never use it. It's locked."

"Does it have a chain?"

"No. Neither does the front door."

Yale thought about that, then announced, "You can't stay here."

"What are you talking about? I have to stay here. This is where I live."

"It's not safe. Somewhere out there, the nut who killed my brother is running loose. You're his—" But she wasn't his widow. She wasn't his anything, thanks to Emmett's phobia about commitment.

Yale went on, "Emma Rose is his daughter. What if the person who killed him comes after her?"

The stark fear in Lexi's eyes made him regret his harsh choice of words. She looked down at her daughter, whose head was snuggled sleepily on Lexi's shoulder. "She's just a baby," she whispered, her face ashen. "You don't think someone would—"

"What about you?" Yale asked, again fighting the urge to go to her. "You and Emmett were together for years. What if the person who killed him decides to come after you?"

"I had nothing to do with anything in Emmett's life that might have been dangerous or illegal, Yale."

"*You* know that, and so do I—because I know you, Lexi," he added at her questioning look. "I know that no matter what my brother was up to, you're an upright person. But you just said yourself that someone broke in and stole Emmett's locked box. You're not safe here."

"It might not have been here. It might have happened at my apartment in the city."

"That doesn't change the fact that this place isn't safe. All a person would have to do is sneak up to the house at night, when no one would see from the road, and lift one of these ground-floor windows. He'd be in in no time."

"He wouldn't have to climb in a window. I rarely lock the doors, Yale. I've always thought Cady's Landing was safe."

"Are you out of your mind? No place is safe these days."

She said nothing, but he could sense the wheels

turning in her mind, see the beginnings of panic on her face.

She stroked Emma Rose's hair. The baby had fallen asleep on her shoulder, and even from a few feet away, Yale could hear the gentle cooing sighs she made in her sleep. The sound tore at his heart.

"You can't stay here," he repeated.

"But . . . where can we go?"

"You can come home with me," he said out of the blue, then immediately wished he hadn't.

There was no way he could go back to his Fifth Avenue loft with Lexi and Emma Rose in tow. What would he tell Justine? He didn't want Lexi and the baby getting mixed up with her . . . or, God forbid, with her father.

No, he couldn't let Franco Di Pierro have any inkling that he still cared about Lexi.

And he did, he realized. He cared a lot. He couldn't let anything happen to her . . . even if he'd never have her again.

"There's no way I'm going home with you," she announced flatly, shaking her dark curls resolutely. "No way."

Even though he knew he should be relieved that her refusal had rescued him from his own blunder, he felt irritated by her attitude.

Not that he was going to talk her into it . . . but he couldn't help asking, "Why not?"

"Because," she said, still shaking her head. "I have no intention of towing the baby and all her gear down to your bachelor pad in the city. We can stay with my parents."

"You don't look convinced of that," he noted, seeing the shadow of doubt on her face.

"It's just that I don't want to worry them," she said. "My mother's been really sick lately."

"I know."

She looked at him in surprise. "How do you know that?"

"Your parents were at the funeral, remember? I spoke to them. Your mother looked . . . she didn't look well," he said, remembering Kathleen Sinclair's gaunt features and painfully thin frame huddled into that huge coat as though she was freezing even though it had been a balmy March day.

"Then you probably realize she's in bad shape, and that my father is very worried about her. We all are."

He nodded.

"Besides, my father lost his job over the summer. He's trying to find something, but the market has been terrible and he's very discouraged. Not all his benefits have carried over, and my mother's medical bills are staggering. My parents have enough to worry about without thinking something might happen to Emma Rose and me."

"I understand."

"If I could just fix the locks on the windows . . ."

"I can help you do that," he said.

"You can?"

"Sure."

"I don't mean to . . . I mean, Yale, it's really nice of you to offer and everything, but you've never exactly been . . . handy."

He was irked at the amused glint in her eyes, but

she did have a point. "I know how to make this place more secure," he said decidedly. "It doesn't take Norm Abram to install a window lock."

Her eyebrows shot up. "Norm Abram? The master carpenter on *This Old House?* I can't believe you watch that show."

"I happen to like PBS," he retorted.

"It's just that . . . Emmett loved *This Old House,* too. He watched it every chance he got. He used to say . . ." Her eyes clouded again. "He wanted to buy a big old house someday. He said he was going to learn how to remodel it and make it into his dream house."

He nodded slowly, watching her. "Was he planning on having you and the baby live there with him?"

"I doubt it," she said, waving a hand in dismissal. "I told you, when Emmett thought of the future, he thought of *himself.* Period." Abruptly, she shoved up the too-long sleeve of her sweatshirt and checked her watch. "It's past five. Do we need to go to a hardware store?"

"We should, if I'm going to fix those windows for you."

"Let's go, then. Everything is going to be closing early, since it's a Saturday."

He shrugged and glanced at the baby sleeping peacefully in Lexi's arms.

"All right, let's go," he echoed, doing his best not to reveal his suddenly overwhelming concern for the child . . . and for her beautiful mother.

* * *

Meredith MacFee looked at the telephone receiver, frowning.

It was ringing.

Just ringing, which was odd, because Yale had never, so far as she knew, gone out and forgotten to turn on his answering machine at home. He was too conscientious.

Thoughtfully, she pressed the talk button, severing the cellular connection, and put the phone down on her polished cherrywood coffee table.

Where could he be?

Last night, before he'd left her in the hotel room—after a peculiarly *unsatisfying* round of lovemaking, she might add—he had told her he'd be staying home tonight to catch up on paperwork.

"With Justine?" she'd asked snidely, slipping her long, bare legs from beneath the cheap hotel comforter and stretching on the bed.

"No." He hadn't even bothered to glance at her nude, fully exposed body. "She has an engagement."

She was pleased, though she knew he didn't love his fiancée. She wondered whether it was possible for Yale Bradigan to love anyone at all. There had been a time—and how glorious it was!—when Meredith had fancied that he had deep feelings for *her*. She had believed that if both their lives weren't so complicated, so filled with other obligations, she and Yale would sail off together somewhere.

But lately, she had begun to suspect that she'd been fooling herself. She had offered to accompany him to Europe this summer, though she'd had no idea how she'd pull that off without Russell getting suspicious. But he'd rebuffed her promptly, saying he needed to be alone, to get over his brother's death.

Just as he'd rebuffed her last night when she'd said, "As long as Justine's busy tomorrow, Yale, maybe I should come over and keep you company. Russell has to deliver a keynote address at a literacy dinner." She'd run her tongue over her lips and added wickedly, "I'll be glad to make your every wish my command, darling."

"You can't come over, Meredith. You know how risky that would be."

"And you know me, darling," she'd pointed out. "I love to take risks. I thought you did, too."

He'd snorted at that, then put on his trenchcoat, picked up his briefcase, and left briskly.

Now she wondered whether he'd decided to go down to the gallery to catch up on his work there, instead of doing it at home.

After a moment's contemplation, she reached for the phone again and dialed. She got his voicemail. Which meant that he could be on another line with a client—unlikely at eight o'clock on a Saturday night—or that he wasn't at the gallery.

If he was there, he'd pick up. Yale was a shrewd businessman; far too shrewd to ever let the gallery phone deliberately go unanswered when it might be someone who wanted to buy some art.

So.

He wasn't at the gallery, and he wasn't home.

Where could he be?

Maybe Justine had changed her plans and the two of them were having a cozy dinner somewhere, she thought jealously.

Or maybe Yale had gone out alone—although that wasn't likely. Not when he could have called her.

No, surely he wouldn't be foolish enough to risk annoying her that way. He was calculating enough to know what would happen if he alienated her.

Meredith hung up, tossed the phone onto the damask couch cushion, and looked restlessly around the den. It was her favorite room among the twelve in the Park duplex; the largest, and yet somehow the coziest.

She had decorated it herself, unlike the rest of the apartment, which had been done by Russell's sister, Lynette, who was a set designer for two New York-based soaps.

The other rooms in the MacFee residence were all lines and angles, glass and marble, leather and iron, black and white. But the den had a homy glow generated by the overstuffed furniture, soft fabrics, and warm colors. There were dozens of variations on the color red here, from the muted pink roses in the Persian rug to the maroon spines among the rows of antique books on built-in shelves by the fireplace.

Meredith's favorite thing in the room—the centerpiece, really—was, ironically, something Russell had picked out.

The painting that hung over the mantel.

It was the one thing that didn't belong here, at least, not in an aesthetic sense. It was modern art, an oil canvas done in swirling shades of blue and gray. The artist had called it *Sky*. According to Russell, it was a masterpiece, having been painted by the sixties pop art icon Devin Tremblay shortly before his death of a heroin overdose.

When Lynette had seen it hanging in the den, she'd turned to Meredith and asked, "Why on earth did you put that in here? It clashes with the color scheme, Meredith."

"Really? I don't think it does," she had informed her sister-in-law sweetly.

Russell had rolled his eyes, distracted, as usual, by a thousand other things. If he was intrigued that Meredith had obviously taken a sudden liking to the painting she had once loathed, he'd said nothing.

There it hung over the fireplace in the room she had begun to think of as her own, even though, technically, Russell was free to use it, too. He did venture into the den when he was researching a case and needed to look something up in one of his out-dated law books. He kept most of his professional references in his midtown office, though, and these days, it seemed, he was rarely home, let alone intruding upon Meredith's cherished domain. She suspected that his time wasn't filled entirely with professional duties and his obligations as a founding member of a literacy task force.

No, it seemed Russell might be involved in certain . . . *extracurricular* activities of late.

For that, she was grateful.

She was free to lounge in solitude on her plush strawberry-colored sofa, to marvel at fate while staring at the painting her husband had bought her as an anniversary gift three years before.

The painting Russell had coincidentally happened to buy from a man who had once been—and would again become—his wife's lover.

Five

"Is this the Moo Goo Gai Pan, or the chicken with Hunan sauce?" Yale asked, peering into a take-out carton.

Lexi turned from the cupboard, where she had been reaching for plates, and checked. "Moo Goo Gai Pan," she pronounced.

"How do you know?"

"I order takeout from the Emerald Palace a few times a week. I recognize everything on the menu at this point."

"You don't cook?"

"Not anymore."

Not without Emmett around to eat with me. She shoved away thoughts of the cozy evenings the previous winter when, attacked by a fervent craving for Italian food, she would cook enormous pots of sauce. She and Emmett would sate their appetites for spaghetti . . . and then for each other, acrobatically making love despite Lexi's increasingly awkward, tremendous tummy.

She felt a flicker of heat at her core and cursed herself for having thought about sex at this particular moment—with Yale Bradigan so close by.

She brought the plates and two forks over to the

tiny table in a nook by the window, then hesitated before setting it. The notion of sharing this tiny space with Yale, of eating a meal here with him, was just too . . . intimate.

The savory aroma of garlic and Chinese spices mingled in the warm kitchen with the musky, heady scent of Yale's cologne. The bulb in the fixture overhead wasn't as strong as it should have been, bathing the kitchen in a shadowy glow. Outside, the wind had kicked up and the windowpanes rattled, making the house seem even cozier. And in the living room, where Lexi had put on the first compact disc her fingers had grabbed, Billy Joel sang about rekindling romance.

Why, when Yale had suggested getting dinner, had she vetoed his offer to take her out to eat? At least in a restaurant, they wouldn't be alone together in this accidentally atmospheric setting.

Actually, she had tried to avoid spending the evening with him at all. She had said she had to get the baby home.

But then he had said he was starving. After all, they had spent two hours driving all over Westchester County, trying to find an open hardware store. By the time they had gone all the way to Pergament, up in Port Chester, Lexi's stomach was actually grumbling, too.

She could hardly expect Yale to spend a few more hours working on her windows, and then another hour driving back down to the city, without stopping to eat.

But why, when he'd said they should just get takeout Chinese, had she been so quick to agree?

Because you liked the idea, for a moment, of eating at home, alone, with him, she admitted to herself. *You let your ridiculous fantasies intrude on reality.*

Fantasies about sharing more than a meal with Yale.

It had been so long since she'd been with a man . . .

So long since she'd been with *him.*

She would never—*couldn't,* no matter how hard she tried—forget what he'd been like as a lover all those years ago.

He was more skilled, when it came to the art of seduction, than any man she'd ever been with—including Emmett.

With Emmett, lovemaking had been too passionate, too heart-rending, to be a flawless, fluid physical ballet. With Emmett, it was more playful—there were times when their noses would bump and they would simultaneously burst out laughing.

And when it wasn't amusing, lovemaking with Emmett had been a breathless, tempestuous event. The stakes had been too high for Lexi to relax and concentrate only on pleasure—especially of late.

Not that she'd rather, under any circumstances, sleep with Yale than with Emmett. The very idea was preposterous—as preposterous as the notion that it was at all possible to sleep with either of them ever again.

Emmett, after all, was . . . gone.

Dead, Lexi. He's dead.

And Yale . . .

Oh, Lord. He was very much alive.

Not that it mattered. She would never allow herself to fall for him again.

Never.

"What's the matter?" he asked behind her, startling her.

"Oh, nothing. I . . . I thought I heard the baby crying," she lied, and cleared her throat nervously, glancing at him.

She couldn't help noticing how broad his shoulders were, how his muscles bulged even beneath the white mesh cotton of his shirt. She wondered whether his chest was still sculpted and hairless, whether his stomach was still hard and lean.

"Do you want me to go check on her?"

"What?"

"The baby?"

"Would you mind?"

Just go, get out of here for a second so I can collect my thoughts and figure out what the hell I'm doing . . .

What the hell you're *doing here, in my house.*

"What do I do if she's crying?"

"Huh? Oh . . . just . . . pat her and tell her everything's okay," Lexi told him.

Even though nothing is . . .

"That's all?" Yale asked.

"That's all. But you know, if it doesn't work, come and get me," she said, realizing that lately, Emma Rose rarely got up after she'd been put down for the night. And if the baby really *had* happened to awaken, it would take a lot more than a simple pat and reassuring words from Yale to get her back down.

When he'd left, Lexi had heaved a quiet sigh of relief and set the stacked plates and silverware down on the table.

She had to calm down.

This was ridiculous, this fantasizing about Yale. She had to put an end to it.

She had to remember the reason she couldn't let him get to her again.

Think of the way it ended, she commanded herself. But she couldn't.

All she could remember, when she thought back over the years to that bittersweet summer, was the way it had begun.

That first night, he hadn't taken her, as all her other dates had, to one of the mediocre restaurants that had lined Main Street in Cady's Landing. No, Yale had taken her into the city.

She remembered being startled when he'd pulled his French vanilla Jaguar convertible onto the expressway heading toward Manhattan.

"Where are we going?" she'd asked, startled.

"You'll see."

She'd never forget that night—how it had felt to be eighteen and driving with the wind in her hair on a warm June evening with the lights of New York City sparkling ahead, promising adventure.

And . . . romance?

"Why did you come over and talk to me on the beach today?" she'd asked him boldly.

"Because I caught sight of you and decided you were the most gorgeous girl I'd ever seen in Cady's Landing," he'd said, turning from the wheel to flash his even white grin at her.

Which, she'd later discovered, was a lie. Emmett had told her that *he'd* spotted her first; that he'd made the mistake of remarking to his brother that she was "hot" and looked like a "wild babe," as he'd put it, and that he was going to talk to her.

And then Yale, being Yale, had made sure he'd got to her first.

And Emmett, being Emmett, had sulked—and then forgotten about her, moving on to some other "wild babe."

For then, at least.

Lexi sighed, remembering how Yale had taken her out to a romantic little restaurant on Mulberry Street in Little Italy. She'd been so impressed with the way he tipped the maitre d' to get a good table, with the way he'd tasted and approved a bottle of wine, the way he'd held out her chair for her and ordered her meal for her.

He made her feel, for the first time in her life, like a woman.

There, in the restaurant . . .

And later, parked near the water in Cady's Landing, in the back seat of his car.

She'd been a virgin, but she'd never hesitated for a moment when she'd realized where her date with Yale was headed. She knew from the way he kissed her. There was never an initial, tentative peck, a testing of the waters—not from Yale. He was a man who knew what he wanted and who always got it.

He had kissed Lexi deeply and thoroughly the very first time, his mouth hot and wet and tasting sweetly of wine and tiramisu. His hands had tangled in her hair, holding her head in place as he'd moved

his tongue into her mouth, sweeping her posses-
sively. Instantly she'd been weak with desire, wanting him—knowing, somehow, exactly *how* she
wanted him, though the sensation was new to her.
It was instinctive, her yearning to have him fill her,
consume her—in a slow, tender, passionate rhythm.

And that was exactly how it happened—not just
once, but again. And then again.

In her inexperience, she'd thought this was how
making love would always be.

She smiled ruefully now despite herself, remembering her disappointment the first time she'd slept
with someone other than Yale.

"Can we do it again?" she had naively asked the
nineteen-year-old cousin of her friend Melissa, after
a frustratingly quick, dissatisfying session of inter-
course.

"Again? Why?" he'd asked, still panting and
sweating profusely.

Baffled, she'd reached down . . . and found . . .
nothing.

"Hey, what are you doing?" he'd yelped, shoving
her hand away.

"Sorry," she'd said with an embarrassed shrug,
missing Yale more than ever, despite all the heart-
ache he'd caused her.

Did he still have that incredible . . . staying
power? she wondered now and felt her cheeks grow
hot.

*It doesn't matter, because you certainly won't be
finding out,* she reminded herself.

She heard his footsteps on the stairs and hurriedly

set the table, turning back toward the counter just as he walked into the room.

"She was sound asleep," he told her, wearing a bemused expression. "Lexi, she's so . . . unbelievable."

"What do you mean?" She paused, watching him, wondering at the enchanted look on his face. She had never known Yale Bradigan to be so—so obviously *awed*.

"I guess I never saw a baby sleeping before. I mean, I was just . . . she looked so tiny and sweet in her little pink pajamas, curled up on her side with her thumb in her mouth. I felt this enormous sense of—" He caught himself, suddenly aware of her scrutiny.

"Sense of what?" she asked softly, touched that this man, who was typically brusque and self-centered, could have such an enchanted reaction to her baby.

"I don't know. Maybe responsibility," he said gruffly. "I just want her to be all right."

Lexi nodded, unwilling to push him into more emotionally intimate territory.

"Can I help get the food on the table?" he asked, walking over to the counter and picking up two cartons.

"Sure." She crossed to the refrigerator. "What do you want to drink? I have . . . beer. Or water, I guess."

"Bottled?"

"Beer?"

"No, I meant the water."

Figures, she thought. "No, tap. But the beer's in

bottles," she said, a little smugly. She pulled one out for herself and twisted off the cap.

"I'll have one, too, I guess," he said, sounding reluctant.

She handed it to him. "I always drink beer with Chinese food," she said.

"You always did."

Startled, she looked up. His expression was fond and faraway, as though he were remembering . . .

Then, abruptly, he frowned and took a swig. "Let's eat," he suggested, and plopped himself down at the table.

She knew she should be grateful that he'd broken the mood effectively for the second time in five minutes. Yale was doing an excellent job of reminding her of all the things she'd never liked about him. He didn't enjoy discussing his feelings, and he had an annoying way of becoming businesslike in the midst of romantic moments, and . . .

And he was a snob who only drank bottled water . . .

You're reaching, she told herself, as she pulled several packets of soy sauce and hot mustard from the bottom of the greasy brown paper bag on the counter. *You want to find things not to like about him, so you're being picky.*

The truth was, she realized as she sat down across from him, Yale was different as an adult from the way he had been at twenty-one, when she'd last known him. He was a little more sensitive and a little more relaxed, and he had a sense of humor.

Sure, this Yale still bore undeniable traces of the arrogant, self-possessed young man he'd once been, but then, those qualities were in the Bradigan genes. Emmett had shared them.

Emmett.

His image careened into Lexi's mind, and she guiltily realized that she hadn't thought about him in . . . what?

Five minutes, Lexi told herself. *It's no crime.*

"Want some of this?" Yale asked, holding up the carton of sweet-and-sour chicken.

"Sure." She lifted her plate and he scooped some on.

"Fried rice?"

"Why not?"

He filled her plate from the containers on the table. He'd insisted on buying enough food to last her a week in leftovers, saying he was really hungry. Lexi had suspected that he somehow knew how bare her refrigerator was.

It was sweet, the way he was serving her. Emmett had never done that, she realized. He had always helped himself and dug right in, often before she was seated at the table.

Of course, Lexi defended mentally, Emmett rarely had enough money to eat breakfast and lunch while he was working his many odd jobs. He was always too hungry to be polite.

But there was something nice, she had to admit, about being with a gentleman again.

Before the thought was completely formed, she scolded herself and tried to sweep it away. She did her best to replace it with a memory of how cruel Yale had been when he'd broken up with her.

But that wasn't necessarily fair. After all, people

changed. There was no reason that Yale couldn't have.

And if he really *was* different . . .

Then there was no reason for her not to be attracted to him.

Yes, there is, she told herself firmly. *He's Emmett's brother, and . . .*

Are you reluctant to fall for Yale out of loyalty to Emmett? she wondered suddenly.

In a way, she supposed she was. After all, she was well aware that the brothers had been at odds all these years, and she had always suspected—or maybe Emmett had implied—that whatever had happened had been Yale's fault.

Yet the other day, Yale had planted the seeds of doubt in her mind. Not just about whatever had happened between him and Emmett.

Yale had pointed out, more than once, in subtle ways, that Emmett had been less than perfect—less than responsible, less than an upstanding citizen, less than committed when it came to his relationship with Lexi.

She realized that she was starting to allow herself to resent Emmett, for the first time since his death. Not for leaving her—he certainly hadn't chosen to die—but for the way he'd treated her when he was still alive.

I deserve to be with a man who lives up to his responsibilities, she thought in surprise.

And she thought about the way Yale had arranged his brother's funeral, how he'd lent her the money to start her business, how concerned he was about his niece's future.

"Lexi?"

"Yes?"

"Why aren't you eating?" Yale paused with his fork midway to his mouth, watching her.

"Oh . . ." She blushed. "I'm sorry. I was just . . ."

"Thinking?" he supplied.

"Yes."

"About Emmett?"

Her eyebrows shot up. "How did you know?"

"You always seem to get this sort of . . . lonely expression when you think of him. I can tell."

"Oh . . ." She didn't know what to say. She couldn't tell him that it wasn't Emmett she was missing just now—that it was him.

She tasted the rice, forcing herself to chew and swallow.

She was no longer hungry.

She reached for her beer and took a long swallow. And then another, despite the knowledge that she'd eaten absolutely nothing all day. She'd get drunk, if she wasn't careful.

And that definitely wasn't a good idea.

Not with Yale so temptingly close . . .

What the hell, Lexi thought recklessly, and drank some more.

Justine let herself into Yale's loft and found everything dark. Which was unusual, because he always left the light under the stove hood on overnight, casting a cozy glow from the kitchenette tucked into the corner of the living area.

She flicked the switch on the wall just inside the door and looked around. Everything looked exactly as it had when they'd left this afternoon. There was her magazine, left on the couch, open to the page she'd been reading. There was the half-empty glass of Evian water that Yale had been drinking from before his phone call.

The call from his *client*.

Yeah, right, she thought bitterly, remembering how he'd boldly lied to her about having to go downtown.

Obviously, he hadn't come home yet.

She'd suspected as much, having called him repeatedly throughout the evening. In his haste to leave, she recalled, he hadn't turned on the answering machine earlier.

Each time she had tried the phone, and heard that endless ringing in her ear, she had grown more infuriated. Her friends at the party had asked her a few times whether everything was all right. She'd brushed them off with curt replies and brooded as she'd watched Angela and the others make fools of themselves, fussing over the male stripper they'd hired.

When the rest of them had gone out dancing to a new club in Brooklyn, she'd left in a cab, a woman on a mission.

Now, standing in the middle of Yale's empty apartment, Justine called, "Yale?"

Maybe he's in bed, she thought vainly, and climbed the stairs to the master suite that overlooked the first floor. "Yale?" she called again, louder this time.

But the room was deserted, the king-sized bed empty.

She glanced at the illuminated face of the digital clock on the nightstand.

It was nearly two in the morning.

Where the hell was he?

And who the hell was he with?

"Lexi?" Yale whispered, and shook her gently.

She didn't stir, curled up on the couch and sound asleep beneath the blanket he'd thrown over her earlier.

"Lexi?" he said, shaking her again.

This time, her eyelids fluttered and she stretched. "Hmm?" she murmured sleepily.

He stood watching for a moment as she burrowed deeper into the cushions. Her breathing starting to grow even again. He wanted, more than anything, to stand here and watch her sleep until morning.

No, what he wanted more than *anything* was to lie down next to her, to mold his body against the soft curve of hers, to run his hands over her, to—

"Yale?" Suddenly, as though a jolt of awareness had just reached her, she jerked awake, her eyes snapping open and looking directly at him.

"Hi." He had to grin at her bewildered expression.

"Oh, my God, what time is it?" She sat up and looked around.

"Late."

"How late?"

"Late. I just finished the windows. They're all

bolted shut. No one can get in here without breaking one." The thought sobered him. "I installed that
new motion detector spotlight outside over the back
steps, too," he told her. "And I put chains on both
the back and front doors."

"You did all that while I was . . . how long have
I been sleeping?"

"About four hours," he said, and she groaned.

"It was those two beers—they knocked me out,"
she said. "The last thing I remember is sitting here
while you were explaining what you had to do to fix
the latches on the bay windows in the dining room."

"They're fixed."

"Oh, Yale, thank you so much for taking care of
all this for me. I can't believe it took hours."

"I can't, either," he said, stretching and yawning.

He checked his watch. The last thing he felt like
doing was going outside, getting into his car, and
driving all the way back to the city.

He was nearly out of gas, too, he suddenly remembered. Great.

"Listen, Lexi, do you know where there's an all-
night service station?"

"In Cady's Landing? Um . . . actually, I don't.
Why?"

"My car's on empty, and I forgot to get gas before we came back earlier."

"There must be one of those twenty-four hour
convenience stores near the entrance to 95. But why
don't you let me make you a cup of coffee before
you go? I don't drink it these days—the smell of it
made me sick when I was pregnant, and I never got

back into it again. But I think my mother brought some over when she gave me groceries last week."

He hesitated, not wanting to waste any more time before getting on the road. But then he yawned again and realized he had better take the coffee. It would be dangerous to drive when he was this sleepy.

"Okay," he said reluctantly. "I'll have a quick cup."

She got up and arched her back like a cat. "Ouch. That couch is about as comfortable as sleeping on a park bench."

He followed Lexi into the kitchen. The small night light plugged into the wall gave off enough of a glow that she didn't bother to turn on the overhead bulb. He watched as she opened the cupboard beside the refrigerator. She stood on tiptoe, looking for something. He noticed the way the sleeves of her sweatshirt brushed her fingertips.

She seemed so tiny, so . . . fragile, he thought, and it was the last word he'd ever have expected to use to describe Lexi Sinclair.

"Do you need me to reach something for you?" he asked, and was dismayed to hear his own voice sounding husky.

"I thought I had a can of coffee up here someplace," she said, her arms stretched over her head as she felt around on the shelf. "I'll get a chair so—"

"I'll get the coffee." He came up behind her and reached past her into the cupboard. As he pushed aside a can of pork and beans and another of canned peaches, he was fully aware of the way there was only an inch or two of space between her back and his front. He accidentally brushed against her and felt himself become instantly aroused.

The clean, herbal scent of her hair reached his nostrils, and as he lowered his hand past her head, he felt a few silky strands tickle his wrist.

He wanted—oh, Lord, how he wanted to bury his hands in that mass of curls, to turn her around and tilt her face up and . . .

"Lexi," he said raggedly, becoming aware of the way she stood motionless in front of him, almost as though she was tensed.

"Yes?" she asked after a moment, her voice strained.

"The coffee . . . I can't find it." He forced the words out when he wanted to say something else entirely.

"Maybe I was wrong about having some," she said, sounding slightly breathless.

Still, she hadn't turned and he hadn't moved. He was essentially imprisoning her against the counter in front of her. She couldn't move without touching him.

And he had never in his whole life wanted anything so badly as he wanted Lexi to touch him.

For a moment there was only silence, and the faint sound of the wind moving through the trees outside.

Then Yale heard a voice.

It was, he realized with a start, his own. Words were spilling from his lips—impulsive words.

"Lexi, I have to go, but before I do, I have to ask you for one thing," he was saying.

"What is it?" Her tone was hushed, as though she knew.

"I have to kiss you. Just once. Please, Lexi . . . it's been so damned long and I know nothing can come of it, but I have to kiss you."

He uttered the fervent plea in a rush, knowing as he did that there was no way he could take it back now. It was out there, waiting to be acknowledged, waiting to be dashed by an indignant rebuttal from the queen of indignant rebuttals.

But Lexi turned slowly, and as she did, her arm bumped against the part of him that blatantly, urgently divulged his desire.

His flesh, beneath the stiff denim barrier, sizzled at the contact, and his breath caught in his throat.

When she looked up her gaze collided with his, and he could have sworn he saw a roguish gleam in her eyes. A gleam that betrayed her naughty secret—that she had touched him deliberately.

Wild with lust, he stared at her.

He waited.

And then she smiled a faraway smile and said, "One kiss, for old time's sake."

He swept her into his arms and his mouth swooped over hers. Her lips parted beneath his, and he tasted her with his tongue, dipping into the moist, welcoming place he had missed more than he'd ever realized. He moaned deep in his throat, and she let out a soft whimper and cupped his face in her hands, forcing him to deepen the kiss.

She let her fingertips roam to the back of his head, holding him to her . . .

As if he would ever let her go now, he thought recklessly.

He ached with a need he hadn't fully comprehended until this moment. It was beyond lust, beyond the carnal craving he'd managed to satisfy, until now, with the willing bodies of Justine and Meredith.

No . . . don't even think of them.

Right now, in this spellbinding moment, there was only Lexi.

And she wanted him the way he wanted her; he could feel her hunger as she pressed into him, wriggling her soft curves against his hard body. She had pulled his shirt from the waistband of his jeans, and her fingertips played over his bare back, sending delicious shivers over him.

He had to have her.

Now.

"Lexi," he whispered desperately, though he knew it was futile, knew she would never let him. "Please . . . I don't want to stop. Please let me make love to you."

Her reply was a single, heated word: "Yes."

Lexi closed her eyes and threw her head back, feeling Yale's hot mouth moving down from her face to nibble the tender hollow beneath her ear, then down along the curve of her throat.

Somewhere in the back of her mind, alarm bells were jangling, warning her that this was wrong, that she should stop.

But she was too far gone to worry about anything but the awesome sensations cascading over her body. No, this wasn't a time for rationalizing; it was a time for *feeling*.

It was all about lust, pure and simple.

Lexi's breasts were crushed against Yale's powerful chest; her hips locked against his. His hands roamed down her back to cup her behind; he shifted, parted her legs, and settled her solidly over his raised thigh. She squirmed against him as if to extinguish the fire that was flaring between her legs, but it only raged more fiercely.

He was lifting her sweatshirt over her head, tossing it aside and then fumbling, for only an instant, with the clasp of her bra. Then he was taking that off, too, and she trembled with anticipation as he held her back and looked down at her.

She looked, too, and wondered fleetingly if he could see the stretch marks that had lined her breasts since her pregnancy. Though the postpartum swelling had long since subsided, her breasts were fuller than they had been before. He used to tease her, all those years ago, about her small bosom. Did he remember that now? Did he notice the difference?

Did he realize that her nipples had shriveled painfully in contemplation of his touch?

Did he know how she longed for his hot mouth to close around her?

He reached out, his gold ring catching the glow from the nightlight, and lightly ran a fingertip down along her flesh, beginning at her collarbone and ending at her nipple. She felt a fluttering below her navel, and she moaned as he stroked the rosy peak, then squeezed it lightly between his thumb and forefinger.

She gasped.

"Did I hurt you?"

"No," she managed to say, then, "Please, Yale . . ." She ground herself against his thigh and tightened her grip on his bare shoulders beneath his shirt.

"What is it that you want?" His breath was hot in her ear, and then his tongue darted out and circled the rim. "Do you want my mouth here? Or somewhere else . . . ?"

Unable to speak, she panted and arched her back, guiding his head downward. He obliged, licking her nipple, round and round, teasing her. He moved to her other breast.

"Oh," she whimpered, moving more fervently to quell the ticklish rippling between her legs.

"More?" He laughed softly, then his lips closed over her breast and he sucked ardently.

Her eyes closed and she focused on the exquisite commotion rising within her as the rhythm of his mouth picked up the rhythm of her thighs. She thrust herself against him, crying out softly in frustration at the unyielding, flat surface of his leg, yearning for more intimate contact.

As though he was reading her mind, he moved his hands down and swiftly unbuttoned her pants, his mouth still working at her flesh. She straightened and he lowered the jeans over her hips. She stepped out of them, and he lifted his head and looked down at her.

She wore a pair of cotton panties, plain white and unembellished, but with a high French cut that curved over her hipbone. She waited breathlessly to see what he would do, unable to tell him what it was that she wanted.

He ran his hand down over the slope of her belly, no longer flat as it had been before the baby, but now rounded in a slight, telltale bulge that was testimony to the changes that had swept her body for nine months. His fingers slid beneath the elastic waistband and then one dipped lower, parting the tender folds of flesh.

He gently sought then finally found her throbbing core. He stroked her and Lexi shuddered at the intense, almost painful rush of pleasure.

"Go on," he crooned in her ear, moving his finger over her, skillfully stoking the heat that built rapidly beneath his fingertip.

"I . . . I can't," she gasped, but it was a lie. She was already on the edge, tantalizingly close to letting go . . .

"You can," he said hoarsely, "we'll go there together."

And then he was sinking to the floor, pulling her with him. He pulled his shirt over his head and threw it aside, and she saw that his torso was lean and tanned and hairless, his muscles rippling as he moved.

He slid her panties off, positioned her on her back, and then moved over her. She opened her legs to him, lifting her hips off the floor to meet him.

But he held off, instead finding her mouth again with his and capturing her lips in a passionate kiss. She moaned, restless with desire, and impatiently tried to unfasten his fly. He laughed and asked in a provocative tone, "Do you want me inside you, Lexi?"

"Yes." She cupped her hands on his behind and tried to urge him closer, but still he held off, teasing her.

"Yale, please . . . I want to feel you . . ."

He tensed at her words, and she opened her eyes. His expression was impenetrable. She suddenly remembered the way he had once asked her, when she was eighteen, to talk dirty when they were making love. She had found it impossible then, had wound up giggling and thwarting his arousal.

But now she wanted to please him, wanted to drive him mad with lust so that he would plunge into her and satisfy her craving.

"Yale," she whispered seductively, as she fumbled at his jeans again, "I know what you need. You need to be inside me, and I need you there . . . now. Now, Yale. I don't want anyone but you."

His enigmatic gaze fastened on her, he reached down slowly and unbuttoned his jeans. He pulled them down, and she saw that he still wore white boxers, Brooks Brothers boxers.

She reached out and slid her hand inside the front opening. She found his taut flesh, felt it spring slightly when her fingers brushed against it. She took him in her hand, stroking him and hearing his breath coming faster.

"Come on, Yale . . . I want you inside me. I can't wait any longer . . . please . . ."

He propped himself on his elbows and looked down at her, and she stiffened in anticipation. She spread her legs further and closed her eyes. She cried out softly as she felt his rigid flesh graze her. But nothing more happened, and she opened her eyes.

"You want me?" he asked, his face flushed, his forehead glistening with perspiration.

"Oh, God, yes," she begged. "Please, now. Please . . ."

The word faded, replaced by a low groan as he positioned himself, then sank into her. One long, deep, satisfying stroke, and then he pulled out again and she shook her head rapidly, clung to his naked shoulders in protest.

"More?" he asked, and she bit her lower lip, nodding.

Again, he thrust into her, slowly, and she shivered inside, hovering on the fringes of gratification as he lifted himself until he was almost, but not quite, withdrawn.

"Again?"

"Yes," she breathed, and he accommodated her, this time driving himself in to the hilt, filling her, hot and pulsating inside her.

Lexi bit back a feral scream at the shattering convulsion that erupted inside her. He moved rhythmically and she quaked around him, borne away on a wave of pure ecstasy.

As though across a great distance, she heard a purring sound deep in his throat, and she realized he was about to come. It excited her further, and as he began to writhe above her, she clutched his backside, urging him in deeper still. He pumped into her, spilling molten pleasure and murmuring her name against her throat.

He collapsed, panting, on top of her, his face buried in her neck. She caressed his hair and felt him still inside her, the insistent throbbing subsiding into a comforting warmth.

For the first time, Lexi allowed herself to collect her thoughts that had been scattered along with their clothes, to acknowledge what had just happened.

She had made love to Yale Bradigan, after ten years of loathing the man, after days of swearing to herself that she would have nothing to do with him—for her own sake as well as for her daughter's . . . and Emmett's.

She hadn't bargained on the force of her own lust, had never anticipated that her self-control would crumble beneath so much as a smoldering gaze from Yale's seafoam eyes.

Yet she should have known . . .

She had been here before; she knew the power of seduction he wielded like a weapon. He had always been able to lure her, with his lips and his hands and his words. Nothing had changed.

And yet . . .

Something *had* changed.

He was different. He was as sensual as he had once been, and he still knew exactly how to touch her, how to send her careening into an earth-shattering climax. But this grown-up Yale was less . . . programmed than he'd once been. She felt as though he was operating on instinct and impulse, where he'd once had a very definite agenda. Her pleasure was no less intense now, but she couldn't help feeling that his own had been more spontaneous this time.

But you've changed, too, she reminded herself. *You've been around the block many times in the past ten years. Your perception of him now, as a grown woman, might be different from what it was when you were eighteen and desperately in love with him.*

Love.

Until this moment, she had proceeded blindly, guided by physical, not emotional, feelings. She had wanted to believe that it was all about passion—about pleasure she had been long denied, in these difficult months since Emmett had died.

But now she had to acknowledge that there was more.

Yes, she cared about Yale Bradigan. It was impossible to hate the man he had become, the man who had helped her in so many ways these past few days. Yes, he was doing so out of a sense of duty, and maybe even out of respect to his brother's memory.

But she admired him for that. It wasn't what she'd have expected from the man she'd seen, only a week ago, as her enemy.

She wondered whether it was her own bitter heart, or Emmett's rancor toward his brother, that had been more responsible for fueling her loathing over these past ten years.

Yes, the man had rejected her as a teenager; true, he might have been responsible for the estrangement with his brother. But those things were a part of the past . . . just as Emmett was. It was over, and Emmett was dead, and now she was alone, except for Emma Rose . . .

And Yale.

Unless he walked out of her life again tomorrow.

All Lexi knew was that she couldn't deny the truth—that she didn't want to let him go.

Six

"Where the hell have you been?"

Yale froze just inside the door of his loft, his eyes fastened on Justine Di Pierro, who loomed before him with her hands on her hips and her dark gaze flashing.

He didn't reply, just looked at her, then finished closing the door behind him. He carried the bulging Sunday *Times,* which he'd just retrieved from his doormat, across the room and put it on the mahogany dining table.

"Yale!"

He glanced up at Justine as he kicked off his shoes, then stooped to pick them up.

"I asked where the hell you've been. It's one o'clock on a Sunday afternoon."

He wondered briefly if she knew he'd been out since yesterday when they'd left together, then dismissed the question as ridiculous.

Of course she knows. You're wearing the same clothes, and she's no fool.

"I have a question for you, Justine," he returned, unstrapping his Tag Hauer watch from around his wrist and tossing it onto the table.

"What?" she asked warily, coming to stand a few feet from him.

She still had on the clothes she'd obviously worn to the party the night before—a black leather miniskirt and navel-baring black top, and sheer black hose and stiletto heels. Her hair was still stiff with spray, and the scent of cigarette smoke and perfume wafted from her. Her eyes were smudged with charcoal liner and mascara, and her complexion, beneath the mask of stale foundation, was pale.

She looks like a dragon lady, Yale thought incredulously—especially when he recalled Lexi as he'd left her, barefoot and wearing an oversized white terrycloth robe, her curls tousled and her face clean-scrubbed.

"I'm wondering what you're doing here, in my apartment, yelling like a shrew," he told Justine. "Unless I'm mistaken, I live here alone and you have an apartment uptown."

"You know damn well that when you gave me the key last year, you said I could come over whenever I wanted. Last night after the party, I thought I'd surprise you. I felt sorry for you, home alone on a Saturday night. But obviously you weren't home, and you certainly weren't lonely. How was your client? Is she a good fuck, Yale?"

He blinked at her choice of words. She might not be the most eloquent woman he'd ever known, but he'd seldom heard Justine raise her voice, let alone speak in coarse language. But she was furious. Rage was evident in her stiff posture; in her gleaming black eyes; in the set of her mouth as she waited for his response.

"As you obviously are aware, Justine, I wasn't with a client. I lied to you yesterday—"

"You bastard—"

"Because I didn't think you'd understand if I told you where I really had to go. But maybe I underestimated you."

"Where were you?" Understanding was the furthest thing from her expression, but at least he had her intrigued. She'd been expecting him to deny the lie, he knew, and now, caught off guard, she had braced herself, waiting for him to explain.

"I was with Lexi Sinclair," he said, and at her blank look, he added, "My brother's fiancée." Which was stretching the truth, since Lexi certainly hadn't been engaged to Emmett. But Justine didn't know that.

Yale knew Justine had little interest in anything that didn't relate directly to her, so she'd probably never paid much attention to what little he had mentioned of Lexi in the past. And she had certainly never laid eyes on Lexi. But that didn't mean she wasn't beside herself with jealousy at the thought of him being with another woman, judging by the way her eyes had narrowed at him.

"Relax, Justine," he said, pulling his wallet and some loose change out of the pocket of his jeans and throwing it onto the table. "She needed help . . . with the baby. My niece," he added pointedly.

"What kind of help?"

"The baby was sick," he said, willing God to forgive him for lying about something like that, "and she didn't have anywhere else to turn. She needed me to take her to the hospital, and then she was afraid to be alone overnight with the baby. So I stayed." The lies slipped effortlessly from him, thanks to years of expertise, and he looked her calmly in the eye as he spoke.

"Why wouldn't you tell me the truth about something like that?" she asked, still looking angry.

"Because lately, I've sensed that you don't trust me, Justine."

She glanced away, looking uncomfortable.

"Anyway," he continued, "I'm the only family Lexi has—"

"You're not family. She wasn't married to your brother yet."

"True, but the baby's still my niece. And I was the only person she could call."

"I thought her parents were at the funeral."

So Justine was sharper than he'd given her credit for being.

"They were," he acknowledged, "but they're out of town."

"So you spent the night with this woman?"

"On her couch," he lied, glad Justine couldn't read his mind and see the images that played there—the memory of Lexi stretched nude in the predawn light that filtered through the windows and over her white iron bed, as he'd explored her body with his fingers and his mouth.

He had lost count of how many times they'd made love, how many times he'd entered her, caught up in renewed passion every time, despite his exhaustion and the warning voices inside his head. They had slept only for an hour or two, drifting off just as the sun had come up, until Emma Rose's insistent cries had roused them.

He looked at Justine, blocking out the memory of the cozy pancake breakfast the three of them had shared in Lexi's kitchen—well, Emma Rose had eaten rice cereal and strained plums while they'd had pancakes, chattering in her highchair and giving Yale delighted smiles every time he caught her eye.

His throat ached suddenly now as he realized that those cherished moments would never be repeated. It was so unfair that he had discovered what he wanted too late. He would never be a part of Lexi's and Emma Rose's lives . . . not the way he wanted to be. Not the way they deserved.

He hadn't told Lexi that.

As he had left, he'd kissed her tenderly, then planted a peck on the baby's dimply cheek.

"Call me later," Lexi had said, "and we'll talk about where to go from here."

For a moment, he'd thought she'd been referring to their relationship. Then he'd realized she was still thinking about the mystery surrounding Emmett's death, which they'd discussed briefly at breakfast.

Yale wished he had never complicated his life by bringing up his suspicions to her. If he hadn't, he wouldn't have seen her after that meeting in the city on Friday, and he wouldn't be half dreading, half looking forward to, the next time they'd be together.

He could have made a clean break, but he'd blown it.

Now he was hopelessly entangled . . . and fully

aware that nothing could come of his newfound feelings for Lexi.

"I'm going upstairs to take a shower," he abruptly informed Justine, and started for the steps leading up to the master bedroom.

"I'll join you," she said promptly, and followed him.

He wanted to tell her to stay away from him, to go home and leave him alone—but he couldn't.

Yale Bradigan had sold his soul to the devil, and he would pay the price for the rest of his life.

On Monday afternoon, bored with the dress department at Barney's, where she was looking for something to wear to her friend Shelby's third wedding, Meredith MacFee decided to pay an unannounced visit to the Bradigan Gallery.

She hopped a cab down Broadway and got out just south of Houston Street. She walked the few blocks over to the familiar brick-fronted building directly across from a trendy new martini bar, tucked between a used bookstore and an ancient vintage clothing boutique. The street was quiet at this hour, except for a bedraggled vagrant who teetered along the curb muttering about the end of the world.

The weather had turned chilly overnight, and now a hint of impending autumn was in the air. As she pulled her black cloak more closely around her, Meredith toyed with the idea of riding up to Windmeadow, her and Russell's estate in northeastern Westchester County, for the coming weekend. The trees would barely have started changing, which meant she could enjoy the country roads without sharing them with the hordes of foliage-seeking urban refugees that would descend by early October.

Yes, and with any luck, Russell would be too busy to accompany her, and Yale would be able to sneak up for a rendezvous.

Smiling at the thought, Meredith stepped into the familiar high-ceilinged space, and her heels made a hollow clicking sound on the polished hardwood floor as she headed briskly toward the back.

Yale stepped out just as she reached the office door, his eyebrows rising slightly at the sight of her.

"Hello, Mr. Bradigan," she said crisply, extending her hand for him to shake as though they were mere business acquaintances.

"You can cut the act, Meredith; I'm here alone," he said, shoving his hands into the pockets of his butter-colored corduroys. With them, he wore an ivory cable-knit sweater, its bulk making him appear even more broad-shouldered than usual.

"In that case," she said, noting the way her voice echoed in the cavernous room, "I'd like a kiss instead."

He obliged, but his peck was perfunctory.

"You call that a kiss?"

"I call this a workday, and a busy one, at that."

She raised an eyebrow and glanced dubiously around the empty gallery.

"I'm up to my scalp in paperwork," he said tersely. "What are you doing here?"

"I tried to call you on Saturday night," she said. "Where were you?"

"Out."

"With whom?"

"Myself," he said, and she could tell by his expression as he looked her serenely and directly in the eye that he was lying.

Yale Bradigan might have been a master in the art of deception, but so was she.

"Really," she said steadily. "And where did you go all by yourself?"

"To dinner. And a movie."

"Oh? Which restaurant, and which movie?"

"Nosy, aren't you?"

"Just curious."

"The Tribeca Grill, and then the revival of *Citizen Kane* that was playing over in the West Village."

She had to admit, it was an ingenious lie on his part. He knew she wouldn't have been out in Tribeca on a Saturday night, and that she didn't really care for current movies, much less classics. She couldn't prove that he hadn't been in either of those places—yet she knew in her gut that he hadn't.

Why was he lying to her?

"Yale," she said, laying a flawlessly French-manicured index finger on his cheek, "I have a sneaking suspicion that you're up to something."

He didn't flinch, and his gaze didn't waver. But then, he was nothing if not imperturbable. That was one of the things that had drawn her to him. He was as icy, inside and out, as she was.

"Why do you say that, Meredith?" he asked, but the moment was interrupted by the street door opening.

They both turned, and Meredith instantly recognized the rotund trench-coated man who stepped into the gallery. He was Franco Di Pierro, Yale's benefactor . . . and future father-in-law.

"And as I was saying, Mr. Bradigan," she said, turning back to Yale, yet conscious of the new-comer's calculating gaze sweeping over her back, "I would appreciate your calling me if you do come across such a painting. My Russell has his heart set on doing something with the wall in our bed-room—our 'love nest,' as he calls it—and I would so love to surprise him for his birthday."

"I'll keep an eye out for you, Mrs. MacFee," he promised, picking up on her cue.

But his light green eyes betrayed an edge that hadn't been there before, and she sensed a new ten-sion emanating from his casual posture.

He was wary of Franco Di Pierro. As well he should be.

"I'll be going, then," Meredith said, buttoning her cloak and turning toward the door. She swept by the visitor with a cordial nod, which he returned. But his attention was focused on Yale.

As Meredith stepped out into the crisp blue and gold September morning once again, she thought, *Tread carefully, Yale. With me, and with him. If you don't, you know exactly what's going to happen.*

Not that she wanted to see any harm come to the man she adored.

But his fate was in his own hands.

He knew that.

And he was fully aware, Meredith knew, that she, like Franco Di Pierro, could be ruthless. She knew his darkest secret, and if she chose to expose it . . .

She just fervently hoped that it wouldn't come to that.

In the sun-splashed nursery, Lexi settled Emma Rose in her crib for a nap and stood looking down at her, over the rail.

The baby, clad in a pink thermal bunny suit that had been a gift from the Sinclairs' next door neighbors, smiled broadly. She didn't look the least bit sleepy now.

"Time for napping," Lexi told her.

Emma Rose raised her little legs, thumping them down hard on the mattress. She opened her mouth to say "gaa," and her pacifier fell out.

"Come on, Em," Lexi said, retrieving it and putting it back in. "It's nap time. Two seconds ago, you were snoozing in my arms."

Emma Rose spit out the pacifier again, squealed, and shimmied excitedly.

Lexi shook her head. "Now you want to play?"

The baby kicked her legs in the air and babbled.

With a sigh, Lexi replaced the pacifier in Emma Rose's mouth and wished she could afford to buy a musical mobile to hang over the crib.

Then she remembered the sizable check she had deposited into her bank account on Friday. Technically, it was supposed to go toward her new business, but . . .

Well, Yale had said to get Emma Rose whatever she needed.

Yale.

The mere thought of him filled Lexi's stomach with darting hummingbirds.

"Go to sleep," she told Emma Rose before slipping out of the room.

She hesitated in the hallway for a moment, then went across to her bedroom. The sheets and quilt were still rumpled. She stood over them, supposing she could make the bed—or change the sheets.

But these were the linens that had been on the bed Saturday night, the ones she and Yale had made love on and tangled themselves in afterward as they'd slept, briefly, in each other's arms.

Last night, when she had gone to bed, she'd caught the scent of his cologne on the sheets. It had wafted around her as she'd tried to fall asleep, reminding her of the passion of the night before.

She had spent all of Sunday wishing she'd been more conscientious about installing a phone, and wondering if he'd have called her if she'd had one.

She had promised him that she'd go into town and call him at the gallery from a pay phone between twelve and one this afternoon. "And if you get the voicemail, that means I'm on the other line," he'd said, "but try back in five minutes. I promise I'll be there, waiting for your call."

They were going to discuss Emmett's death, she knew—try to come up with a strategy to find out more about it.

In the hours since Yale had left Sunday morning, Lexi had tried to focus on Emmett, tried to brainstorm for clues and figure out what could have happened.

But every time she pictured Emmett's face . . .

well, it wasn't his face at all. Because she wasn't
seeing it framed by a long mane of tawny hair, but
by the short, conservative cut that belonged to Yale.
And she wasn't thinking back over the months, trying to remember the things Emmett had said, the
people he had seen, the places he'd gone.

No, she was thinking back as far as a few hours,
recalling the magic Yale had worked on her body.
He had been as magnificent as she remembered,
yet in a different way. His lovemaking had been
less mechanical, and more . . . emotional? Could it
be? Had Yale Bradigan been transformed into someone who actually *cared?*

It was as though this man was somehow a com-
bination of the best parts of both Emmett and Yale.
He had Yale's level-headed responsibility, but Emmett's warmth and passion. And while he had displayed shades of that familiar icy detachment, it had
been far less intimidating than she remembered, and
had melted completely the moment their lips had
met.

Well, you've grown up and changed, Lexi reminded herself. *Maybe Yale did, too.*

Maybe Emmett, too, would have become a mature, responsible person if he'd had the chance.
Maybe his daughter would have transformed him
in the way Lexi had never been able to.

No, she told herself, glancing at the photo of Emmett that sat on her dresser. His hair was shaggy,
falling into light green eyes that were more turbu-
lent than the sea. *No, Emmett was Emmett. He gave
you what he could, and he'd have done the same
for Emma Rose. But it wouldn't have been enough.*

Lexi sighed and reached down to pull the rumpled sheets off her bed. But as she lifted the top one, Yale's scent filled her nostrils once again, and instead of tugging it free from the mattress, she brought it to her face, inhaling deeply.

No matter what Yale had done to her in the past . . .

No matter what she had promised herself about her future . . .

No matter what had happened to Emmett . . .

Nothing changed the fact that Lexi was falling for Yale again, falling hard and fast, the way she had so long ago.

She desperately wanted to believe that this time things would be different.

And she desperately wanted—needed—to obliterate the nagging little doubt in the back of her mind, the one that told her not to get involved again, not to trust him again.

But she couldn't erase it . . .

So she chose to ignore it.

And she left the sheets on the bed.

"That should do it," Franco said, leaning back with a grunt and folding his hands behind his head.

Yale nodded and glanced over the list of figures he'd scribbled on the pad. They had just gone over the fiscal budget for the gallery, at Franco's suggestion.

"What do you think?" Franco watched him from beneath his heavy-lidded dark eyes. He was sitting in the black leather chair beside the desk in Yale's office, the chair that belonged exclusively to him. Yale had never dared sit in it with Franco present; when he wasn't around, Yale had tried it and found it top of the line.

Just like everything about his future father-in-law—his fine Italian leather shoes and custom-made suits; his salon-dyed black hair that betrayed not a hint of gray; his capped white teeth; his lime-scented imported cologne.

Franco Di Pierro was an imposing man; a no-nonsense man whose deadly steel core was barely concealed beneath a genial facade.

"What do I think?" Yale echoed. "I think this will be perfectly satisfactory, Franco."

"Good." The man's eyes gleamed, and he leaned forward and steepled his hands beneath his fleshy chin.

Yale closed the pad and set it aside on his cluttered desk. Tomorrow, Gina, the bookkeeper Franco had hired, would be in, and he would go over the new figures with her.

"How are you treating my princess?" Franco asked suddenly.

Yale's heart collided with his rib cage, and he had to force himself to say steadily, "Like gold, Franco. How else would I treat her?"

"Good." Franco nodded thoughtfully, and Yale's mind raced frantically, wondering if he had somehow found out . . .

"I took her down to the San Genarro festival last night," Yale said.

"She told me."

"She did?" Yale tried not to look alarmed.

Justine had left his loft only at nine this morning, when he'd departed for the gallery. She had been headed in a cab to the midtown ad agency where she worked as a secretary. With rush-hour traffic, she couldn't have arrived there much earlier than nine-thirty. Franco had unexpectedly walked into the gallery just before eleven, and he'd presumably driven all the way from his home in Bensonhurst.

He must have left right after Justine had called him.

What had she told him?

Relax, Yale told himself. Justine might have been suspicious when he'd first arrived home yesterday afternoon, but he'd done more than enough to dispel that.

Hadn't he displayed undivided interest in everything she'd said, even when he was going out of his mind with boredom as she discussed her clothes, her nails, her hair?

Hadn't he taken her downtown to the Italian festival when all he wanted to do was put on sweatpants, sit alone at home, and daydream about Lexi?

Hadn't he fervently made love to her in the shower, and then again last night—even though he'd closed his eyes the whole time, pretending she was someone else; a brown-eyed beauty with silken curls and luscious curves, with a throaty voice that begged him . . .

"Yale," Franco's voice distracted him, and he snapped to attention, "you seem a little . . . distant today."

"Distant?"

The man was watching him intently, and Yale forced a grin, a casual shrug.

"I am distant, Franco," he said, shaking his head. "My mind is somewhere else. I just . . . I can't stop thinking about Justine."

His future father-in-law's eyebrows shot up in a surprised, pleased expression. "Why is that?"

"She and I had a wonderful time together yesterday, and last night . . . and I can't believe the wedding is still so many months away. I can't wait until I can call her my wife."

"In that case, arrangements can be made," Franco told him. "We can move the wedding up a few months—"

"No," Yale said instinctively, then realized his protest had been too quick, too vehement. "No, we can't get married any sooner. There are too many details; Justine would have a fit if she had to rush. She wants everything to be perfect. And I want to marry her on Valentine's Day, the way we planned. It's the most romantic day of the year, Franco."

The man nodded, again looking pleased. "It'll come soon enough, Yale. Then my Teeny will be your bride . . . but she'll still be my baby. *Capisce?*"

Yale nodded. He got the message, had gotten it all along.

If anything ever threatened Justine's happiness . . .

If Yale ever dared to betray her . . .

Franco would have no qualms about making his Teeny a widow.

* * *

Meredith stepped out of the cab in front of her Park Avenue building and wondered what she was going to do with herself for the rest of the day.

She wasn't in the mood for shopping, or visiting, or lunching.

What she *was* in the mood for would have to wait, since Yale was otherwise occupied, and presumably would be for the rest of the workday.

She swept into her building, greeted the doorman, and went up to the duplex she shared with Russell on the twentieth floor.

It was grand, even by Meredith's standards. She had grown up in a townhouse on East Thirty-seventh Street, where her father, a physician, had his offices on the ground floor. Meredith had attended the finest private schools, and had spent weekends and summers at her parents' East Hampton estate, where she'd learned to ride—and to socialize and shop.

She had been a lithe, beautiful girl who was always a little too restless for her own good. She had been smoking and drinking by the time she was twelve and had lost her virginity the following year with her best friend's older brother. Bored with the guys in her crowd, Meredith had fantasized about the long-haired bad boys who hung out in the East Village. She had even slept with a few by the time she'd graduated from high school . . . but most of them were too bleary-eyed and out of it from drugs and alcohol to prove very exciting.

Her mother's heart had been set on Meredith attending her alma mater, Wheaton—an all-girls' college. The next four years had been disappointingly chaste, save the semester she'd spent in Holland.

She had worked as an assistant editor at a fashion magazine when she graduated; her parents had paid the rent on her one-bedroom apartment on Gramercy Park. She dated constantly, and slept around, by her friends' standards. And yet she never met anyone terribly exciting.

She had known Russell MacFee since those East Hampton summers of her teenaged years; his family had a house down the beach from hers. They had never dated, since Russell was Meredith's friend Shelby's boyfriend. But by the time they reached their midtwenties, he and Shelby had long since parted. And one night, Meredith bumped into him at a party and decided he was appealing, in a buttoned-down kind of way.

They had slept together that first night, and it had been surprisingly good. Russell was in law school, but he always made time for Meredith back then. They were engaged by the time he graduated at twenty-eight, and they married a year later.

Now, a decade after that, they had become stereotypes: Russell, the workaholic Manhattan divorce attorney; Meredith, the bored socialite wife. They had everything that money could buy, but nothing that it couldn't.

The maid was dusting the sprawling living room when Meredith walked into the house. "Hello, Mrs. MacFee," she said politely.

"Hello, Joanne. Don't bother doing the den today. I'm going to be spending the afternoon in there."

Meredith deposited her bag and cloak in the foyer closet. In the master bedroom, she swiftly changed into a pair of black leggings and matching turtleneck that clung to her slim figure. She inspected herself in the mirror, decided that she didn't look a day over twenty-five, and then headed straight for the rose-colored room at the back of the apartment.

Once inside, she closed the white-paneled door behind her, then locked it after a second's thought. Not that Joanne was prone to barging in, but Meredith distinctly wanted to be alone with her thoughts of Yale.

She stretched out on the damask sofa and glanced at the painting over the fireplace, with its field of smoky blue and gray swirls. So bland, she'd thought, when Russell had presented her with it, proudly telling her it was a masterpiece by Devin Tremblay.

You call that a masterpiece? she had asked, making a face at it.

But now she was fascinated by the canvas. It was a complex conglomerate of veiled lines and icy tones . . . so very like the man she adored.

So different from his twin brother.

She recalled the first time she had met Emmett Bradigan. He had been twenty-one and free-spirited; she had been thirty and newly married to Russell.

In a cliché that now seemed almost laughable, Russell had hired Emmett to wallpaper the master bedroom and bath. Meredith had been enchanted by the rugged, long-haired young workman, who invariably wore tight jeans and a t-shirt that revealed a muscular upper body.

It hadn't been hard for her to seduce him. She was ripe for pure sex, having discovered that Russell's libido seemed to have waned the moment they'd returned from their honeymoon. Meredith had always had an insatiable hunger when it came to lovemaking. And Emmett had the adventurous panache and the stamina of youth.

The two of them had spent long afternoons making love in the disarray of the master bedroom. In the back of her mind, Meredith supposed she had wanted Russell to walk in and discover them. In those days, she still loved him—or thought she did. She had probably thought that finding her with another man would shake him up enough to revive their marriage.

But that hadn't happened.

For a while, she was happy with her young lover. Long after he'd finished working on the bedroom, they had continued their affair, meeting at his shabby, cluttered Queens apartment and making love on his sagging boxspring and mattress, laughing as it squeaked and groaned beneath their weight.

But eventually, Meredith had grown wistful. Emmett, with his moody good looks and his rebel wardrobe, wasn't the kind of man she could be with forever. He was too impetuous, too irresponsible. He lacked the refinement that went along with money; and that, she realized, was more important to her than she'd ever realized.

If only she could find a man who had Russell's sophistication and debonair attitude toward women; but Emmett's youth and good looks and libido.

She never dreamed that such a man actually existed.

But she found him, the day she showed up at Emmett's apartment unannounced.

Yale had been there, newly graduated from RISD, and fresh from a job interview, clean-cut and wearing a well-cut dark suit.

Meredith had declared to herself, the moment she saw him, that she would have him. But she had been careful not to let on . . . in front of Emmett, that she found his brother captivating.

And Yale hadn't let on, either, when she'd slipped her phone number into his pocket the moment Emmett had turned his head.

He had called her that night, and they had met surreptitiously a few hours later, at an Upper East Side bar that Emmett would never have set foot in.

Now, as Meredith lay on the couch remembering that first long-ago night she and Yale had made love, she felt her body tingling all over. She leaned back against the cushions, closed her eyes, and again felt his strong hands roaming over her naked body, felt his hot, wet tongue gently probing her most secret places.

She squirmed, pressing her bottom into the soft cushions, recalling the things he had done to her.

From that first night, she had been hooked on Yale Bradigan.

He was everything she had always wanted in a man—daring and passionate in bed, yet urbane and conservative everywhere else. Somewhere in the back of her mind, Meredith supposed she had known he was using her, yet she hadn't cared. As long as he was where she wanted him to be, when she wanted him, she could care less about his motives. That was how it had been back then, and that was how it was now.

It had been Meredith who had arranged Yale's first job, as an assistant at a well-known downtown gallery owned by a friend of a friend. He had been an ambitious young man with big dreams of owning a gallery of his own someday; she had promised to do everything she could to help him achieve that goal. In return, she wanted nothing more than his time and attention—and, of course, his exquisitely endowed body.

She ran a hand lightly over her breasts, and felt her nipples tightening beneath the two layers of fabric that separated them from her fingers. She was vaguely aware of heat building between her legs as she thought again of what a magnificent lover Yale was.

He had possessed a startling finesse that went well beyond his years. When she had taken up with him again a few years back, she had wondered whether his bedroom talents had waned in his absence.

They hadn't; not then. But lately, he had been a little too preoccupied for her taste. Granted, he had more than enough reason to be worried about something other than sex . . .

But don't think about that now, she commanded herself. *Think about how he* was . . .

A delicious pressure was building at her core, and when she squeezed her thighs together, it grew more urgent.

Meredith tilted her head up and focused her eyes on the painting over the fireplace.

With one perfectly manicured hand, she lifted the elastic waistband of her cashmere leggings away from her flat belly; with the other, she slid down, down, past the top of her silk panties. She gasped softly at the contact of her icy fingers on the hot, tender flesh that waited, but she rubbed anyway, in a precise rhythm.

She stared at the blue and gray painting, but she was seeing Yale Bradigan, feeling his breath hot and panting against her thighs. Her own stroking hand became his unrelenting tongue.

She quivered, feeling herself nearing release.

Yale . . .

Her breath caught in her throat and her body was racked with a violent, awesome spasm, and then another, and another.

Oh, God, Yale . . .

Meredith lay utterly still when it was over, savoring the brief fulfillment of an appetite that lately seemed more ravenous than ever.

Please, Yale, she thought fiercely, *please don't force me to destroy you. All you have to do is stay with me and make me happy, and I'll keep your secret forever.*

"Hello, Yale?"

"Lexi . . . hi."

She pressed the receiver to her ear and frowned. He didn't sound as excited to hear from her as she had been to call him.

"I'm calling you," she said, trying to quell her uncertainty, "the way you told me to."

"How's Emma Rose?"

"She's fine." She glanced down at the baby, who sat with her legs dangling in the cheap umbrella-style stroller Lexi had bought over the summer for twenty dollars.

"Good. Where are you?"

"At a phone booth in front of the Emerald Palace on Main Street," she said, glancing up at the restaurant and remembering Saturday night, when she and Yale had laughed and kidded around while they were ordering their dinner to go.

Suddenly, it seemed ages ago.

"Listen, I know you're at work, and I won't keep you," Lexi said, and paused, half-expecting him to protest. But he didn't, and her heart sank as she rushed on, "I wanted to tell you that I just came from the phone company, and I made arrangements for a hook-up. It should be on first thing tomorrow. Do you want the number?"

"All right, hang on . . ." There was a shuffling sound, and then he said, "Go ahead."

She gave it to him, then said, "And the other thing is that I thought of something—about Emmett . . ."

"What?" he asked, sounding interested for the first time since he'd picked up the phone.

"There's this friend of his—his name's Joe. Joe Parker, and he bartends downtown, at the Wet Dog Tavern in the Village. I thought I might give him a call and see if he knows anything about Emmett."

"Good idea," Yale said.

Lexi thought he seemed slightly disappointed that she didn't have something more concrete to report.

"I think he'll be able to tell us some things we don't know. I mean, if anyone knows what Emmett was up to, Joe's the one," she said, a bit defensively.

"Good. See what you can find out and then get in touch. I have a customer right now."

She swallowed hard. "Okay."

She hung up after a brief, hollow goodbye.

Emma Rose was grinning up at her, and Lexi mustered a weak smile to give her in return.

What she wanted to do was sob.

It was clear, from Yale's aloof tone, that he didn't care about her, clear that what had happened between them on Saturday night had been nothing more than a casual encounter.

How could you have been so stupid?

How could you have thought it was anything more?

How could you have let yourself fall for him again? Didn't you learn the first time that Yale Bradigan is nothing more than a self-centered, devious lout?

"But he seemed so different," Lexi whispered faintly, oblivious to the traffic on Main Street, and to Emma Rose's delighted babbling.

She had honestly believed he had changed.

And you were obviously wrong, she told herself miserably.

In the back office, Yale hung up the phone and stood up.

He stuck his head out the doorway and peeked around the corner into the empty gallery. Satisfied that he was alone, he returned to his desk and once again lifted the receiver.

His mouth was set grimly as he dialed, then listened to one ring, two rings, three . . .

There was a click, and then a familiar voice said, "Wet Dog Tavern, Joe speaking."

Seven

Lexi flipped onto her stomach and closed her eyes, wanting nothing more than to drift off to sleep. It was well past three in the morning, and Emma Rose would be crying for her bottle in a few short hours.

Sleep, damnit, she commanded herself, and punched the pillow beneath her head.

But she had been trying for hours, tossing and turning in the dark bedroom on the bed where only two nights ago she and Yale Bradigan had made passionate love. It had been a mistake not to change the sheets this morning, but it was too late now. She stored the spare linens on the top shelf in the closet in the nursery, and if she went in and started rummaging around there now, the baby would wake up.

So she was stuck trying to sleep as the lingering remnants of Yale's scent assaulted her nostrils, reminding her of what they had done together—and of what could never be.

Lexi was furious with herself for ever imagining that Yale had changed, and that she might have a future with him.

How could she have forgotten the difficult lesson she had learned at eighteen?

She had spent that summer falling in love with the Golden Boy of Cady's Landing and had been certain he felt the same way. He had wined her and dined her and made love to her every chance he got. Those few months were an awakening, for Lexi, an introduction to a world she'd never realized existed.

Yale made her feel like a woman—not only that, but like *his* woman. For that carefree interlude when he was on break from school, he was attentive and romantic and, after dark when they were alone, lustful.

When September came and he departed for Providence, she had cried.

"Don't, Lex," he had said, wiping her tears from her cheeks as they stood beside his packed Jaguar. "I'll call you tonight, when I get settled. And I'll send you a train ticket to come up and visit me next weekend."

"But what am I going to do until then?"

"Dream of me," he'd said, kissing her gently on the lips, then opening the car door and slipping behind the wheel.

"Yale, do you promise?" she'd asked hurriedly, wanting to clutch his sleeve and beg him not to go.

"Do I promise what?"

"That nothing will change between us?"

He had stared at her for a second, a second she hadn't recognized as ominous. Not then.

Now, looking back, she knew what he must have been thinking.

That she was out of her mind if she thought he, Yale Bradigan, was going to maintain a relationship with a hometown girlfriend when he had dozens of eligible women to chose from at school.

But that day he had merely smiled and said, "Of course nothing will change, Lexi."

"I love you, Yale," she had said as he'd started the motor and pulled away.

She had never known whether he'd heard her or not.

There had been a phone call that night, as he'd promised.

But his end was filled with the background chatter of his roommates' voices and loud music and doors slamming—and hers was filled with silence. She couldn't think of anything to say besides "I miss you," and he couldn't talk, he said, because there was no privacy in his rented apartment.

"I'll call you tomorrow," he'd said cheerfully before hanging up.

"And you'll send me the train ticket, right?"

"Right," he'd promised, but he'd sounded distracted.

The phone call had never come.

The ticket had never come.

He had taken a coward's way out, Lexi thought, bitter even now, after all these years, after all that had happened since.

He had simply shut her out cold, not calling, not writing, not caring. It was easier that way, easier for a man like Yale, who hated emotional scenes.

Still, she hadn't been able to believe, at first, that it was really over, that their passionate romance could actually end that way. Lexi had told herself, in those early days after he'd left for school, that he was simply too busy to get in touch, or that he'd tried to call when no one was home.

But then, after she'd left a half-dozen messages with his roommates, who always sounded amused when she told them her name, she began to realize the truth. Yale wasn't going to call her back, and he wasn't going to invite her to visit him in Providence.

He was gone for good.

He had cast her off without an explanation, the way a child would discard a clingy neighborhood pest.

In the weeks that followed, Lexi had run the gamut of emotions: bewilderment, hope, shame, denial, fury, sadness, resentment, disbelief, disgust . . . and finally just a deep-seated pain that had taken root and dulled her emotions.

The ache had stayed with her for months.

It had been Emmett who had picked up the pieces, who had broken down her walls and taught her to love, to trust, again.

Now he, too, was gone forever, and she was alone.

Not alone, she reminded herself, rolling over to her other side and closing her eyes. *You have Emma Rose, now. She needs you.*

She smiled at the thought of her beautiful baby girl.

For her sake, she would look to the future and forget about Yale.

And for her sake, she would find out what had really happened to Emmett.

On Tuesday afternoon at three o'clock, Justine Di Pierro stuck her head in the door of her boss's office. He was about to shoot a Nerf basketball through the hoop above the window.

"Uh, Marty?" Justine asked, tugging her short red skirt a little lower on her thighs.

He turned and saw her, and grinned. His eyes traveled appreciatively down her body and came to rest on her legs in their sheer black hose.

"Justine. What's up?"

"Here's the rest of that presentation I typed," she said, handing him the document. "I have to leave early today, remember?"

"Oh, right. What was it again . . . a doctor's appointment?"

"Yeah," she lied, and cleared her throat. "So if you don't need me anymore, I'd better get going."

"No problem. Good luck," he said, and she could feel him watching her as she headed for the door.

Marty had been ogling her for a year now, ever since he'd joined the ad agency as a senior account executive. But Justine didn't mind. Not really. She knew she looked good; why wouldn't he notice?

Yale doesn't seem to notice anymore, she told herself, then shoved that troubling thought out of her mind.

Back at her desk in the secretaries' bay, she turned off her computer and grabbed her black leather shoulder bag.

"Where are you off to?" Monique, who sat across from her, asked.

"Doctor appointment," Justine replied with a wink.

"Oh, I forgot all about that. Have fun. I'll cover the phones for you."

"Thanks. See you tomorrow." Justine sailed out to the elevator.

Out on East Forty-Eighth Street, she donned her ubiquitous dark sunglasses and headed toward Fifth Avenue.

Ten minutes later, she was stepping into Mimi Milano.

The bridal salon was one of the most exclusive in the city. Justine had impulsively called for an appointment yesterday morning after leaving Yale's loft, and been told there would be a two-week wait. But all she'd had to do was call her father to remedy that. Franco Di Pierro was always willing to pull a few strings for his baby girl.

So, here she was.

As she walked into the hushed world of white tulle and satin roses, she felt her stomach fluttering in excitement—and maybe something more. Something she didn't want to acknowledge.

"Yes, may I help you?" asked the perfectly coiffed sales assistant, who wore a thousand-dollar fuchsia designer suit with gold buttons.

"My name is Justine Di Pierro, and I have a three-thirty appointment."

"Of course, Ms. Di Pierro. My name is Deirdre, and I'll be assisting you. Let's see . . ." She flipped a page on a pad behind the desk and said, "Your wedding date is Valentine's Day, correct?"

"Correct."

"And who is the lucky bridegroom, and what does he do?"

"His name is Yale Bradigan," Justine said smugly, "and he owns an art gallery downtown."

He's a helluva a catch, she added to herself. *And now he's all mine.*

So why did she feel vaguely concerned? She had been dodging misgivings ever since Sunday afternoon, when Yale had reappeared after spending the night at Lexi Sinclair's house up in Westchester.

Justine wanted to believe that it was platonic.

And he'd certainly gone out of his way to please her on Sunday, making love to her against the slick tile wall in his steamy shower stall, and then again later that night in his king-sized bed.

She had almost dared to think that the old Yale was back . . . the one she had fallen for long before his brother had been killed, long before her father had become involved in the gallery business.

But something had been distinctly different about him yesterday, something she couldn't put her finger on.

And in the back of her mind, a shadow was starting to loom over the fairy-tale wedding she had been planning and envisioning ever since they'd gotten engaged last Christmas.

Don't be ridiculous, she told herself. *He won't back out on you, especially after you've bought the dress. You've already ordered the invitations, and called the caterer . . .*

As if those were the only reasons Yale Bradigan couldn't call off the wedding.

No, Yale was bound to go through with it because his very life depended on it.

So why couldn't Justine seem to relax?

"And you would like to look at our selection of gowns, correct?" Deirdre was asking.

Justine nodded, shifting her mind back to the row of plastic-draped silk and lace confections along the far wall of the salon.

Deirdre went on, "Allow me to remind you that all of them are Mimi Milano originals and are one-of-a-kind creations. Do you know what you have in mind?"

"Yes," Justine said decisively, shoving aside every shred of doubt. "I know exactly what I want. Something dazzling and extravagant . . . something fit for a princess who's marrying the man of her dreams."

And he will marry me, she told herself grimly. *He has no choice.*

Yale saw Meredith before she spotted him. She was seated at a small table toward the back of the bar.

Tonight, she was a brunette, he noticed acidly. Her wig was short and curly, and with it she wore ridiculous dangling earrings and a pair of oversized horn-rimmed spectacles. He happened to know that her vision was twenty-twenty, so the glasses were obviously part of her disguise.

Wondering why she never seemed to feel foolish

darting around town in one crazy get-up or another, he started toward her table.

"Can I help you, sir?" asked the pretty blond hostess, who materialized from her station near the restaurant entrance.

She gave him a smile he recognized as flirtatious, and he was distinctly aware of Meredith shooting daggers in the young woman's direction.

"I'm just meeting someone in the bar, actually," Yale told her. "And I see her right over there. Thank you anyway."

"You're late," Meredith greeted him. "I'm on my second martini."

"You're lucky I managed to meet you at all," he responded, sitting across from her. "I just received several new paintings, and I have a lot of work to do."

"Mmm," she said blandly, sipping her drink.

He ordered an iced tea, and saw Meredith raise an eyebrow.

"Why are you on the wagon tonight?" she asked when the waiter had left.

"I just told you, I have a lot of work to do."

"Oh, let's celebrate. Russell is away on business . . ."

"And . . . ?"

"Oh, for God's sake, Yale, you know what I mean."

He was distinctly irritated with her. The last thing in the world that he wanted to do was spend the night with Meredith MacFee.

And yet there was something pathetic about the way she sat here, looking slightly drunk and wearing that wig that made her look like a throwback to the seventies. When he had recently asked her about the disguises, she had told him they made her feel provocative and daring. It was so *Meredith* of her to say that.

You call more attention to us, if anything, when you're dressed like that, he'd told her.

He glanced around to see if anyone seemed to be noticing them now. The after-work crowd of young professionals at the bar was busy with two-for-one margaritas and the free chicken wing and mini-eggroll buffet. The couple at the next table a few feet away seemed first-date nervous and focused on making what appeared to be a stilted conversation.

"If I must spell it out for you," Meredith said, looking exasperated with his wandering gaze, "you can come back to the apartment with me for the night and make passionate love to every inch of my body."

He couldn't resist asking, "And why would I do that?"

She regarded him narrowly. "Don't play games with me, Yale."

"I'm sorry, Meredith, but you make it so easy."

There was a moment of silence as they locked gazes. Hers, behind those clear glasses, was darkly pensive.

He shifted uncomfortably in his seat and was relieved to see that the waiter was approaching with his iced tea. As soon as he'd departed, Yale squeezed the lemon, took a sip, and looked up again at Meredith.

"Sometimes I wonder," she said slowly, "if you underestimate me, Yale."

"Why is that?"

"You seem to have adopted a rather cavalier attitude toward me lately. It's almost as though you've forgotten that I'm in a position to annihilate you." Her words were matter-of-fact.

He felt a chill slipping down his spine. "And how would you do that?"

"I know your secret, remember?" she said levelly.

He hesitated, took another drink from his glass. The icy liquid made his throat ache.

"Meredith," he said in a low voice, aware that the couple at the next table had run out of conversation and might very well be eavesdropping, "You can't be threatening to tell Justine—or Franco . . ."

"Tell them what?" she asked, feigning innocence with a shrug.

"About us," he hissed. "I know you're not that reckless . . . or that stupid."

She threw her head back and laughed. "Oh, you poor naive darling," she said, shaking her head. "Not *that* secret. Do you think I want to get myself killed along with you?"

He swallowed hard and wished he had ordered liquor after all. "What . . ." he began, and cleared his throat, casting a glance at the next table. He said more quietly, "What secret are you talking about, Meredith?"

"Oh, don't play dumb. You know exactly what I'm talking about, Yale. And you know *exactly* what will happen to you if I chose to betray you."

She leaned toward him, affording him an unobstructed view of her bare breasts inside her low-cut black cashmere top.

"But of course," she went on, "I won't do that. Not as long as you keep me content."

The Wet Dog Tavern was a small dive of a bar, but it was in a prime location in the heart of the Village, on Thompson Street, just off Bleecker.

Lexi had been there a few times with Emmett, but not in over a year. And never in the afternoon.

It was just past two on Wednesday when she got there, and the place was empty except for two tie-dyed NYU types having beers and leaning on the jukebox in the corner.

Lexi immediately spotted Joe Parker, sitting on a stool behind the bar and smoking a cigarette. He was a shaggy-haired, brawny man who had to be around forty. His age and the difficult life he'd led showed in the weary lines around his eyes, though from a distance he didn't look more than twenty-five.

Joe was a real dead head, according to Emmett, having followed the Grateful Dead on tour whenever he had the chance. He still dressed the part, wearing tattered jeans and a long smock-type shirt, and a headband tied around his graying hair.

He had a tattoo of a ball and chain on his forearm. Emmett had once told her Joe had been in and out of prison when he was younger—"nothing serious; small-time con stuff, Lex"—and that he'd gotten the tattoo as a constant reminder that he never wanted to go back there. He was determined, Emmett had said, to live a clean life.

"And he has ever since I've known him," Emmett had said.

Back then, a younger and perhaps more liberal Lexi hadn't been at all bothered by the fact that Emmett's best friend was an excon. Now, thinking of Emma Rose, she felt a twinge of doubt.

And she thought of Yale, who would undoubtedly judge Joe Parker a loser based on his appearance alone.

Well, Yale's nothing but an opinionated snob, she told herself, and was determined to keep an open mind about Joe, just as Emmett had always done.

"Lexi Sinclair!" he called, spotting her and standing. He came around the end of the bar and opened his arms.

"Hello, Joe." The few times they had met, he had been busy working the bar and hadn't said more than a few words to her. But now he greeted her like a long-lost friend, grabbing her in a bear hug.

"You look good," he said, pulling back and studying her.

"Thanks." But she knew she didn't. She hadn't slept very much this week; the makeup she'd applied had made her look pasty and didn't conceal the purplish trenches beneath her eyes.

She was wearing a pair of old black leggings, a snug black turtleneck, and chunky-heeled black boots—all remnants of her pre-motherhood days in New York. But nothing fit the same—the sweater seemed to strain over her maternity-enlarged breasts, and her no-longer flat stomach seemed too rounded for comfort in the clingy stretch pants. The boots still fit the same, yet she rarely wore anything but sneakers these days, and the heels had made her legs ache when she'd walked over from the Astor Place subway stop.

"How's the baby?" Joe asked in his perpetually scratchy voice, motioning for her to take a seat at the bar.

"She's fine . . . my parents are watching her," Lexi replied, climbing onto a stool. She set her black leather shoulder bag next to her and looked at Joe. "How have you been?"

"Couldn't be better," he said, retrieving his half-smoked cigarette from the ashtray behind the bar.

Now that we've totally recapped the telephone conversation we had the other day . . . Lexi thought.

"What can I get you to drink?" he offered. "Want a beer?"

She hesitated. It was too early for that . . . wasn't it?

Oh, what the hell.

"I'll have a Rolling Rock," she told him, thinking that someone like Yale would probably think it was bad form to drink beer in the middle of the afternoon in a seedy bar.

To hell with Yale.

Joe opened two bottles and plunked one down in front of her. He drank from the other, then took a long drag from his cigarette.

She took a sip of the icy beer, then leaned her forearms against the bar. "Look, Joe, I told you I need to talk to you about Emmett—"

"I know, Lexi, and I'll answer whatever questions you have. But I don't see what I can tell you that you wouldn't know yourself. You lived with him."

"I never *lived* with him," she pointed out. "He kept his own place, Joe. He always needed that space, and now I'm wondering why."

Joe shrugged. "He was a private guy."

"Yeah, but why?"

"A lot of people are like that. It doesn't mean they're involved in anything shady."

"No, but Joe, I can't help but think that Emmett might have been. Somebody killed him."

He nodded soberly. "I'm not arguing with you, Lexi."

That took her by surprise. "The other day on the phone, you didn't say you thought he'd been murdered, too."

"There were people sitting right here at the bar in front of me then. I couldn't talk. But now I can," he cast a glance at the two guys in the corner, who were engrossed in a conversation of their own, "and I'll tell you that there's no way Emmett's death was accidental."

She realized that part of her had been expecting Joe to dispel the notion that Emmett had been murdered. Yale's hunch was one thing—he hadn't seen his brother in years, so maybe he was wrong. And Lexi herself had kept wanting to believe that the fire had been an accident.

But Emmett's closest friend had also drawn the conclusion that it was no accident. That meant someone had deliberately stolen her child's father away, had robbed little Emma Rose of the chance to bond with a man who might possibly, after all, have been a good Daddy.

You'll never know what would have happened, Lexi told herself, and felt her loss more acutely than ever.

She thought of what Emmett had said to her the first time she had timidly broached the subject of marriage, well over a year ago.

"Are you crazy? Why would you want to marry a guy like me? Life sure as hell wouldn't be a bed of roses with me, Lexi, and you know it."

She had pressed the matter against her own better judgment, and he had run scared. They had stayed broken up for several months, and Lexi had told herself it was better that way. She had always known Emmett wasn't the marrying type and had never thought she was, either. But as her thirtieth birthday approached, she found herself secretly yearning to settle down—yearning, even, for the kind of lifestyle she had always scorned, for the Brady Bunch world where she'd grown up.

Emmett Bradigan didn't fit that hokey suburban picture, and anyway, she was convinced she'd lost him forever.

But then, on a rainy June evening, she had come home from the night shift at the telemarketing firm where she was working to find Emmett at her apartment.

He hadn't said a word, had simply led her into the bedroom. Candles flickered on every surface, and a sweet fragrance wafted to her nostrils.

"What is that?" she asked, then saw her bed. The

white quilt was strewn with rose petals—thousands of rose petals.

"Maybe I can make your life a bed of roses after all," Emmett had said softly. "I'm not saying I'll get married . . . but I'm lost without you, Lex."

And he had made sweet, sensual love to her. She would never forget the feel of the slippery, silky rose petals against her naked skin, or the way he had stayed inside her afterward, stroking her face and whispering in her ear, telling her how much he had missed her, how glad he was to have her back in his arms.

Nine months later, their daughter had been born—the daughter Lexi had named Emma Rose . . . after her father, and after the magical night when she had been created by two people who were very much in love.

No, there was no way of knowing what would have happened if Emmett hadn't been murdered.

"Who killed him?" she asked Joe, trying to keep the tremor from her voice. She swallowed more beer, felt it simultaneously chilling and warming her insides.

"You tell me, Lexi."

"If I knew, I wouldn't be here. What makes you so sure he was killed?"

"They said the fire started when he passed out, drunk, smoking a cigarette. And I'm *positive* the guy was off cigarettes *and* booze," he replied promptly. "He came in here a lot in the last few months before he died, and never once did he order a beer or bum a bugle from me."

Bugle. That was what Emmett had always called

his cigarettes. Lexi smiled briefly at the bittersweet memory.

"He quit smoking when I did," she told Joe, "because of the baby."

"I know; he told me. He said the smell of smoke made you sick, and he said he couldn't stand to see you like that."

"Emmett said that?"

"Sure. What, you think he wanted you retching your guts out?"

"No, it's just . . ." *It's just that he wasn't very good at showing his concern,* she thought with a pang. She'd never realized that it might really have bothered him to see her heaving over the toilet every morning.

"If he was going to fall off the wagon or start smoking bugles again, Lexi, he'd have done it here. He seemed pretty stressed out those last few months, but he never ordered anything more than a Coke, and like I said, he never lit up. Not when everyone around him was smoking and drinking."

"Why was he so stressed out?"

Joe shrugged. "A baby on the way'll do that."

"It had to be more than that," she said. "I thought he was preoccupied, too, but it didn't seem to have anything to do with the baby. Whenever we talked about that, he seemed to forget whatever was bothering him. And anyway, I saw him feeling the pressure a lot of times *before* the baby was on the way."

"Well . . ." Joe seemed on the verge of saying something else, but he couldn't seem to bring himself to do it.

"What is it? Joe, come on, tell me whatever you're thinking."

"Emmett liked to gamble," he said reluctantly.

She blinked. "You mean like, casinos? Vegas? Or . . . Atlantic City?"

"No. I mean, he had a bookie."

"Oh." Why was she surprised? "You think his death had something to do with that?"

Joe shrugged and stubbed out his cigarette, which he'd smoked down to the filter. "I'm just telling you, he gambled. Big time. And he *lost* big time, too."

"I can't believe I didn't know this," she murmured, shaking her head. Then she thought, *what am I talking about? Of course I didn't know. I didn't know a lot of things about him.*

She had been bracing herself, waiting for Joe to tell her about another woman, or about a secret drug habit. Gambling was mild in comparison . . . unless it had led to his death.

"Lexi," Joe said, in as gentle a tone as his raspy voice would allow, "I'm not saying that Emmett's gambling debts had anything to do with his death. But if I were you, I'd check into it."

"How?"

Again Joe shrugged.

"Do you know who his bookie was?" she asked bluntly.

"Nope." He lit another cigarette.

She looked carefully at him, trying to catch his eye, but he was focused on putting his lighter away and taking a deep drag, then blowing twin streams of smoke through his nostrils.

Something told Lexi he was lying.

"Come on, Joe, who was the bookie?"

"I told you, I don't know." He shifted his gaze restlessly to the two guys standing by the jukebox, then back at her.

There was nothing for her to do but take a last drink of her beer, then stand and pick up her bag. "Thanks for helping me, Joe."

"No problem, Lexi. You just keep me posted, okay?"

"Sure." She waved and left, wondering what he was hiding.

Checking her watch as she paused on the corner of Thompson and Bleecker, she saw that it wasn't even three yet. As long as she was in the city, she had made plans to meet her friend Anita Mangione for drinks. But that wasn't until five, when Anita got out of work.

What was she going to do to kill time for the next two hours?

She could just walk around the Village. She used to love to poke around the shops on Saint Mark's Place.

A thought was forming in the back of her mind. She tried to shove it away, but it was insistent.

Reluctantly she dug through her purse for the business card Yale had given her last Friday.

His gallery was no more than a ten-minute walk from here, if she headed straight down Thompson to SoHo.

So what? That doesn't call for you to drop in on him.

But he'd asked her to tell him what she'd found out from Joe.

And despite her personal unwillingness to get any more deeply involved with Yale than she already was, she had to concentrate on what was important: finding Emmett's killer.

She headed south down Thompson Street.

Meredith sipped the last of her martini—dry, two olives—and stared bleakly out at the deserted street, lost in thought.

"Can I get you another drink?" the bartender asked, suddenly appearing at her table, startling her.

"Oh . . . I suppose. Yes, that would be fine," Meredith told him, then turned back to the window as movement outside caught her eye.

It was nothing but a young couple walking their dog. The woman had a pink streak in her blond hair, and the man had a shaved head. Both were dressed entirely in leather.

Yale, in his conservative Brooks Brothers wardrobe, was so out of place in this neighborhood, Meredith mused. He was out of place in the eclectic SoHo art world, period. Yet he knew exactly what he was doing when it came to his business; the consummate professional, he fit in seamlessly at openings and industry gatherings. She had seen him in action.

Part of what had always drawn her to him was the paradox created by his conservative appearance and level-headed demeanor, and the unconventional career he had chosen. Even Russell had commented, "He looks like one of us, not like one of them"—*them,* of course, being the flamboyant, black turtleneck and wire-rimmed glasses-clad denizens of the downtown scene.

Russell, of course, had no idea that his wife was screwing Yale Bradigan. Not that he was likely to care either way. Their marriage had been "in name only" for years. She suspected he had a mistress of his own, and she was welcome to him . . . provided, of course, that he could get it up at all these days.

Really, Meredith, how coarse of you, she thought, picking up her second martini the moment the waiter had set it down in front of her.

But it was true. Russell had been nearly impotent, where she was concerned, for years. He had told her, on their honeymoon, that there was something wrong with her voracious sexual appetite. He'd also told her there was something wrong with the fact that she had no desire to have children . . . something they'd failed to discuss until their wedding night.

She had to assume that his diminished sexual interest in her was directly related to their failure to see eye to eye on the child issue, since they had happened simultaneously.

"We can have kids," she had told him, "when *you* can lug them in *your* body for almost a year, then squeeze them out through the pinhole in your dick."

He had cringed at her language, then told her that there was nothing to worry about; that pregnancy and childbirth were the most natural things in the world.

"Everyone does it," he'd said.

"Not everyone," she'd shot back. *"I* have no intention of sacrificing my body to be used as an incubator for nine months, then capping it off with excruciating torture to get the thing out of me. And I have no desire to spend the next twenty years raising rug rats."

"We'll get a nanny," Russell had protested.

But she had been adamant. She wondered, occasionally, why he never bothered to end their marriage. But then, why bother? As a divorce lawyer, Russell spent every day immersed in acrimonious settlement battles. Why would he want to wage one of his own?

And anyway, they were compatible on a strictly social and domestic basis. They both disliked movies and the theater—Russell often referred to the entertainment world as "vulgar and boorish." They both loved art, classical music, fine dining, and museums. Their circle of friends was largely made up of the privileged Manhattanites they had known all their lives, many of whom had intermarried, just as the MacFees had.

Yes, life with Russell was comfortable, and Meredith saw no need to rock the boat.

So long as she had Yale.

It sickened her to think she was blackmailing him into being with her, but what option did she have?

She needed him, *had* needed him ever since she'd first become involved with him over a decade ago. Back then, he'd needed her, too—had needed her money, and her praise to feed his ego, and her connections in the art world.

But now she was losing him the way she had the first time, and she had no idea why.

Back then, it had been obvious.

She had, simply put, gotten herself knocked up.

Of course, Emmett had no idea she was seeing Yale, who had made her swear she'd never allow his brother to find out.

She'd had no intention of telling either of them about the baby, but Emmett had found the home pregnancy kit in the wastebasket.

His reaction had been shock—followed by the natural assumption that the child was his, and that she was going to have it.

The latter had infuriated her, and the moment she'd done so much as suggest that she might not go through with the pregnancy, Emmett had informed her that it was his child, too, and that he deserved to be involved in the decision.

"You have no right to tell me what to do with my body!" she'd shrieked at him.

And he'd had the *gall* to argue with her, enraging her so thoroughly that she had spontaneously told him that the baby probably wasn't even his.

"I thought you and Russell don't sleep together anymore," he'd responded, looking startled.

"We don't."

"Then whose . . . ?"

She shouldn't have told him. She didn't know why she had told him. Out of spite for his controlling attitude about her pregnancy, she supposed.

She had always been aware that Emmett would be hurt if he discovered that his brother was sleeping with her behind his back, but never had she imagined the depth of his devastation. The look on his face had been one of disbelief, then of utter pain.

An only child herself, Meredith hadn't comprehended the bond between Yale and Emmett, hadn't realized how deeply they cared about each other—nor how brutal Yale's betrayal had been. Looking back, she had often wondered why Yale had allowed himself to get involved with her in the first place if he cared so much about his brother.

She wanted to think she was simply irresistible, that Yale had been as attracted to her as she was to him. Flattering herself, Meredith had told herself, often, that Yale was, quite obviously, insanely jealous that Emmett had her—a beautiful woman of impeccable breeding and great wealth.

But deep down, she had always known that his reasoning was probably more complicated than she would ever understand. Yale was competitive, ambitious, even ruthless when it came to business. She had seen evidence that he was the same in his personal life. It stood to reason that his identical twin would be both his closest ally and his foremost nemesis.

She had never found out what had happened when Emmett had confronted Yale about his relationship with her, but she could imagine.

The two brothers had never spoken again.

Not to each other.

They had both refused her phone calls. And when she'd lost the baby the day after the scene with Emmett, she'd felt nothing more than relief that the decision had been made for her. The baby wasn't meant to be . . .

And she and Emmett weren't meant to be, either.

Back then, she had struggled to accept the same truth about her relationship with Yale. She had put him out of her mind and moved on, taking other lovers over the years and using them, physically, until she tired of them and discarded them.

But there was never another Yale.

Fate had brought him back to her.

Fate, and Russell. She hadn't been aware, when he'd bought her the Tremblay painting, that Yale was the gallery owner who'd sold it to him. She'd found out only when she and Russell had bumped into him, purely by chance, on Central Park South last year—about six months after he'd given her the painting.

"Yale," Russell had suddenly called at a passerby, and the mention of the name on her husband's lips had instantly caused Meredith's heart to leap.

Surely it can't be the same man, she'd told herself before turning to see who had caught Russell's eye.

It was him.

How Meredith had managed to regain her composure she would never know. But she pasted a cool smile on her lips and greeted him politely, as though she were meeting him for the first time.

He, too, displayed the pleasant detachment with which one might treat a total stranger. But his eyes betrayed the slightest hint of intrigue when his gaze met hers.

It was enough to allow her to find the nerve to show up at his gallery the following morning. To her amazement, Yale hadn't turned her away; nor had he seemed surprised to see her.

No, he had been pleasant, chatting amiably with her the way a person did when he was catching up with an old friend. He told her that he'd realized who Russell was when he'd bought the painting, but of course, hadn't let on. And when she asked, he told her he was alone in the gallery; no, there was no one working in the back office.

"Yale," she had said promptly in a "let's cut the chitchat" tone, "I would love to unbutton those khaki pants of yours, and I'd love to pull them down around your ankles."

He regarded her calmly with those light green eyes of his, and she hadn't been able to read his expression.

So she'd gone on, emboldened by the fact that he hadn't rebuffed her, that his gaze was riveted on her face. "I'd love to reach inside the boxer shorts I know you're wearing. I want to touch you . . . Right here and right now."

"No," he'd said, shaking his head and seeming to snap out of whatever spell he'd been under.

At that, she'd been ready to leave, thinking, *You can't blame a gal for trying.*

But he'd said, in a low voice, "I'll meet you later."

Those words had sent a thrill through Meredith. She had won him back.

Later, she would discover that he and Emmett had never made amends, though Yale made it clear that he didn't want to discuss the past.

She also discovered that he was about to become

engaged, to Justine Di Pierro. She sensed he didn't love her, and pressed him on his motives for the marriage. Naturally he hadn't revealed a thing. It wasn't until much later that she'd pieced together the big picture.

Yale had had the misfortune of having what he'd intended to be a one-night stand with the only daughter of Franco Di Pierro, a key figure in Brooklyn's notorious Volarro crime family. It hadn't taken much digging for Meredith to discover that whatever Franco's baby wanted, she got.

She, like Meredith, wanted Yale.

Her powerful daddy had seen to it that she got him. It didn't take much imagination for Meredith to picture how he had done it.

Meredith knew that Yale owed the career success he had always longed for to his future father-in-law's connections and financial backing as well as to his own business savvy. Franco had become Yale's behind-the-scenes partner in the gallery business, propelling him to the forefront of the Manhattan art world.

After Franco had come on board, Yale's career had skyrocketed. He became known for selling works by well-known modern artists as well as by promising newcomers, all at fair prices.

In payment for achieving his goals as a premier gallery owner, Yale was duty-bound to marry Franco's daughter.

Meredith knew that he didn't love Justine. Nor did he love Meredith. Yale Bradigan loved only himself.

But that didn't mean Meredith was willing to lose him.

She narrowed her eyes, focusing again on the window. Across the street, the familiar brick-fronted gallery was quiet and appeared empty. Inside, she knew, Yale was undoubtedly doing paperwork in his back office. Whenever a customer walked in, he came out and she had a perfect view, through the plate glass front window, of what went on.

So far, Meredith hadn't seen anything out of the ordinary.

But she was certain, based on how preoccupied he'd been lately, that Yale was up to something.

Sooner or later, she would find out what it was.

All she had to do was wait . . .

And watch his every move.

In the back office of the gallery, Yale picked up the file folder marked *Rothman*. Daryl and Bebe, two of his wealthiest customers, had visited the gallery this morning. They wanted something "pastel and seafaring" to hang in the new beach house they'd just bought in Quogue.

He didn't have anything suitable among the paintings he had on hand, but he had promised them that he'd do his best to find it. He scribbled a note, tucked it into the folder, and replaced it in the wooden cabinet beside his desk.

Yale implemented a hands-on business acumen, keeping individualized files on each of his customers. In them, he noted their decor and taste, as well as what kind of pieces they ideally sought. Whenever he came across something that was suitable, he notified the customer, and, invariably, made a sale.

He glanced at the large oil canvas he'd received this morning from a trendy twenty-two-year-old painter whose works were selling rather well. It would be perfect for David Levine, a Staten Island stockbroker who wanted something modern, with browns and blacks, to fit into his paneled study.

Yale opened the second drawer of the cabinet and was about to pull out the folder marked *Levine* when a high-pitched buzzer announced that someone had entered the gallery.

He ran a distracted hand through his hair, shoved his chair back, and stepped out of the office.

"Hello, Yale."

The sight of Lexi Sinclair took his breath away. She looked windblown and her cheeks were red. She was dressed, head-to-toe, in clingy black—a turtleneck that outlined the swell of her breasts and leggings that hugged the curve of her hips and the tiny bulge of her tummy.

Yale remembered all too clearly how he had stripped her clothes away and explored every inch of that extraordinary body of hers, stroking her and tasting her . . .

Don't, he cautioned himself, but he was helpless. He couldn't seem to erase the memory of the stolen interlude they'd shared on Sunday, couldn't even seem to find his voice or think clearly.

"I just saw Joe Parker," she said, walking toward him, apparently oblivious to his flabbergasted state.

"Joe Parker?" he managed to echo.

"Emmett's friend," she told him, coming to a stop a few feet from him. Up close, he could see that her expression was sharp and wintry. "He told me something that I think might interest you."

"What's that?"

She hesitated, looked around.

"It's all right," he assured her. "There's no one else here."

"Emmett might have had a gambling problem," she said succinctly.

"How do you know that?"

"I just told you. I saw his friend Joe. He said Emmett had a bookie, and that he lost regularly. Do you think he could have been in over his head in debt? I know he had an addictive personality—"

Yale snorted at that, and she glared.

"I also know," she continued, "that if he *was* in over his head, there's no way he could have bailed himself out."

"So you think—what?"

"That he might have borrowed money from someone to pay off his debts—namely, a loan shark. But of course, he couldn't pay him off, either, and he got himself killed."

He raised his eyebrows, impressed at her concise conclusion. "You sound pretty sure of yourself, Lexi."

"It makes sense."

"It does." He couldn't seem to shift his mind back to Emmett's murder. All he could think was that he wanted her, all of her, body, heart, and soul.

How could he have thought he could live without her?

Because you have to, he reminded himself. *There are too many reasons why she can never be yours.*

"That's all you have to say?" she was asking him. "That it makes sense?"

"No, I just—" He broke off, shook his head, knowing he had far more to say, but that it didn't matter. Nothing mattered except the fact that he was going to lose Lexi—yet again.

"Let me guess," she said, her jaw rigid and her eyes flashing. "You were just thinking of something else. Like how you wish I hadn't barged in here. Like how you can get rid of me without coming right out and ordering me to leave."

"No, Lexi, you couldn't be further from the truth. I don't want you to leave. I never want you to leave me . . ."

He saw the impact of his words on her face: first disgust, then, as it dawned on her that he was sincere, disbelief.

"What do you mean?" Her voice was almost a whisper.

"I don't want to let you go," he said raggedly, "but I have no choice. Lexi, I want nothing more in the world, at this moment, than to haul you into my arms and tell you that I'll always be there for you."

She shook her head. "Don't lie, Yale," she said, though her eyes betrayed that she wanted desperately to believe him. "You've always had a smooth line. You've always been able to get me right where you want me. You know what buttons to push. But this time—"

"No," he said, reaching out and touching her

sleeve. "Forget about the past, Lexi. I was young then, and I didn't care about anyone but myself. I've changed, and I—"

"What about the other night, then? You took what you wanted, and then you left me, and you had no intention of anything more. When I called you the next day—*because you asked me to,* remember?— you were cold and you all but told me to get out of your life. Are you going to deny that?"

"No."

She blinked.

"I didn't want to get involved with you, Lexi— you're right. But not because I don't care. God," his voice cracked and he cleared his throat. "I care about you more than I've ever cared about anyone."

There was a moment of silence as she surveyed his face.

"Then why . . . ?" she asked, looking bewildered.

"If I get involved with you, we'll both be in danger," he said. "You, and me . . . and Emma Rose."

"What are you talking about, Yale?"

"Lexi, I'm engaged." The words sounded as hollow as he felt.

She looked stricken, then regained her composure. "I'm very happy for you," she said stiffly.

"Don't be. In a few months, I'm going to marry Justine Di Pierro." He said it with significant emphasis and waited to see if the name registered.

"Di Pierro?" she echoed blankly. "Is that supposed to mean something to me?"

He sighed. "Franco Di Pierro is a very prominent member of the Volarro crime family in Brooklyn."

"You're involved with the Mafia." She said it flatly, and shook her head. "Yale—"

"Lexi, believe me, it's not something I was even aware of when I first—*dated* Justine," he told her. "I had no idea who her father was . . . not until it was too late. Now I owe him my career."

"And if you don't marry his daughter . . ."

"That's not an option," Yale said. "I have to marry her. Franco is ruthless. He'll kill me if I don't."

"I see."

"And if he ever got wind that there was someone else . . ."

Lexi nodded.

He watched her intently, wondering what she was thinking.

"Yale," she said finally, "it's best this way— knowing that I *can't* be involved with you, that an affair could be deadly. Because I can never seem to control myself where you—*and* your brother— are concerned. And I always end up getting hurt."

"I don't want to hurt you, Lexi," he said softly. "Ever."

And then he did something that was foolhardy and reckless, yet something he couldn't refrain from doing.

He pulled Lexi into his arms. She gasped a protest in the moment before his lips touched hers, but it was lost as he swept her into a heated, thorough kiss. He poured his every tattered emotion into that kiss, showing her what he felt for her, telling her the things he couldn't say.

When it was over, he released her and saw that

her face was flushed and her eyes were filled with tears.

"You shouldn't have done that," she told him in a strained voice, pressing a fist to her reddened mouth.

"I know . . . oh, God, Lexi, I'm sorry," he said, distraught that he had placed her at risk.

His gaze turned toward the door. What if Franco had walked in on them?

But there was no one there, and the street outside was deserted as well.

"I have to go," she announced, pulling his attention back to her face. She appeared more in control, and her tone was carefully indifferent.

"You should," he agreed, hating himself for what he had done to her, for what could have happened.

"What about Emmett?" she asked.

"What about him?" he responded automatically, before realizing what she meant. "Oh . . . look, we have to talk. But not here, and not now. Not after . . . *that.*"

She nodded. "If you don't want to pursue this, Yale, I can look into it on my own," she said.

"No!" he protested, so forcefully that she looked startled. He softened his voice. "Lexi, he was my brother, for God's sake. And he was murdered. I have a right to investigate what happened. No one will question that. We'll get together and talk about it."

"I don't think that's a good idea."

"If we're only talking, there's no danger," he pointed out. "I promise that's all that will happen. We'll talk. I'll come up to Cady's Landing this weekend. Look, I'll tell Justine all about it, so it'll be out in the open, okay?"

She hesitated. "For Emmett's sake, okay. But, Yale, so help me, if you lay a hand on me—"

"I won't, Lexi," he promised. "I swear."

But it'll be the hardest thing I'll ever do, he added to himself.

"Come on Saturday, then," she told him, and headed for the door.

"I will."

He watched her leave. As soon as the door had shut behind her, he let out a shaky breath.

That had been an incredibly close call. What on earth had possessed him to kiss Lexi here in the gallery, when Franco or Justine or anyone else could have walked in on them?

But it's okay, he reminded himself. *You were lucky this time. Nobody saw.*

Shaking his head, he walked back to the office.

Eight

On Saturday morning, Lexi found herself singing as she straightened up the living room.

She looked at Emma Rose, who was playing with a plastic measuring cup in her bouncy seat, and asked, "What's wrong with me, Em?"

Emma Rose, busy with her makeshift toy, ignored her.

Just like I'm going to ignore any attraction I have for Yale, Lexi promised herself. *And I'm not going to be happy just because he's coming over here today. I know it's not because he wants to see me.*

The news that he was engaged had come as a shock—and, in a sense, as a relief. Now that she knew he was off-limits, it would be easier to resist those old feelings that kept rearing up . . .

If only it were that simple.

Yale wasn't just engaged—he was going to marry a Mafia princess. The implications made Lexi shudder. If he wasn't careful, he'd end up—

The way Emmett had.

She shook her head to block out the morbid thought. She couldn't bear to consider the notion that something might happen to Yale, too.

As for herself and Emma Rose—they'd be fine,

so long as she and Yale kept their relationship strictly platonic.

There was no way Lexi was going to risk her daughter's life by falling in love. Period.

She rearranged the throw pillows on the sagging couch, then brushed some crumbs off the coffee table into her hand. She dumped them into the potted philodendron on the wide windowsill and glanced out to see the familiar black car just turning into the drive.

"He's here, Em," she announced, and told herself that her heart hadn't just fluttered with excitement. No, and she wasn't weak-kneed at the thought of being close to Yale again.

Remember what this visit is about, she commanded herself. *You have to talk about Emmett's death. It's up to the two of you to find out what happened. No more distractions.*

She scooped the baby out of her seat and carried her to the front door.

"Hi," Yale called, taking something out of his trunk. He slammed it shut with his elbow, and saw that he had two large white shopping bags in his hands.

"What's that?" she asked as he walked up to the steps.

"Just some stuff I picked up at F.A.O. Schwarz," he said. "I had a lunch at the Plaza yesterday, and since it's right across the street, I did some shopping for my niece."

"Yale . . ." Lexi shook her head at him as he planted a kiss on Emma Rose's head.

"What?"

"I don't want you to do that."

"Do what? Buy toys for my niece?" He frowned. "Look, Justine picked most of this stuff out."

"Oh." Lexi nodded, trying to act as though the mention of his fiancée hadn't sent her spirits tumbling.

"Over lunch, I told Justine that I was coming up here today—just like I said I would. She's the one who suggested I bring something for the baby."

"Oh," she said again.

"Actually, she wanted to come along and meet you, but she had a bridesmaids' luncheon—her cousin is getting married next weekend."

Lexi nodded, wondering why he was telling her all this. He sounded so casual, as though he and Lexi always chatted about the woman he was going to marry. As though the thought of him with someone else—whether he loved her or not—didn't make Lexi feel sick to her stomach.

As though she wasn't standing here so attracted to him that just being near him made her body tingle in intimate places.

She tried not to let her gaze rest on his full lips, struggled not to remember how they had felt against her own mouth and her naked skin.

She did her best to ignore his broad chest and shoulders and not think of how he had looked bare; all lean, hard flesh and rippling muscles.

She forced her eyes from dropping lower, couldn't let herself recall the exquisite pleasure she had felt the moment he'd entered her, moved inside her and on top of her so that there was nothing but him . . .

"So, why don't we go inside and show Emma Rose what I bought her?" Shattering her erotic daydream, Yale transferred one of the bags to his other hand and opened the door for her.

Lexi stepped inside, and he followed. "The place looks nice," he said, glancing around.

"Thanks. It's kind of bare . . ." She shrugged. "But we'll buy more furniture and stuff for the walls as soon as my business takes off. I've been placing orders for basket supplies with my wholesale place. That's my makeshift home office."

He put the packages on the couch and looked in the direction she was pointing, at the dining room table. It was cluttered with papers and order forms and catalogues. "You need a desk," he observed.

"This is fine for now. We never entertain dinner guests or anything, so . . ."

Emma Rose squirmed in her arms, babbling at Yale.

"Hi, sweetie. Look what Uncle Yale bought for you," he said, rattling the bags.

Lexi knelt on the floor with the baby on her lap, and Yale plopped himself down beside her. Surprised, she realized that she had never seen Yale Bradigan sprawled anywhere, let alone on the floor. He was prone to sitting properly, with both feet on the floor and his posture rigid.

Now he looked utterly comfortable and casual—down-to-earth, even. He was wearing jeans again, this pair a little more broken-in than the brand new ones he'd had on last week. With them, he wore a custard-colored sweatshirt—not a ratty old college one like she was wearing, but, Lexi noticed, a heavy cotton one that bore a Ralph Lauren logo and had to have cost at least a hundred dollars.

So much for down-to-earth.

"Go ahead," he urged, handing Lexi a bag.

Reluctantly, she peered inside. It was filled with gaily wrapped presents.

It took nearly a half hour to work through the piles of gifts Yale had bought. Emma Rose squealed in delight every time Lexi helped her tear into a package, though she seemed far more interested in the crumpled wrapping paper and cardboard boxes than in anything that was inside.

When they were finished, Lexi and Emma Rose had accumulated a pile of dolls and teddy bears and puzzles and plastic toys and blocks and rattles. There was an electronic music machine and a spinning top filled with bright balls and a complete set of toy musical instruments, everything from a tambourine to a drum.

"Yale," Lexi said, shaking her head, "you shouldn't have done this."

"Why not? She's my niece, and she doesn't—"

He cut himself off, and Lexi looked sharply up at him.

"She doesn't what?"

"Nothing."

"She doesn't have anything, is that what you were going to say?"

"No," he said, but she saw him steal a glance at the plastic measuring cup Emma Rose had tossed onto the floor beside the bouncy seat.

Lexi was furious. "You think that my daughter

is destitute, don't you?" she accused, putting the baby in her seat and standing up.

Yale scrambled to his feet, too. "I never said that."

"Then why did you go and buy out the whole toy store for her?"

"Because I can afford to . . . and because I *love* her," he said, and the emotion choking his voice made Lexi freeze.

He loves her.

The knowledge should have touched her, should have warmed her. Instead, she was suddenly, irrationally, consumed by jealousy.

He loves my daughter, but he doesn't love me. He'll never love me.

She swallowed hard over the lump that had risen in her throat.

Yale bent and began picking up the discarded wrappings that were strewn all over the floor.

After a moment, she joined him in silence, and together they gathered all the paper and cardboard into the two white shopping bags.

"I'll put these in the kitchen," Lexi said.

He nodded. "Can I take her out of her seat?"

No, she wanted to say. *No, you can't touch her, and you can't love her, because it's not fair.*

Then, in disgust, she commanded herself to grow up. *How can you begrudge your daughter an uncle who loves her? An uncle who's the only link she'll ever have with her father?*

"Sure," she said quietly, and headed toward the kitchen.

She spent a long time putting the paper into the

recycling bin outside the back door, and then longer
still pouring two glasses of the iced tea she'd made
that morning. She'd even run out to the Food Em-
porium for sugar and a lemon, remembering that
Yale had always liked his tea "sweet and sour," as
he used to say.

Now she painstakingly cut the lemon into wedges,
and she thought about what had just happened.

She decided that she ought to be glad. She should
want Yale to love his niece—

No, I do want him to love her, she argued with
herself. *It's not that.*

She wanted her daughter to have a male role
model. Oh, Lexi's father was around, but he was
getting up there in years, and he was growing increasingly subdued, worrying about Lexi's mother.

She didn't like to think about what lay ahead. It
was going to be tough for all of them.

Emma Rose needed all the family she could get.
And Yale was her family. His Bradigan blood ran
through the baby's veins.

Wistfully, Lexi squeezed a wedge of lemon into
his iced tea, then stuck another on the rim of the
glass.

You're lucky Yale cares about Emma Rose, she
told herself, picking up both glasses and turning
toward the living room. The alternative—his not
caring at all—would be far more cruel.

Besides, she knew better than to think she and
Yale could make a relationship work, even without
his being engaged. She would never trust him again,
not entirely.

She left the kitchen, resolving to put her own

messy feelings aside and concentrate on the real reason for Yale's visit.

"What do you think about what Joe Parker said?" she asked abruptly, returning to the living room and unceremoniously setting the two glasses down on the coffee table.

Yale looked up. He was seated on the couch, holding Emma Rose on his lap.

"I taught her how to say hi," he told Lexi. "I can't believe it. She said hi."

"No, she didn't." Lexi sat cross-legged on the floor opposite him. "She can't talk yet. She's way too young."

"But I kept looking at her and saying hi, and she finally smiled at me and said hi. I swear, Lex, she really—"

"Sometimes she accidentally makes a sound that sounds like a word," Lexi interrupted with a shrug. "She does it all the time."

"Oh." He appeared deflated.

Lexi immediately regretted her attitude, knowing how badly Yale wanted to have made a discovery about his niece; knowing she could have gone along with it, acted as though he really had taught her to say hi.

Her matter-of-fact dismissal had been mean-spirited.

What's the matter with you? she scolded herself.

"But you know, Yale," she said quickly, "she really is going to start talking in a few months. And then she'll be echoing everything you say."

He contemplated that, sitting with the baby's hand

wrapped lovingly around his index finger. Then he
said, "So you think I'll be around in a few months?"

What was that supposed to mean, Lexi wondered.
Was he implying that he was going to play the love
'em and leave 'em routine with her daughter, the
way he had with her?

"No," she said tersely. "I think you're going to
forget all about her. I think you're going to get married and move on and never look back, and I—"

"Whoa, Lexi, hang on there. I wasn't asking if
you thought I'd still care about the baby. Of course
I will. I won't hurt her. I promise you that."

I don't make promises . . .

No, Lexi told herself, Emmett was the one who
had said that—not Yale.

Yale had never made promises, either, not back
when Lexi was young and in love with him and
desperately longing to hear him promise he'd always be there for her.

Just as she'd later longed for Emmett to vow the
same thing.

The Bradigan men didn't make promises unless
they could keep them.

Now Yale was promising to be there for her
daughter.

And if he said it, then he had every intention of
doing it.

She shoved aside the nagging thought that she
had sworn she'd never trust him again.

"What I meant, Lexi, was—are you going to let
me be a part of her life?" Yale asked, watching her
closely. "You kept insisting that you didn't want me
around."

"I changed my mind."

"Why?" He was watching her carefully, bouncing the baby slightly on his knee.

"Because I can tell that you care about her," she said honestly. "And you're the only family she has on her father's side."

"I thought that didn't matter to you."

"Well, it does," she said, lifting her chin.

He watched her for a moment, then shook his head. "You know, Lexi, you could make life a lot easier on yourself if you wouldn't be so damn prickly about everything. Lighten up."

. His words provoked her, and she was about to spit out a retort when she saw that he was grinning at her.

She couldn't help grinning back. "I guess I have been kind of cranky," she admitted.

"Cranky? You? Of course not," he said, and she had to laugh at his expression.

"Okay, I'll be nice. I promise."

"Nice? Hey, I wouldn't want you to change that drastically," he said in a teasing tone.

Emma Rose looked at the expression on his face and giggled.

"What are you laughing at?" Yale asked her, jiggling his knee. The baby squealed with delight.

For a few minutes, he played with Emma Rose. Lexi watched as he tickled her and lifted her high over his head, making airplane noises. The baby laughed so hard she couldn't catch her breath, and Yale finally lowered her and said, "Okay, simmer down, little girl."

He cuddled her against the soft cotton sweatshirt

that covered his chest, and within moments, Emma Rose's eyelids were fluttering closed.

He looked expectantly at Lexi. "Do you want me to put her upstairs in her crib?"

"You can if you want to."

"Can I just hold her and let her sleep on me for a little while?"

She eyed her daughter, contentedly cradled in Yale's strong arms. "Sure," she said, and chased away the first thought that entered her mind . . .

You lucky kid.

But it was useless to keep longing for what could never be.

Useless to think that Yale might make a good father someday.

It won't be to Emma Rose, she told herself firmly.

"Yale, we have to talk about Emmett," she said, getting back on track.

He nodded soberly, his eyes clouding over. "Tell me everything Joe Parker told you."

"I already told you most of it."

"Tell me again."

So she did.

And he appeared to be listening, but he didn't seem thrown by anything she said. It was almost as though he had mentally drifted behind that familiar wall of detachment.

She found herself wondering, not for the first time, why he was so eager to solve the mystery of his brother's death. After all, he and Emmett had been virtual strangers over the past decade.

"What do you think?" she asked when she was

finished and he sat there, absently stroking the sleeping baby's head.

"I don't know."

"You don't know . . . what?"

"I don't know whether it was the gambling that got him in trouble."

"Well, don't you think we should find out?"

"You're getting all irritated with me again," he observed with a calmness that made her even more annoyed.

"Well, you're the one who brought up the fact that Emmett might have been murdered in the first place," she pointed out, struggling to sound unruffled, "and now you're just sitting there not saying anything, like you want me to magically solve the mystery."

"I'm absorbing everything you said. This isn't a cut-and-dried Nancy Drew case, Lexi. My brother was a complicated man. He traveled in rough circles, and he was probably involved in a lot of shady things you didn't know about."

"Well, whatever I knew about him was far more than you did." She hated herself for sounding so spiteful. "You didn't bother with him for years, and now that he's gone, you're feeling guilty, so you—"

"I *don't* feel guilty," Yale cut in. "What happened between my brother and me was complicated, Lexi. And no, I didn't bother with him for years. But in the end, he was still my brother—my twin. Part of me. And I have to find out what happened to him."

She stared at his stoic face, wondering why he could never let go and show the emotion he had to feel inside.

"Okay. Let's not get into what happened between you and Yale. I know you're not going to tell me."

"Maybe I should tell you."

She blinked.

"It was over a woman," he said, looking down at Emma Rose's peaceful little face.

"You fought over a woman?" Her mind whirled. Could it have been over *her?* She remembered that Emmett had said he had spotted her first, had pointed her out to Yale. Then Yale had moved in and stolen her away.

Maybe that was why neither brother had ever been able to commit himself to loving her. Maybe they both had too much guilt over their rivalry to—

"She was a wealthy married woman," Yale said, and Lexi's wandering mind slammed to a halt.

"Her name . . . well, her name doesn't matter," Yale went on, seemingly unaware of what she had been thinking. "But she was beautiful and sexy and worldly, and she seduced my brother when he was twenty-two. I think she liked that he was rough around the edges . . . for a while. Then she got tired of him."

"And she dumped him for you."

Yale shrugged. "She didn't dump him. She kept seeing him, kept sleeping with him. And with me. I knew about him. He didn't know about me. It was a low-down thing for me to do."

"Why did you?"

He didn't answer right away. Lexi wondered about the nameless, faceless woman who had had such an impact on both Emmett and Yale that they had forsaken each other because of her. What magical power had she possessed that Lexi herself didn't?

"It's pretty simple, I suppose," Yale said finally. "Money, power, and lust. She had the first two, and we shared the last."

Lexi nodded, trying to shut out the vision of Yale, naked and entangled with a strange woman, doing things to her that Lexi wanted to think only the two of them had shared.

And Emmett, too, had been captivated by this woman.

If he was twenty-two at the time, that made it only a year or so before he'd become involved with Lexi.

Had he been on the rebound?

She thought back to the night she had turned twenty-one, the legal age for drinking. Her friends had taken her out to Pappy's, a popular Irish pub in Cady's Landing. After drinking one vodka-and-tonic after another, she had found herself glancing up to see Yale watching her from the other end of the bar.

Her heart skipped a beat, and in her alcohol-fogged mind, she had wildly thought that she still loved him.

But then she had seen that his golden hair fell past his neck and he wore a black leather jacket. And the glint in his light green eyes told her that it wasn't Yale, after all.

It was his twin brother, Emmett.

Emmett, the rebel.

Lexi knew what the people of Cady's Landing thought of him. Local gossips had a field day with the motorcycle-riding, hard-drinking, brooding rogue. Emmett had been branded a troublemaker early in life, thanks to his sharp tongue and cocky grin.

And Lexi knew what his twin brother thought of him. Yale had never made any pretense where his brother was concerned. He loved him, but he was disappointed that he had barely gotten through high school and had dropped out of college. He supported himself doing handyman jobs and spent most of his nights partying. And, Yale had scoffed, he was under the delusion that he was going to become a great writer—a joke, because Emmett had never applied himself to anything in his life.

That night in the pub, Lexi thought about what Yale had said about Emmett, and what Yale had done to her, and she made up her mind on the spot.

She was going to get Emmett Bradigan to spite his brother.

She hadn't bargained on falling in love with him.

Now, she wondered again why he had been so willing that long-ago night. Was he on the rebound from the married woman who had betrayed him? Was he, too, trying to spite Yale?

"How did Emmett find out about you and . . . that woman?" she asked Yale.

"She got pregnant," he said grimly. "He accidentally discovered that she was and assumed the baby was his. She told him it might be mine."

Lexi flinched, knowing what that must have done to Emmett. He had always been so competitive with Yale, had always been aware that Yale had succeeded wherever he had failed.

"He confronted me," Yale went on, his tone wooden, "and I didn't know what to say. He kept telling me to deny it. I couldn't. He—we fought. Physically. He jumped on me and started beating on me, and I gave it right back to him. Finally, we broke it off and stormed off in opposite directions."

"And you never spoke to each other again?"

"No." Yale shook his head and met her gaze. "We never did."

"You never thought, even once, that you should have made a move to patch things up?"

"Of course I thought it."

She kept her composure though she wanted to lash out at him again, saying quietly, "But you were waiting for Emmett to approach you first."

"I didn't say that," Yale told her.

"Then what? It was up to you to apologize, Yale. You're the one who betrayed him."

There was a long silence, her words hanging in the air between them.

She waited for Yale to turn into his old sardonic self, to argue with her, to tell her to mind her own business . . .

None of those things would have surprised her.

What he said next, with his head bowed, did.

"You're right, Lexi. I should have. I don't know why I didn't. And now it's too late. I've lost my brother forever."

When he looked up at her, she was startled to see tears and sorrow in his green eyes.

Before she could stop herself, she was beside him on the couch, gently touching his hand. "I m sorry," she said.

"So am I. I miss him, Lex."

No one in the world felt Emmett's loss as acutely as she did. But, Lexi realized, as she stared at the stark loneliness on his face, Yale shared her grief. In the end, it didn't matter that he and Emmett had been estranged for a decade. He had lost a part of himself, his other half.

He cleared his throat hoarsely, and Lexi realized that his eyes were still locked on hers. She felt powerless to break the connection.

The only sound in the room was the baby's soft cooing as she slept in Yale's arms.

Mesmerized, Lexi saw Yale's face moving closer, saw his mouth parting slightly. A shiver of anticipation slid through her. She heard a hushed whispering sound and realized, just before he kissed her, that a sigh had escaped her.

His lips met hers gently, and Lexi was lost in the sweet sensation, in the magic that had always lingered between them.

She reached up to caress his face, and he shifted closer to her, deepening the kiss.

The baby stirred on his lap then, breaking the spell instantly.

Lexi pulled back and gasped, realizing what they were doing. "My God," she said, standing and backing away from the couch. "We can't do this."

"Lexi—"

"Please," she said, and held out her arms. "Just give me Emma Rose. She . . . she needs to take her nap."

He nodded and handed the baby, who was now

whimpering, over. "Lexi, I didn't mean for this to happen. It just—"

"You have to go."

"I know." He stood. "But . . . are you all right?"

"I'm *fine,*" she said sharply. "Just, please, get out of here."

She avoided his gaze, afraid of what she might see there—and of what her own eyes might betray.

"I'm going," he said, taking his keys out of the pocket of his jeans. "I'll see you, then, Lex," he said, and bent toward the baby.

Lexi flinched and cradled her closer.

Startled, Yale glanced up at her. "I just wanted to kiss her goodbye."

"Just go."

"All right, then . . ."

She didn't watch him leave, just stared down at Emma Rose, comforting her, quieting her, rocking her back to sleep.

A moment later, the door had slammed behind him.

Emma Rose jumped, immediately opening her mouth in a pitiful cry.

"It's all right, sweetheart," Lexi said, rocking the baby in her arms.

But it wasn't.

She should have known better than to see Yale again, for any reason. Instead, she had overestimated her willpower and underestimated the strength of her feelings for him. How easy it had been to become caught up in his spell once again, wanting him so desperately she had forgotten that she was risking her very life, and her daughter's.

One thing was certain.

She was never going to see Yale Bradigan again.

She heard his car start, and wandered back to the living room to watch him drive away. She put Emma Rose over her shoulder and patted her back, but her daughter continued to weep inconsolably.

"It's all right, Em, it's okay. You're all right," Lexi said over and over, stroking her fine baby hair.

As the sleek black Lexus headed out through the twin stone columns at the entrance to the driveway, it was all she could do not to burst into tears herself.

She swallowed hard over the lump that had formed in her throat and was about to turn away from the window when she heard a sound that made her stop.

A car had started up somewhere nearby . . . which was odd, because the Worths, who owned the estate, were out of the country until the first of October, and the caretakers didn't come on weekends.

Lexi frowned and leaned closer to the window just in time to see a silver Mercedes come barreling out of the thicket of bushes that edged the property directly across the road. It took off speeding in the same direction Yale had gone, and Lexi glimpsed a flash of a woman's red hair and dark glasses behind the wheel.

Was she tailing Yale?

Lexi glanced at the bushes where the car had been. There was no reason for anyone to park there. The land belonged to Abercrombie Stables, which was situated on vast acreage that included wooded trails and open meadows and a creek. The main buildings were on the opposite side of the property, nowhere near here.

Whoever had been driving that car was obviously following Yale.

All the windows in her house were open and the screens were on. It wouldn't have been difficult for someone to creep up to the place and eavesdrop on her conversation with Yale.

Before that eerie realization could sink in, another disturbing thought struck Lexi.

The windows weren't that high off the ground. Anyone standing outside could have seen in . . . and witnessed them kissing.

Lexi's first thought was that she had to call Yale and tell him what had happened.

Then she remembered the vow she had made only moments before.

Should she keep the woman in the Mercedes to herself?

What if Yale's in danger?

If he was, it was his problem, she told herself stoically. She couldn't get involved and put herself at risk, too. She had a baby to worry about.

But you're already involved, she reminded herself. Whoever was spying on Yale had followed him here and knew where she lived.

Lexi put Emma Rose down in her seat and was immediately met by a squawked protest.

"Just a minute, Em," she said, and turned back to the window.

She lowered it and secured the latch Yale had installed just last week. Then she did the same with the rest of the windows on the first floor, all the while telling herself that she was being paranoid, that she was letting her imagination run away with her, that she and Emma Rose were perfectly safe.

But deep inside was the helpless realization that it probably wasn't true. They might very well be in danger.

And Lexi had no idea what to do about it.

"Just think, the next shower will be for you, Justine!" trilled Taffeta Martinelli, who was Justine's favorite among the "cousins" she had known all her life.

Justine and her mother were seated at a card table in the smoky church basement recreation room with Taffy and her mother, Donna. The shower was almost over, thank God. It was the last place Justine wanted to be this afternoon.

"That's right, Teeny," Carmella Di Pierro said, patting her daughter's arm. "You'll be the next bride. Just a few more months and we'll be doing this for you."

Justine nodded and pretended to concentrate on Angela, who was exclaiming over the automatic bread making machine she had just unwrapped.

"Have you picked out your gown yet?" Taffy asked, nibbling on a round white Italian almond candy she'd plucked from the fluted paper cup on the table. She was always talking about how she was on a diet, but she ate more than anyone Justine knew. Everything about Taffy was big and round—her stomach and her face, even her brown eyes that perpetually looked surprised.

"Actually," Justine told her, "I just ordered it from Mimi's this week."

"You mean you're getting your dress from Mimi Milano?" Gloria, another cousin who was seated at the next table, poked her head over Taffy's shoulder and raised her plucked eyebrows. "It must have cost a fortune."

"You know Franco," Carmella said with a shrug. "He doesn't mind. Not when it comes to his Teeny."

"He'd buy you Princess Di's wedding dress if you wanted it," Gloria said enviously. Her father, Uncle Carl, was such a tightwad that his nickname was Carlo the Scrooge.

"A lot of luck it brought Princess Di," Taffy commented with a grin.

"Never borrow a wedding gown from someone whose marriage didn't take," Donna agreed. "You can wear mine, Taffy, since Santo and me are so happy."

"Ma, what's up with you? How come you have such a thing about your wedding gown?" Taffy rolled her eyes. Everyone knew she had been named after the fabric her mother had worn on her wedding day. Donna had always been a little strange, but Justine liked her.

"Because the day I married your father was the happiest day of my life," Donna told Taffy. "I wish you would find someone wonderful to marry, like Angela did. And like Justine did."

"How am I supposed to land someone like Yale Bradigan?" Taffy retorted, looking down in dismay at her roly-poly figure stuffed into a gold lamé dress. She dropped the handful of candy she was holding into the paper cup and pushed it out of reach.

"You're so lucky, Justine," Gloria said wistfully.

Aunt Donna nodded. "I hope you're as happy with Yale as I am with my Santo."

So do I, Justine thought. But she wasn't so sure. She couldn't imagine Yale calling her by a cute nickname the way Uncle Santo called Aunt Donna "Duckie Dear." And she couldn't imagine him playfully grabbing her butt or asking her to rub his feet, the way Uncle Santo always did with Aunt Donna.

"What's Mr. Wonderful doing with himself today?" Taffy asked Justine, starting to reach again for the candy, then pulling her hand back as if she'd just remembered her diet.

"Why?" It came out more sharply than Justine had intended.

"Just curious, that's all," Taffy said with a shrug. "Why? Sore subject?"

"Of course not. He's visiting his niece up in Westchester."

Carmella's eyebrows went up. "I thought he didn't have any family."

"He doesn't, really, now that his brother's gone." Justine hadn't bothered to tell her about Yale's hospitalized alcoholic mother.

"What brother? What happened to him?" Aunt Donna asked.

"He was killed in a fire," Justine said shortly. "Back in March."

"So he has family other than the brother?" Carmella asked again.

"He just has this niece—his brother's kid."

"The brother was married?"

"No, Ma, it's an illegitimate kid. She lives with her mother up in Cady's Landing, and Yale went to visit her."

"How come?" Taffy asked, as Carmella's eyebrows rose up even further, but she didn't say anything.

"Why wouldn't he want to visit his niece?" Justine asked. It was what she'd been telling herself ever since yesterday afternoon, when Yale had told her about it over lunch at the Plaza.

She had tried to take it in stride; had even suggested going over to F.A.O. Schwarz to buy presents for the kid. Yale had suggested that she come along, and when she'd reminded him she had Angie's shower, he had seemed surprised.

But Justine found herself wondering . . .

What if he'd purposefully picked Saturday to visit because he knew she had other plans?

What if . . .

Oh, Lord, what if Yale was involved with Lexi, his niece's mother?

She couldn't help remembering the fleeting look that had crossed his face when he'd mentioned her name. It had been sort of . . . wistful.

Was Yale cheating on Justine with his dead brother's girlfriend?

Nah. He wouldn't be that stupid.

Would he?

"Justine?"

She blinked. "Yeah?"

"What are you, on another planet? I've been talking to you for like, fifteen minutes," Taffy said.

"Don't exaggerate, Taffeta," Aunt Donna chided.

"Okay, two minutes. I was asking you if you're going back to Angie's after the shower to look at the gifts."

"I'm looking at them now."

"I mean, close up."

"No, thanks. I have stuff to do later," she replied succinctly, watching Angela hold up a dual-control electric blanket for everyone to see.

"Like what?" Taffy wanted to know.

Justine shrugged. She wasn't about to say, *Like figure out what the hell my fiancé is up to.*

But that was exactly what she had in mind.

The first thing Yale did when he walked into the loft was check the answering machine.

According to the digital display, there was one message.

Who could it be?

Lexi, he thought, as he pressed the play button and heard the tape whir as it rewound. *Please let it be Lexi.*

All the way home, he had been haunted by the image of her face, of how right it had felt to kiss her. He knew he couldn't have her, that it would be best to sever his connection to her. Yet he couldn't help longing to hear her voice.

Still, the call was far more likely to have come from Justine. Or from Meredith, who had been making herself scarce all week, for some reason.

There was a beep, and the message played back.

"Yale, this is Franco. I just got my hands on another Edward Parker Rand landscape for you. Call me when you get in."

That was all.

Yale frowned. He didn't feel like talking to Franco about business. He wouldn't care if he never laid eyes on another painting again. The same went for his future father-in-law . . . and his future bride.

If only Yale could take Lexi and Emma Rose and whisk them off someplace where the three of them could be together.

But that was impossible. There was no place they could go where Franco wouldn't eventually find him. He could never live a life where he always had to look over his shoulder. And he couldn't bear the thought of anything happenings to Lexi or Emma Rose.

Barring a miracle, he was going to marry Justine and spend the rest of his life with her . . .

And wondering what it might have been like if he had been able to marry the only woman he had ever loved.

Meredith tossed her horseshoe-shaped Tiffany key ring on the marble-topped foyer table and started briskly toward the bedroom.

"Meredith? Is that you?"

"Russell!" She stopped short as he poked his head out of the study. "What are you doing home?"

"I live here, remember?" He was impeccably dressed, as usual, in navy chinos, a pressed white oxford shirt, and tassel loafers. He had a pen tucked behind his ear and he wore his glasses instead of his contacts, which he did only when he was busy working at home.

Meredith tried not to look disappointed to see him. "I thought you were spending the weekend in East Hampton with your mother."

Or so he had claimed.

"She came down with a bug," Russell replied, running a distracted hand through his short, pale blond hair.

Meredith considered that. Her mother-in-law, a notorious hypochondriac, was always coming down with something, so that wouldn't be surprising. On the other hand, she had suspected that Russell was really sneaking away for a weekend with his mistress, whoever she was. Maybe she was the one who'd come down with something.

"I thought you were spending the weekend up at Windmeadow," Russell said in turn.

"I was going to, but . . ." *But I'm too busy stalking my lover, who's involved with another woman.*

I just spent the last two hours stuck in traffic on the Hutchinson Parkway, wondering about the beautiful brunette I saw him with, first kissing at the gallery the other day, and now at that shabby little house in the country.

"Anyway," Russell went on, not waiting for her to finish her sentence, "I just made a distressing discovery."

"What's that?"

"The Devin Tremblay has been stolen. I haven't even had time to call the police yet."

For a moment, Meredith didn't have a clue what he was talking about. Then she realized—the painting. She had never connected it with the artist; only with Yale.

"It hasn't been stolen," she told Russell, her mind racing. He was so rarely at home; he spent little time in the study when he was. She hadn't thought he'd notice it was missing.

"It hasn't been stolen? What are you talking about? Where is it?" he demanded.

"I brought it to John Treadwell."

Russell frowned at her mention of the renowned art expert. "Why?"

"I wanted him to take a look at it."

"For what reason?"

Meredith studied him for a long moment. Then, on a whim, and because she couldn't come up with an alternative, she decided to tell him the truth.

"Because," she said evenly, looking her husband in the eye. "I have reason to believe that the painting is a fake."

Nine

"Lexi!"

She had just stepped inside the door of El Rio Grande restaurant off Third Avenue when she heard someone calling her. She turned and saw Anita Mangione waving at her from the bar. The place was still populated by a waning Monday midtown lunch crowd, and she had to elbow her way over.

"Hi," she said breathlessly when she reached Anita, who gave her an affectionate squeeze. "Sorry I'm late."

"No problem." Anita grinned. "But I just ordered my second margarita, so I might not be able to carry on much of a conversation by the time our food comes."

During the ten minute wait for a table, Lexi sipped a Dos Equis beer, flashed new photos of Emma Rose, and caught up on gossip with her friend.

She had met Anita, who was a secretary for a public relations firm, during a long-term temp assignment three years earlier. Lexi had been instantly drawn to Anita; everyone was.

She had the looks of a model, thanks to her high cheekbones and luminous chocolate-colored eyes, svelte six-foot figure, flawless ebony skin, and short, chic black hair. She was the kind of friend who would listen sympathetically to your problems, and make her own few foibles into funny, self-deprecating stories. She was happily married to Dominic Mangione, a dashing Italian businessman, and they lived in a rent-controlled duplex in Chelsea that had a fireplace, a garden, *and* a balcony.

Lexi often teased Anita that she lived a charmed life, to which Anita always replied, "Girl, my first twenty-five years were hell. I deserve a little bliss."

When they were seated and had ordered, Anita said, "So tell me, Lexi, what really brings you into the city so soon after last week's visit? I know it's not just to have lunch with me—not that I'm not delightful company and all that."

Lexi smiled, then said, "Actually, I just spent the last three hours hiking all over the Upper West Side, dropping in on all of Emmett's old haunts."

"What old haunts?"

"You know, that billiard hall on Amsterdam, and a few bars, and two coffee places where he used to go listen to poetry readings all the time." Lexi reached for a tortilla chip and dunked it into the guacamole the waiter had brought.

"And you were looking for . . . ?"

"Some kind of clue," she said around a crunchy mouthful.

Last week when they had met for drinks, Lexi had told Anita that Yale suspected Emmett had been murdered. Anita, who had long known the saga of Lexi and the Bradigan brothers, had been wary. Not just because Lexi was poking her nose into possible danger, but because she was entangled with Yale again.

"Did you find anything?" Anita asked, stirring the melting lime-colored slush in her salted glass.

"No. Except that everyone I spoke to mentioned that Emmett had seemed a little preoccupied lately. And that no one had seen him light a cigarette or order anything stronger than a Mountain Dew."

Anita contemplated that. "What's your next step?"

"More of the same. This afternoon I'm going downtown. There are a few bars and restaurants in the Village and SoHo that I want to check out."

"Are you going to see Yale?"

"No."

"Good."

Lexi raised her eyebrows. "Why do you look so relieved?"

"Lex, he's trouble. You've said it yourself for as long as I've known you. And I don't care what you tell me, people don't change their entire nature in the course of a few years."

"You're right," Lexi told her, nodding. "They don't, and Yale certainly didn't. Even if he had, it wouldn't matter, because getting involved with him could be deadly."

"What?"

Lexi filled her in about Justine and her Mafia daddy.

"You have to stay away. Don't think you're strong enough to resist him, girlfriend," Anita told her. "When I was married to Jermaine, I knew he was dirt. But no matter how badly he treated me, he had this ability to turn around and sweet-talk me until the day I filed for divorce and refused to see him ever again."

Lexi nodded, familiar with the details of Anita's disastrous first marriage to an abusive womanizer.

"Stay away from Yale, Lexi," Anita said. "He's trouble."

"I know, and I intend to. But I have to find out what happened to Emmett. I need some kind of closure, I guess."

The waiter appeared, bearing two plates laden with succulent Mexican food.

For the next half hour, Lexi tried to concentrate on eating and on Anita's cheerful chatter. But she kept picturing Yale's face, even as Anita's warning echoed in her mind.

Stay away from him . . . he's trouble.

And she knew it was true.

But it didn't erase the memory of the man who had cuddled her daughter, awed by her sweet innocence. Or the man who had tenderly made love to her in the darkest hours of the morning, bringing her back to life after months of dull loneliness.

That man was someone she could trust.

Someone she could love.

"Okay, Meredith, what is it?" Yale set the beer he'd just bought down on the table and unceremoniously plopped himself down across from her. They were in a Houlihan's on Fifth Avenue. Though the place was virtually deserted in the middle of the afternoon, he had found her in disguise and

tucked away in a secluded booth, sipping her ubiquitous martini.

"Is that how you greet me?" She didn't look surprised, though. No, there was something different
about Meredith today. He had heard it in her voice
when she'd called to ask him to meet her, and now
he saw it in her face.

She was masquerading as what she had once
called a Florida babe—a tanned blond bombshell.
She wore a long, curly flaxen wig, and her face
was unnaturally sun-kissed for autumn in the Northeast, apparently thanks to a liberal coating of bronz-
ing gel. Her clothing was pastel—a peach sweater
and pale yellow pants—and she wore lots of gold
jewelry.

"Tell me whatever it is you have to tell me, as
long as it's so important you had to drag me away
from the gallery in the middle of a busy afternoon."

She made a face at that, and he bristled. "I told
you, Meredith, I'm in the middle of setting up a
sculpture exhibit, and I've had browsers all day,
and—"

"I think once I've told you what I have to say,
you'll agree that it couldn't wait, Yale."

He nodded impatiently. "Go ahead."

"First of all, on a hunch, I took the painting that
Russell bought from you last year to an art expert."

A faint warning bell went off in his mind.
"And . . . ?" He prodded.

"And, Yale, it's a fake."

The words slammed into him like a rolling piano.
He stared at her.

"You look stunned," she observed, resting her

chin on her hand and regarding him across the table. "Hmmm. I wonder . . . Is this one of your carefully staged deceptions, or is your surprise authentic?"

"Meredith, I had no idea that the Tremblay was a fake." His mind was whirling.

She pursed her lips. "The way I see it, if my painting is not authentic, chances are that a lot of others in your gallery aren't, either. And if that's the case . . . you're a fraud."

"Meredith—"

"I just wonder," she mused thoughtfully, "if you're an unwitting pawn in your future father-in-law's game."

Her allusion to Franco sent a chill down Yale's spine. "Of course I'm unwitting, Meredith," he said, trying to stay calm. "You can't think I *knew*—"

"I know you well enough to be fully aware that you're capable of a scam like this, Yale. Ever since the first day I met you, when you were nothing more than a kid, really, you have been greedy and cutthroat and self-absorbed. And now you're entangled with a woman whose father makes you look like a philanthropist. If he dangled an opportunity in front of you—the chance to become wealthy and successful, even if it wasn't by scrupulous means—well, I have a hard time imagining that you wouldn't have taken it."

"How *dare* you insinuate that I'm in on this, you—"

"Ah-ah-ah, I'd watch my mouth if I were you, Yale," she said with maddening aplomb. "This isn't the only dirt I have on you. In fact, this is nothing."

He bit back a curse and forced himself to sit back

in his chair, to regard her with renewed composure. "What is it that you hope to achieve, Meredith?"

"It's simple," she said. "I want you."

"You have me."

"No, I don't. I never did. I have your body to screw when you feel horny, and I have your company when I drag you to see me, but I don't have you."

"You know about Justine, Meredith," he said in a barely controlled tone.

"I'm not talking about Justine."

He stared at her, wondering if she could possibly know about Lexi. But that was impossible . . .

"Even before there was Justine, I never had you, Yale," she said after a moment, her expression cryptic. "You were using me ten years ago, for my money and my connections and for sex, because I was far more experienced than the college girls you were used to. But I suspect that the main reason you used me was because you knew your brother had me. And whatever Emmett had, you wanted. The same went for him. It was some sick childhood competition."

"No, it wasn't," he said, though he knew she was right. "I cared about you then, and I do now."

She laughed.

He set his mouth grimly. "You know that things are complicated now. You're married—"

"In name, yes. You know Russell means nothing to me. You know I'd leave him without looking back if you could ever detach yourself from your lifestyle and come away with me. We could live in Europe. Or the Caribbean."

"I'm getting married," he continued, as though she hadn't spoken. "I give you what I can—"

"Lately, you give me nothing. Ever since your brother—you've kept your distance. Not that I blamed you."

"Thank you for having the grace to allow me to grieve—"

"Grieve?" she echoed, bobbing an incredulous brow at him.

He wanted to slap that look off her face. Instead, he took a long swallow of his beer, then wiped his mouth with his sleeve.

She raised an eyebrow. "How crass of you, darling," she commented, gesturing at the wet spot on the cuff of his white dress shirt.

"Damn it, Meredith, will you stop with that attitude? I'm upset. We're talking about my brother, who happens to have died."

"Not *died,* Yale," she said, wearing a smirk. "He was murdered, my dear. And *you,* if you'll recall the unfortunate details, happen to be the one who killed him."

The Purple Cat was a small café on Lafayette just north of Houston Street. Lexi had been there several times with Emmett. He loved the eclectic decor and the cozy wrought-iron tables and the blues music playing in the background.

As she stepped over the threshold, she was struck by a sudden, overwhelming longing for him, and a wave of grief so unexpected and intense that tears sprang to her eyes.

She wanted him back desperately, yearned to see that devilish grin of his and that lazy, sexy gleam in his eye. She longed to smell his special Emmett scent of leather and smoke and his own musky essence. She ached to run her hand along his stubbly cheek—he'd always hated to shave—and tangle her fingers in his untamed mane.

Oh, God, what am I doing, going on without him? she wondered frantically, as she hesitated in the doorway.

The desolate feeling had been building all day, growing particularly acute in the few hours since she'd left Anita. She wanted to release the strained throbbing in her throat, to let out an anguished sob.

But somehow, she managed to get hold of herself. She reminded herself that he was gone forever, and that he hadn't been perfect.

That always helped—thinking of the hard times. And there had been many.

He was immature and selfish, she thought, *and messy, and irresponsible, and unreliable . . .*

And he would have been long gone by now, anyway, even if he had lived.

She looked around the café. Most of the tables had lone occupants, mainly students or arty types who were immersed in books or newspapers. There was a hand-holding couple in one corner, and a frazzled-looking mother with an infant who was sobbing on her shoulder.

Suddenly, all Lexi wanted to do was go home to her daughter and forget about solving the mystery of Emmett's death. What did it matter? she wondered wearily. He was gone, and nothing was going to change that.

She contemplated leaving right now and catching

a rush-hour train back up to Westchester. She had told her parents she wouldn't be back to get Emma Rose until later tonight, but they'd probably be glad to see her earlier.

Kathleen had looked more ill than usual this morning, and Scott's eyes had been lined with concern. Lexi knew it couldn't be easy on either of them, caring for a baby all day, but they had told her to take her time and get all her errands done.

Of course, they had no idea what she was really doing in the city today. She had told them she was ordering supplies for her basket business, feeling guilty for lying, but what else could she do? She certainly wasn't going to worry them with the news that she had taken it upon herself to investigate a possible homicide.

"You can just sit anywhere," called a jeans-clad waitress, who had noticed Lexi standing just inside the doorway of the café.

She hesitated only a moment longer, then headed for a table. After all, she was already here. She might as well order—not that she drank coffee these days, but she could use something hot and soothing—and ask her round of questions.

Then she would go home and forget all about Emmett.

And Yale, who haunted her thoughts even more relentlessly.

"Can I help you?" asked the waitress, flipping her brown braid over her shoulder and pulling a pad out of the apron around her slim hips.

"I'll just have a cup of decaf," she said.

"Hazelnut or regular?"

"Hazelnut. And I need to ask you some questions. Have you been working here a while?"

"Yeah."

"Would you possibly recognize someone who came in here last winter and spring?"

"Whoa, I haven't been here that long. Just a month."

Lexi sighed. Apparently, in this transient business and neighborhood, more than a week or two was considered "a while."

"You know who you need to talk to?" the girl asked. "Lenny."

"Lenny?"

"The owner. He's *always* here."

Lexi looked around. "Where is he now?"

"He ran across the street to get cigarettes. But as soon as he comes back, I'll have him come talk to you. What are you, a detective or something?"

"Or something."

The girl didn't press her, just said, "Cool," and left to get her coffee.

A moment later, the door opened and a man walked in. He was youngish, dressed in baggy flannel and denim, with a frizzy black ponytail and round gold-rimmed glasses. Judging by the hard pack of Marlboros in his hand and the purposeful way he strode toward the kitchen, Lexi sensed that he was Lenny.

Sure enough, a moment later he had returned, tailed by the waitress. They both stopped in front of her table. "Tess said you need to speak with me," he said, indicating the girl, who set a cup of

coffee in front of Lexi, smiled, and turned toward
a newcomer at a nearby table.

"I had a few questions," Lexi told Lenny. "Do
you have a second?"

"Yeah, sure." He sat across from her and took
out a cigarette. He lit it without asking if she
minded, and puffed on it. Marlboro had been Emmett's brand, Lexi remembered, and the smell of
the smoke threatened to trigger another bout of sor-
rowful nostalgia.

She reached for her bag and turned her attention
to Lenny. "Are you here all the time?"

"All the time."

"So you might recognize someone who had come
in here before?"

"I recognize you."

"You do?" She had only been there a few times.

"Sure. You were here with that blond guy . . ."

"Right . . ."

". . . the one with the identical twin brother."

Her heart skipped a beat. "How do you know
about that?"

"Because the two of them were here together a
couple of times last winter."

"Are you feeling all right, Bunny?" Justine asked,
regarding Yale carefully.

"I'm fine."

She shrugged and bent her fingers toward her
palm, studying the fresh tomato-colored manicure
she'd gotten during her lunch hour this afternoon.

Yale sat beside her on the couch, pretending to

read *Art News*. She knew he was pretending because he hadn't turned a page in over half an hour, since she'd arrived at his apartment. He seemed to be staring blankly at the page, stewing about something.

Justine sighed and checked her watch. Nearly seven-thirty. "Do you want to go get dinner now?"

"I told you, I'm not really hungry."

"That was a while ago," she pointed out. "I thought you might be ready now."

"I'm not."

She started to chew her lower lip, then remembered her lipstick and stopped. "Well, maybe I should just go home."

He shrugged and she wondered if he'd heard her. "Yale?"

"Hmm?"

"Do you want me to go home?"

"If you want to."

"Of course I don't," she said, exasperated. "We were supposed to be going out to a romantic dinner tonight, remember? You promised. Then, when I showed up here, you looked surprised to see me, like you'd forgotten all about it. Now what's your problem?"

"I'm sorry, Justine," he said, blinking as though he'd just snapped out of it. "I'm just not . . . feeling great."

"Are you sick?" She reached out and laid her hand across his forehead.

He grimaced.

She frowned.

"Your hand is cold," he said.

Her fingernails appeared blood-red against his skin. "You look pale," she observed. "But you don't feel hot."

"Maybe I should just go to bed."

She turned her bottom lip under in a pout.

He didn't seem to notice, so she said pointedly, "I was really looking forward to dinner tonight."

"Okay, fine. Let's go," he said abruptly, tossing the magazine aside and standing up. He tucked his starched white shirt more snugly into his light-weight wool dress pants.

"You have a stain on your cuff," Justine said, grabbing for his wrist to show him.

He flinched as though she'd reached out to slap him.

"God, what's wrong with you, Yale?" She studied his face. "You look terrible."

"I told you, I feel terrible."

She watched him for a moment, trying to ignore the voices in her head. The ones that were urging her to go ahead and do it. Go ahead and confront him with the suspicion that had been eating away at her since last week, the one she shoved aside every time it nagged at her consciousness.

When ignoring it didn't work, she had tried to disprove it, looking for evidence at every turn that she was wrong. But she could no longer ignore the facts. She couldn't go on denying the truth.

Not when Yale's cold indifference was staring her in the face.

Not when he recoiled whenever she reached out to touch him.

"Does the way you feel have anything to do with the woman you've been seeing?"

She caught the shocked, guilty expression that darted into his eyes before he could wipe it away.

"Woman?" he echoed, frowning, as though he hadn't the faintest idea who or what she was talking about.

Dismayed, Justine realized she had hit pay dirt.

How dare he lie to me? she raged inside. *How dare he see another woman?*

She glared at him. "Don't play dumb with me, Yale."

"What do you mean? I don't know what you're talking about."

"Yes, you do. It's written all over your face."

And it was, she thought, staring at him. He was doing his best to appear innocent, but she'd caught him off guard. A flicker of guilt edged into his eyes before he looked away from her.

Justine burst into tears. "How could you?"

"How could I what? Justine . . ."

She felt his hands on her shoulders and shoved him away. "Don't touch me. How could you betray me like this?"

"I haven't betrayed you, Justine. I haven't done anything. I don't know what you're talking about."

"Yes, you do," she sobbed. "You've been so strange lately . . . for the past few months. I should have guessed sooner . . ."

"Guessed what?"

"And then, when you didn't want me to come with you to Europe in July—"

"I needed to be alone after my brother—"

"I should have known . . ."

"Known *what?*"

He was doing his best to sound confused and act innocent, but Justine saw right through it. She was on the right track. She had never seen him this way. He was thoroughly rattled.

Well, he should be.

"Daddy isn't going to like this," she told him, sniffling and wiping at her eyes.

He froze.

Good.

"Justine, what are you talking about?" Yale asked in a low voice.

"I'm talking about my father. When I tell him that you've betrayed me—"

"I *haven't* betrayed you!"

"You're lying!" she screamed at him. "You don't love me, and you don't want to marry me. You're going along with it only because of my father—because he's done you favors, helped you get your business off the ground. But once he hears what you've done—"

"I haven't done anything! Justine, be reasonable."

She laughed in his face. "I am being reasonable, for the first time since I met you. I don't want a man who doesn't want me."

"Of course I want you. I'm going to marry you. I love you, Justine."

Too little, too late, she thought, and shook her head.

"No, you aren't going to marry me," she said

calmly, though deep inside, her heart and soul were writhing in pain. "You'd have to be alive for that."

The phone started ringing as soon as Lexi had put the sleeping baby down in her crib.

The sudden shrill sound startled Lexi, who gasped, and woke Emma Rose, who screwed up her round little face as though she was going to burst into tears.

"Oh, no, no, sweetie, it's all right," Lexi said, grabbing the pacifier and popping it into her daughter's mouth. Emma Rose promptly closed her eyes again and sucked contentedly.

Lexi hurried down the stairs as the phone rang a third time. It had to be her parents. She had realized, as she was driving home from their house, that she had forgotten the diaper bag there.

It was no wonder. She had been completely distracted ever since her conversation with Lenny at the Purple Cat Café.

"Hello?" she said breathlessly, snatching the phone up in the middle of the fourth ring.

"Lexi!"

Yale's deep voice charged into her. She jumped and dropped the receiver as though she'd been electrocuted.

She could hear him calling her name as the phone dangled from its cord, banging against the table leg.

With trembling hands, she retrieved it. She was about to hang it up when she heard him call out, "Lexi, please, whatever you do, you have to listen to what I have to say."

She hesitated, then put the receiver to her ear and said, "I don't want to talk to you."

"Please, Lexi, it's life or death."

He sounded desperate.

Her heart strained, and she fought the urge to ask him what was wrong, whether he was all right. Despite everything, she had feelings for him . . .

Feelings that refused to be shattered.

But she couldn't let him trap her again, couldn't let him win her over with his charm, couldn't let him use her own helpless attraction against her.

The truth was that Yale Bradigan was a selfish, conniving monster.

And he had lied to her.

Lenny had told her that he'd seen both Emmett and Yale in the café several times in January and February. He identified Emmett from a photo Lexi carried in her wallet, and he swore, over and over, that yes, he was certain he'd seen Emmett with someone who looked exactly like him. He'd even said that the other brother was the total opposite in appearance—short hair, business clothes, conservative, polished.

"He acted like a snob," Lenny had said, when Lexi kept pumping him for information.

A snob. That was Yale, all right.

Lenny had said that the brothers had met there several times, and appeared to be going over some kind of papers. More than once, they had seemed to be arguing. And no, he had never been able to overhear anything they'd said.

Lexi had left the café in a daze. Why had Yale lied about seeing Emmett? And Emmett had kept it from her, too. What was going on? Why had the two brothers been in contact?

She had to uncover their secrets.

She had to face the likelihood that Emmett's death was somehow connected to those mysterious meetings with Yale.

She didn't want to consider the notion that he might have had something to do with Emmett's death.

Not only did it fill her with horror, it didn't make sense. After all, he was the one who had brought up the subject to Lexi, who had suggested that they investigate it. Why would he have done that if he was involved somehow?

One thing was certain . . . until she found out exactly what had happened, she couldn't trust him.

"Lexi?" he said in her ear. "Are you still there? Lex, please, you have to hear me out. I have to tell you something important about—"

"No," she cut him off curtly, and hung up the phone.

A moment later, as she sat there hugging herself, a fist clamped over her trembling mouth, it rang again.

Upstairs, she heard the baby wake with a startled cry.

"Damn you," she cursed Yale, and grabbed the receiver. She held it for only a second before slamming it down to break the connection.

Then she quickly lifted it again, heard the dial tone, and left it off the hook.

*T*ε*n*

Justine was about to open the door to Yale's apartment with her key Tuesday morning, but thought
better of it. She knocked, and as she waited, again
rehearsed the speech she had prepared.

*I'm sorry I threatened you on Saturday. I have
no intention of telling Daddy what happened. I
should have listened when you said you haven't
cheated on me.*

It was what she desperately wanted to believe.
She had spent the night convincing herself that she
should believe him. He was going to be her husband; didn't that mean she needed to learn to trust
him?

If he said nothing had happened, Justine decided,
then nothing had happened.

She would forget their confrontation and move
on.

The alternative was out of the question.

Part of Justine loved and respected her father for
his fiercely protective nature. Part of her feared
what he was willing to do on her behalf.

If she told Franco she suspected Yale had cheated
on her, he would have Yale killed, just like that.

She knew it, and Yale knew it.

The bottom line was, no matter what Yale had done, Justine loved him. She couldn't stand the thought of losing him.

She had chosen to believe him.

She knocked again, wondering if he was still asleep. It wasn't even seven o'clock yet. She hadn't slept all night, and had gotten dressed and hopped into a cab as soon as it was light.

She waited, then looked down at the key in her hand. If he was home, the chain would be on.

Of course he's home, she told herself. *Where else would he be at this hour?*

After a moment's consideration, she inserted the key into the lock and turned it. She pushed on the door, fully expecting it to be jerked to a halt by the chain.

But the door swung open, and there was no chain, and there was no Yale inside.

His keys weren't hanging on their hook in the hall, which meant he was out.

Maybe he just went to get the paper, Justine told herself, then remembered the *Times* she had stepped over on his doormat.

Maybe he wanted coffee or a bagel from the deli.

She hurried up the stairs to the master bedroom and saw that his bed didn't appear to have been slept in.

But she didn't want to believe he hadn't been home all night. She didn't want to think that he might have gone to *her,* that right at this moment, he might be lying naked in her arms, sleeping, or worse . . .

He just went out to get coffee, Justine told herself

again, ignoring the fact that he always kept gourmet coffee on hand and that he wouldn't have left the paper lying in front of his door if he'd gone out.

She returned to the first floor and settled down on his couch to wait.

Lexi's hands shook as she pulled the sheaf of light blue cellophane up over the handle of the white wicker basket. She fastened it with a teddy-bear-patterned bow she had made earlier, fumbling with the coated wire as she wound it around the bunched plastic wrap.

"There," she said aloud, holding the basket up to show Emma Rose, who was lying on a quilt on the dining room floor. "What do you think, sweetie?"

Emma Rose smiled up at her, then raised her arms to be picked up.

"Not yet, Em. Mommy's busy right now."

She had been working on the baskets all morning, filling them with sample items she had bought last week at Caldor's. She was planning to bring the finished samples around to local hospital gift shops tomorrow. She had done three of them now—two with get well themes, and the one she'd just completed for a newborn boy.

She had expected the work to keep her distracted so she wouldn't think about Yale. But while her hands were busy, her mind was, too, spinning with wild speculation.

More than once, she'd been tempted to call him, to confront him with what she'd discovered yesterday.

But she always stopped herself, knowing any contact with him would be dangerous.

She was just reaching for the next basket, a natural wicker one interwoven with pink ribbon, when a knock at the front door made her jump.

Frantically, she wondered if it was Yale.

She couldn't answer it.

But the car was in the driveway. He would know she was home.

What if he came around the side of the house and saw her through the windows?

She would hide.

"Come on, Em," she whispered, stooping and picking up the baby.

She crouched and ran into the kitchen, and looked around in a panic. If he came to the back door, he would see her through the window.

Where could she go?

She heard footsteps coming around the side of the house.

She was trapped.

Her heart pounded wildly in her ears, and the baby squirmed in her arms, whining a protest.

"Shhh, Em," Lexi whispered, ducking against the side of the refrigerator, which was just out of the line of vision from the door. "Stay quiet, sweetie."

A shadow fell across the kitchen floor, and there was a knock.

Oh, Lord. What if he broke in? What if he—

"Lexi?"

She cried out in relief.

It was her father.

"Daddy," she called, and came around the refrigerator. She hurried to the door and saw him frowning at her through the glass.

"Where were you?" he demanded, stepping into the kitchen. "I was getting worried."

"I . . . I was busy with the baby. I couldn't get to the door right away."

"The whole house is shut up tight as a drum," Scott said, pointing to the closed windows. "It's eighty degrees outside. Why don't you open it up? The windows are screened, right?"

"Yeah, I just didn't think of it." Lexi shrugged. The baby squirmed in her arms and babbled at her grandfather, who seemed to notice her for the first time.

"Hi, honey, he said, holding out his arms. "Come and see Gramps."

Lexi handed Emma Rose over and busied herself at the sink with her back to her father so he wouldn't see how badly shaken she was.

"So what's up, Dad?" she asked, running the water.

"I just came to see if you're all right. Your mother has been trying to call you since last night. You left the diaper bag at our house."

"Oh, I . . ." Lexi had forgotten all about it. She turned and noticed that it was draped over her father's shoulder. He balanced Emma Rose on his hip and handed it to her.

"Thanks," she said, putting it on the counter. She turned back to the sink.

"When your mother couldn't get through last night, we figured you were on the line with someone, and we gave up and went to bed. But this morning she started trying at seven, and it's been busy, so—"

As he was speaking, he had stepped into the dining room. He cut himself off suddenly, and Lexi realized he must have spotted the receiver still dangling from its cord in the hallway.

"Why has the phone been off the hook, Lexi?" Scott asked.

"I just . . . I needed to concentrate on work," she said lamely. "I've been really busy trying to get these baskets done."

He said nothing, and she turned to look at him. He met her gaze sternly.

"Something's wrong, isn't it?"

"No, Dad, everything's fine." She turned back to the sink again.

"No, it isn't. When you came back last night, I could tell you were upset. What happened in the city yesterday?"

"Nothing."

"Does it have something to do with Yale Bradigan?"

Startled, she glanced at him. "Why would you say that?"

"Just a hunch. And it looks like I'm right. Stay away from him, Lexi. I never liked him. He's the kind of guy you can't trust as far as you can throw."

She was surprised by the vehemence in her father's voice. Scott Sinclair was a genial type who liked almost everyone. Yet Lexi thought of him as an excellent judge of character. On the rare occasions when he was turned off by someone, there was usually good reason.

Never before had Scott voiced any kind of opinion on Yale. The fact that he was doing so now chilled her to the core.

What if Yale really had been involved in Emmett's death? Could he possibly be capable of . . .

Murder?

No. Yale couldn't have killed his own brother. He couldn't have killed anyone.

Then why are you afraid of him? she argued with herself.

I'm not. I'm afraid of whatever it is that he's hiding.

I'm afraid of the fact that he would blatantly lie. To me.

"Lexi?" her father prodded.

"Don't worry about Yale, Dad. He's not a part of my life." *Any more.*

"Good."

"How's Mom?"

Scott's expression clouded over. "Not so good. She's been in a lot of pain."

Lexi nodded, her heart twisting in anguish at the thought of her mother suffering. "Can't they do anything for her?" she asked. "Give her some medication, or something?"

Her father shrugged. "She goes back to the doctor tomorrow. We'll see."

"It'll be all right, Dad," Lexi said, and he nodded, though they both knew the words couldn't have been further from the truth.

It would never be all right again, not where her mother was concerned.

She wondered how much time Kathleen had left.

The mere thought of losing her tore into Lexi's gut, made her feel sick.

She watched her father, saw the way he was absently stroking Emma Rose's hair, knew what he was thinking. That he didn't know what he was going to do, how he was going to go on without his wife.

Lexi thought of the hollow ache that had grown inside her since Emmett had died, thought of all the things she would never be able to share with him, all the times when she had needed him, over the past five months, and he hadn't been there.

She couldn't imagine anything in life that could hurt more than losing someone you loved.

When does it get easier? she wondered. *When do you start living again?*

Involuntarily, she conjured the image of Yale, of how he made her feel every time he kissed her, of the rapture she had known when he'd made love to her after so many months of her being untouched and alone.

No, she warned herself, *you can't think that he's the answer, that he can make you miss Emmett any less.*

She realized then that maybe it wasn't Yale she was drawn to; maybe it was just that she longed for someone, anyone, to fill the gaping hole Emmett had left behind.

Her father exhaled heavily, a dark, melancholy sigh that told Lexi he was well aware of what lay ahead.

She wanted to comfort him, but there was nothing to say. She couldn't reassure him that the pain would fade with time, not when her own hadn't. If anything, it seemed to have grown more intense.

Oh, Emmett, she thought wistfully, *what I wouldn't give to have you back . . .*

But it was no use wasting her time wishing for the impossible.

Emmett was yesterday.

She had to concentrate on getting to tomorrow without him.

And, she reminded herself firmly, without Yale.

At a little past three on Tuesday afternoon, Meredith arrived at the familiar gallery just off Spring Street.

She had taken a cab right to the door today; the weather was too oppressive and muggy for her to walk over from Broadway, as she usually did. It was unusually warm for this time of year, and the sky was a gauzy gray color that seemed to be shielding something ominous.

A storm is definitely brewing, Meredith thought, as she crossed the sidewalk to the gallery door. According to this morning's *Times,* Hurricane Helga, which had tormented the Florida panhandle over the weekend, was supposedly making its way up the East Coast, bringing nasty weather toward New York.

She pulled the knob and found the door locked. That was strange. Frowning, she peered through the glass and saw that the place looked deserted. The track lighting in the high ceiling was turned off, and the office in back looked dark, too.

Where was Yale?

The place was always open at this hour on a weekday.

Meredith slowly turned away, puzzled. She thought back to yesterday afternoon, when she'd left him after their chat at Houlihan's. He had grown subdued the moment she'd brought up his brother.

She had been fully prepared to have him confront her, telling her she had no proof that connected him to Emmett's murder.

Then she would have laughed in his face.

Did he think she was foolish enough not to have secretly taped the conversation they'd had back in March, when she'd convinced him, subtly of course, that he had to get rid of Emmett?

Not that she wanted to use it.

That, or the information she had discovered about the painting being a fake.

The last thing she wanted to do was ruin Yale Bradigan.

No, scratch that. The *last* thing she wanted to do was lose him. She would do whatever she had to— including threatening him with blackmail—to keep him.

There was no good reason why they couldn't go to Europe together, or to the islands, or wherever he chose, and start a new life where no one would ever find him. If he didn't agree to come with her . . .

With a sigh, she looked around. The street was deserted, of course; this neighborhood wasn't exactly teeming with activity this early on a weekday. She'd have to go back over toward Broadway to find a cab.

As she walked, she thought that it was a shame

it had come to this. She had never wanted to see anything bad happen to Emmett; she didn't want to see anything happen to Yale now.

But it's their own fault, she reminded herself. *Both of them.*

Emmett shouldn't have poked his nose where it didn't belong. Everything would have been fine if he and Yale had stayed strangers, the way they had for the past ten years.

But no, Mr. Irresponsible had gone and borrowed money from a loan shark to settle his gambling debts. Then, of course, whatever great scheme he'd had for paying off the loan had gone awry. So what did he do? He'd come running to his rich brother after ten years of estrangement.

Thanks to fate, Meredith had been in the gallery that day, otherwise she might never have known what had happened.

It had been late November, and she'd wanted to say goodbye to Yale before leaving for the Thanksgiving cruise she and Russell always took. She had been in disguise, of course, and was waiting for Yale to finish up his work in the back office when the door opened and Emmett Bradigan had strode into the gallery.

The sight of him, after so many years, had nearly caused Meredith to lose her composure. But she had stayed cool, pretending to examine a plastic sculpture.

Thanks to the paper-thin wall of the office, she had overheard the entire conversation, beginning with Yale's shock at seeing his brother again, and his growing anger as he'd realized why Emmett was there.

He needed money. A lot of money. And he knew Yale had it.

The cold-hearted bastard had turned his brother down, of course. Meredith could just imagine how Yale had probably looked at Emmett with scorn as he said, "You've made your bed, now lie in it."

She could imagine the rage Emmett must have felt, the despair when he realized there was nowhere else to turn. He must have been at the end of his rope if he'd gone crawling back to Yale.

Meredith had been waiting, listening for Emmett to protest his brother's refusal, when the door to the office had opened suddenly and Emmett had come barreling out. She'd turned her face away, terrified that he would recognize her despite her disguise.

He had stormed out of the gallery without another word.

Of course, Yale had refused to discuss what had happened, even though he knew that Meredith had overheard the whole confrontation.

It wasn't until a few months later that she had learned that Emmett *had* recognized her that day in the gallery.

Not only that, but he'd put two and two together and followed them all over town, snapping photos of their trysts.

Quite simply, he had blackmailed Yale into giving him the money, threatening to deliver the photos to Franco Di Pierro if he refused. It seemed Emmett had some underworld connections and knew all about Yale's engagement to Justine, and what would happen if his future father-in-law found out about his affair.

Yale had assured Meredith that he had everything under control. Emmett had his money, so he had no reason to go to Franco.

"What are you, a fool?" Meredith had raged. "He might not use those photos now, but what about down the road? He can take you for every cent you're worth, then hand over the pictures anyway. Franco will have us both killed."

"Franco won't find out. I should never have told you any of this."

Not that he'd had a choice. Meredith, who had a way of popping up at opportune times, had overheard Yale's end of a heated telephone conversation with Emmett. Her name had been mentioned several times. Yale had had no choice but to tell her what was going on.

He hadn't wanted to look at the big picture, to reach the conclusion that was so obvious to Meredith.

But suddenly one day, he saw the light. She had no idea what had caused him to change his mind.

He was the one who had come up with the idea of using a hit man. Meredith hadn't thought it was a good idea to get anyone else involved but suspected he'd realized he was too weak to do the job himself.

Meredith had believed that as soon as Emmett was out of the picture, life would get back to normal.

But after the deed was done, Yale had changed. He seemed preoccupied, withdrawn, as though he was having a hard time living with the knowledge of what he had done.

She knew better than to bring up what had happened; he had warned her, the day before the murder, that he didn't ever want to discuss it again.

That was why Meredith was shocked that he hadn't responded with fury when she'd mentioned it yesterday.

There was a moment when she'd seen a flicker of rage in his expression, but he had quickly lowered the veil that always hid his emotions. He had stood and left without saying anything other than that he would think about what she had said.

Maybe she shouldn't have threatened him.

It's his own fault, she thought again.

He had driven her to it, had infuriated her with the way he had been carrying on with his dead brother's girlfriend behind her back. Did he think she was a blind fool, like Justine? Did he think she wouldn't find out, that she wouldn't dare to do anything about it if she did?

Meredith reached into the pocket of her black cloak and felt for the photograph she had tucked there before leaving home this morning.

The photograph that showed him kissing the beautiful brunette Lexi Sinclair.

She wouldn't resort to using it unless she had to. Hopefully Yale would come to his senses before then, would tell her that whatever she wished was his command.

Then she would tell him the details of her plan. How the two of them would run away together, how they would live, happily, for the rest of their lives in a place where Franco would never find them.

If he really cared about her as he said he did, he would do it.

And if he turned her down . . .

Meredith patted the photograph in her pocket.

Now all she had to do was find Yale.

And she had a pretty good idea where he might be.

The clock on the mantel in Yale's apartment struck six, shattering the silence.

Justine glanced up, noticed that the room was growing dark. She had been sitting here for hours, waiting . . .

Thinking.

And realizing that she was a fool.

Yale didn't love her.

He didn't want to marry her.

And he was having an affair behind her back.

She knew who he was seeing, too. She had been over everything they'd done, every conversation they'd had during the past few months. And one thing kept coming back to her.

Lexi Sinclair.

His dead brother's fiancée.

She remembered how Yale had lied to her about going to visit her, and how he'd spent so much time picking out toys for her daughter that day. At the time, Justine had told herself that it was sweet, the way he was seeing to it that his niece was taken care of.

Now she suspected what his real motives had been.

Winning over the child's heart, just as he'd won over the mother's.

"Damn you to hell," Justine whispered, shaking her head at the empty room. "How can you have done this to me? How can I have been so stupid?"

She stood abruptly and crossed over to the wet bar between the two floor-to-ceiling windows that overlooked the shadowy, rainy street below. She poured herself a Scotch in one of his etched crystal highball glasses and downed it.

After refilling the glass, she stared out the window, wondering moodily why Yale chose to live in this dreary neighborhood, with its drab, gloomy buildings that had once been factories and warehouses. True, SoHo was chic. Block after block of filled gourmet grocery stores and nouvelle cuisine restaurants and trendy boutiques. But Justine had never wanted to live here after they were married.

She would have preferred a co-op on the Upper East Side. Or even buying a house in Bensonhurst, near her parents. Not that she could envision Yale fitting in there.

Well, she didn't fit into his world, either. She didn't know anything about art, she thought bitterly, and she didn't like eating arugula and capers, and she didn't wear retro clothes.

She finished the second glass of Scotch and blinked back tears, turning away from the window.
Damn it.

She still wanted to be Yale's wife, regardless of their different worlds. He was the kind of man she had always dreamed of marrying. A man who had class. And culture.

And a mistress.

Justine wiped at her eyes, pouring more Scotch into her glass.

She would be drunk by the time he came home . . . *if* he came home.

The thought that he might not show up, that he might spend the night with *her,* caused a rush of bile to rise in Justine's throat. She swallowed it with another gulp of Scotch, then turned away from the window. Her gaze rested on the telephone.

Fury mingled with hazy confusion in her mind as she tried to decide what to do.

It took only a few moments.

Then, on wobbly legs, Justine walked unsteadily over to the phone and lifted the receiver. The alcohol might have numbed her doubts, but it hadn't caused her to forget the information she had filed away long ago, just in case.

The special phone number.

The one her father had given her to use in emergencies, for his beeper, "in case you ever need me, Teeny."

I need you now, Daddy, she thought blearily, as she dialed.

It was nearly nine when Lexi came back downstairs after several hours and found the entire first floor dark.

How could she have forgotten to turn on the lights?

Because it was still light out when you took the baby up, she reminded herself.

She turned on lamps as she moved back through the house to the kitchen, trying not to let the shadowy rooms spook her. She hesitated in front of the telephone table, contemplated putting the receiver back into its cradle.

But if she did that, Yale would call her.

And she didn't want to talk to him ever again.

She would change the number first thing tomorrow, get an unlisted one. Maybe she would look for a new place to live, so that he wouldn't be able to bother her.

She walked into the kitchen and saw that it was still a mess.

Emma Rose had finally gone to sleep after an unusually fussy evening. She had screamed ever since she'd finished her dinner, giving in to fits of wailing throughout her bath and her nightly bottle and Lexi's attempts to soothe her with a lullaby.

She had to be teething, Lexi knew. The baby was at the right age, and she had been sucking on her fist for several days now, occasionally probing her lower gums with her tiny index finger. Lexi had offered her a chilled teething ring earlier and had given her acetaminophen, but nothing had seemed to help.

Certainly the storm that had blown in just after dark hadn't made Emma Rose—or Lexi—any calmer. The house shook in the wind, and a hard rain pattered against the windows, punctuated by bursts of thunder and lightning.

Not the kind of night you wanted to be alone in an old house in the middle of nowhere, Lexi thought, as she turned on the tap at the scarred porcelain sink. The pipes creaked and groaned and it took forever for the water to grow hot. She washed Emma Rose's baby bowl and spoon, and the bowl and utensils from her own solitary dinner of Campbell's tomato soup.

Back when Emmett was around, she used to buy the family-sized can, and they would have it for dinner on cold, rainy nights, along with grilled muenster cheese sandwiches.

Lexi had both cheese and bread in the house for a change, and she'd been starved when dinner time had rolled around. But she hadn't been able to bring herself to make herself a grilled cheese sandwich to eat with the soup. It would have been too powerful a reminder of Emmett.

What she wouldn't give to have him here with her tonight. Stormy nights had always seemed cozy when Emmett was around, not threatening the way this one was.

I miss you so much, damn you.

Why don't you at least haunt me? I wouldn't be afraid if you did. I swear. You can do the whole routine, rattle chains and moan, whatever.

Just come back, will you? Visit me. Even for a little while.

But she had never been able to count on Emmett to be there for her when he was alive. Why did she think he might show up, now that he was dead?

The thought amused her, and she allowed a tight, bitter smile to cross her lips as she turned off the water and dried her hands.

She left the dishes to drain in the wire rack on the linoleum-covered counter, then looked around the kitchen. The rain-dotted windows reflected the room, and she wished, for the first time, that they had shades, or even venetian blinds, which she'd always hated. At least that way, she'd know nobody could see in.

The very notion that someone might be out there in the storm, watching her, made the hair on her arms stand up.

Hastily, she flicked off the light over the sink and stood looking out into the dark, windy yard. Ancient trees swayed and rustled overhead as the rain made a sifting sound in the leaves and grass.

There was no one there, of course.

Not even Emmett's ghost.

Sighing, Lexi returned to the dining room and surveyed the basket-making materials spread out over the table. She had made a mess on the floor with the colored shredded paper she was using as filler. It was going to take her forever to sweep the floor, since she didn't own a vacuum cleaner.

But it would be worth it. The finished products were beautiful, she thought proudly, surveying the row of cellophane-wrapped baskets on the floor beneath the windows. She'd made seven of them in all, for different occasions. First thing tomorrow morning, she would ride over to the hospital gift shop and show them to the manager.

She needed, more than ever, to make this business venture work. There would be no more money coming in from Yale. Even if he tried to send it, she couldn't take it.

She wouldn't have anything to do with a man she couldn't trust, no matter how destitute she was.

Outside, there was a sudden ear-shattering boom

that made her jump and flutter a hand against her pounding heart.

"Just thunder," she told herself.

She debated turning on the stereo to create some reassuring background noise, but then realized she wouldn't be able to hear Emma Rose if she woke up.

Anyway, stop being such a baby, Lexi told herself.

She tried to ignore the eerie feeling that was stealing over her.

She started putting away the supplies she'd scattered all over the room, putting scraps of ribbon into a plastic bag, lining up the scissors and tape and glue and stapler, neatly stacking the how-to craft books she'd checked out of the library.

That done, she decided it was time to stop prolonging sweeping the floor. It had to be done before tomorrow, since Emma Rose was sure to find a way to grab hold of some shredded paper and shove it into her mouth.

Lexi remembered that the broom was still in the front hall, just inside the door, from when she'd swept the steps yesterday. Humming to herself in an attempt to overcome her growing uneasiness, she walked back through the living room to the hall.

There was no overhead light there, and it was dark enough so that she could see out the large window in the door. She glanced out into the night as she reached for the broom, then did a double take.

What she saw made her gasp.

A shadowy figure stood on the other side of the glass, watching her.

Eleven

Yale checked his watch as he walked briskly toward his loft building. It was just nine o'clock. He tucked his hand back into the pocket of his trenchcoat, and his fingers grazed reassuringly against cold steel.

The rain was coming down in chilling sheets around him and had been ever since he'd left the small apartment above the Wet Dog Tavern. But it had been impossible to get a cab on Bleeker Street. And anyway, he needed the walk, to clear his head.

To think about Lexi.

He'd been trying to reach her all day, but her phone was still busy—still off the hook, of course, ever since last night.

Then, he had been prepared to spill his guts to her.

Now, he wasn't sure what he'd say if he got through.

He couldn't tell her the truth . . . or could he?

How would she react to his secret?

How do you expect her to react? She certainly won't be understanding, welcoming you back into her life with open arms.

Not Lexi. She would be furious, shocked, wounded, bewildered . . .

No, he couldn't tell her the truth.

He longed to see her again, just one more time before he left.

Joe was going to help him get out of town. He'd spent the day making arrangements for Yale to stay with some friends of his at a fishing cabin up in the woods in Maine. They were going to set up a new identity for him, get him safely out of the country, into Canada, and then overseas. Joe had all the right connections, thanks to the years he'd spent in prison. His friends could help anyone vanish . . . anyone, that was, who had a tremendous amount of money.

And Yale, of course, did.

He didn't want the new life to be permanent. If part two of his plan worked, he would be able to come back eventually, to claim what was rightfully his.

He thought about the warning Joe's gravelly voice had tossed after him as he'd left the apartment. "Watch your back, buddy."

Yale had met that with a casual wave and a "See you in a little while" on his way out the door, but Joe's words still echoed in his head.

Watch your back.

He was in danger, and he knew it.

But he couldn't lie low in Joe's stuffy apartment forever, trying to absorb the shattering events of the last few days and wondering about his future. He could no longer delay escaping the web of secrets and lies that surrounded him.

With Joe's help, he finally had a plan. It was time to put it into action.

Even though it might mean leaving Lexi and Emma Rose behind forever.

He walked up the steps and unlocked the double front doors of the building. Standing beneath the shelter of the small overhang above the stoop, he looked over his shoulder. The street, shrouded by a curtain of steady rain, appeared to be deserted. Yet Yale knew that someone could be crouching inside one of the parked cars that lined the curb, or lurking in an alley or in the shadows of a doorway.

His hand tightened on the revolver tucked into his pocket. Joe had insisted he take it, calling him a fool when he'd tried to refuse.

"Do you have a death wish?" Joe had asked.

He hadn't answered.

But what he'd wanted to say was, *Maybe I do.*

Not that he was going to sit around and wait for the inevitable—for some hired thug, or Franco Di Pierro himself, to strike.

But before he left New York, he needed the locked metal box he'd stolen from Lexi's apartment. It was hidden in the loft.

He knew he was risking his life going back for it.

But he had to do it.

In that box was his only chance of someday returning to Lexi and Emma Rose.

He walked up the dark flight of stairs toward his apartment door, wondering if someone was waiting for him inside.

In his gut, he didn't think so. Franco wouldn't

think he'd be foolish enough to risk coming back
to his apartment. He'd think Yale was already safely
out of town, and he'd be trying to track him.

Yale thought about Meredith as he felt around in
his other pocket, the one without the gun, and retrieved his keys. He wondered, as he had been since
last night, how Justine had found out about them.
He could have sworn she was fumbling around,
merely guessing . . . yet maybe he was wrong.

Meredith had said she wouldn't be stupid enough
to reveal their affair, knowing that her own life
would be at risk, too.

But then, she was a shrewd woman. A woman
who had been deeply hurt by the fact that Yale
Bradigan no longer cared about her. And she knew
about the art. Had she somehow used that information to protect herself?

Another thought occurred to Yale as he put his
key in the lock and turned it.

*What if Justine hadn't been referring to Mere-
dith?*

*What if she had somehow found out about him
and Lexi?*

He had spent the last twenty-four hours assuring
himself that she hadn't, that there was no way.

Meredith didn't know, either, though he had suffered a moment of panic yesterday when he'd
thought she'd somehow figured it out.

No, there was no way anyone could be aware that
he and Lexi—well, that they had feelings for each
other.

Justine and Meredith couldn't read his mind.

And there had been only that one stolen passionate interlude . . .

The memories of those precious moments in
Lexi's arms last weekend made him tremble even
now. Again he longed for one more chance to see
her, to tell her the things he should have said so
long ago . . .

To confess the truth, painful as it would be for
her to accept.

But it was too late now.

For all he knew, someone might be shadowing
him already, just waiting for the right moment to
strike. He couldn't risk leading them right to Lexi.

As the bolt slid open with a click and Yale pushed
the door open with his left hand, the fingers of his
right closed over the revolver and drew it out of
his pocket.

Just in case, he told himself, stepping over the
threshold.

You have to make this fast. Just get the box and—

He froze just inside the door, suddenly sensing a
presence.

He held his breath and slowly steadied the gun
in front of him as his eyes scanned the room.

It was dark . . .

But there in front of the window, was the silhouette of a person.

Just as Yale aimed the weapon, she spoke his
name.

And he realized it was Justine.

"What are you doing here?" he asked warily,
lowering the gun but keeping it ready.

"Waiting for you," she slurred, and he realized she was drunk.

He crossed the room and switched on a lamp on an end table beside the couch. Then he turned to look at Justine.

She was a mess. Her dyed blond hair, usually teased and sprayed into place, appeared matted and straggled across her face. Her eyes and cheeks were smeared with black eye makeup and looked swollen—telltale signs that she'd been crying.

Despite the knowledge that this woman had undoubtedly issued his death warrant, Yale found himself pitying her.

"Justine," he said quietly, "are you okay?"

She met his question with a staccato, bitter laugh, instantly destroying the aura of vulnerability and obliterating his sympathy.

"What do you care?" she asked, stepping closer to him.

He caught a whiff of alcohol on her breath and saw that she was having trouble standing without wobbling.

"Justine, I care about you," he said, moving to steady her by grabbing her shoulders.

She jumped back, shrieking, "Don't you dare touch me!"

"Justine—"

"Why aren't you with *her?*"

"With who?"

"Don't pretend you're so innocent. You know who I'm talking about." Glaring, she spat a single word at him, one that caused his heart to ice over instantly.

Lexi.

How could she know?

He couldn't waste time wondering. The realization that Justine knew about Lexi sent alarm bells screaming through his mind.

Lexi was in danger.

Lexi and the baby.

He had to get to them.

"Damn you!" he hollered at Justine, advancing on her.

She immediately crumbled, confrontation giving way to cowering as she tried to step away.

"What did you tell your father?" he demanded, backing her into a corner between a ficus tree and a pedestal that held a bronze sculpture.

"Nothing," Justine said. "I didn't tell him anything, I swear."

But she was lying. He knew it, could see it in her eyes.

For all he knew, Lexi and Emma Rose were already . . .

No, he couldn't bear to think about them being hurt. He had to believe they were okay.

"Yale," Justine said in a high-pitched, liquor-blurred voice.

He pierced her eyes with the hatred that suddenly boiled over inside him, and in a single, impulsive movement, reached blindly for the sculpture on the pedestal.

In his rage, Yale fully intended to wield the heavy bronze in a crushing, deadly blow to her skull . . . but his senses took hold at the last second, and he realized, in horror, what he was doing.

You can't do this, his mind screamed, and he lowered the sculpture, trembling.

Justine, seeing his movement, flinched violently backward as if to protect herself. She stumbled over the huge porcelain pot that held the ficus tree and her head slammed into the wall. She went down in a heap at Yale's feet.

For a moment, he was too dazed to react. Then he set the sculpture on the floor and bent over her crumpled form. He felt for a pulse point at her neck and found one. She was out cold, but alive.

Yale breathed a sigh of relief. Lord knew he'd wanted to kill her, for what she might have done to Lexi.

But he wasn't capable of murdering anyone.

With a shudder, he turned and raced for the door. With the storm, traffic would be light, but the roads would probably be a mess. He might make it to Lexi's within an hour, maybe less.

He stopped only long enough to retrieve the metal box from its hiding place inside the oven, which he never used. Then he took the steps to the street two at a time, fervently praying that it wouldn't be too late.

So this was Lexi Sinclair, up close and in person.

Sheltered from the downpour by the small sloping roof above the doorstep, Meredith stared at her through the glass. Her gaze swept over Lexi's tumble of unkempt dark curls, her baggy gray sweatshirt that had stains—probably spit-up, she thought distastefully—on the shoulders. Her pale face was devoid of makeup, with eyes that were rimmed with bags . . . and filled with terror.

"It's all right," Meredith called, pasting a reassuring smile on her face. "Can I talk to you for a minute?"

The woman hesitated, then reached toward the door.

Meredith assumed she was going to open it, but she must have flicked a switch instead, because suddenly, the doorstep was bathed in yellowish lamplight.

Meredith blinked against the glare, knowing it was her turn to be scrutinized. She kept her expression friendly, even as she wanted to barge through the door and shake the bitch who had stolen Yale away from her.

It was a fluke that Lexi had shown up in the front hallway the moment before Meredith was going to ring the bell. She had lost her edge, been caught off guard before she could prepare herself, mentally, for what she knew she had to do.

Lexi abruptly reached out and opened the door a crack, and Meredith saw that the chain was still on.

"Who are you?" Lexi called above the wind and rain, a waver in her voice.

Meredith hesitated. "I'm a friend of Yale's . . . I've come to warn you about him," she added after a moment. "Thank God I've reached you in time."

She saw the expression that crossed Lexi's face and knew she had said the right thing.

The door was closing again, but sure enough, it was only momentarily. Now it was open wide, and Lexi was running a hand through her hair in a gesture that had little to do with awareness of her looks, and everything to do with weariness and nerves.

"Come in," she said, gesturing, and Meredith stepped over the threshold.

Lexi closed the door behind her, shutting out the storm. She folded her arms across her chest as though the damp chill had crept inside, and looked Meredith in the eye.

"What's your name?" she asked with surprising directness.

Taken aback, Meredith didn't have time to come up with anything but the truth. "It's Meredith MacFee," she said, and extended her hand.

Then she noticed the flicker of recognition in Lexi's eyes.

"So you know who I am," she said, dropping her arm to her side. She shook the rain out of the long, dark curly wig she wore—one startlingly similar to Lexi's hairstyle and shade.

She thought about the times she had worn it as Yale had made love to her and wondered if he had ever imagined that she was Lexi. The thought sickened her, and renewed hatred filled her gut.

Lexi was nodding. "Yale told me about you."

"What did he say?"

"That you were involved with him, and with . . . Emmett." The pain etched in her face was raw, yet she made no move to break eye contact with Meredith.

"That was a long time ago," Meredith said after a moment, shifting uncomfortably.

"I know. You were the reason Yale and Emmett were estranged."

"Yale told you?"

Again Lexi nodded, but she said nothing.

"You never knew—Emmett never told you about me?" Meredith had always wondered whether he'd dwelled on what had happened, or whether he'd put it behind him and forgotten any feelings he'd ever had for her. He had been so different from Yale; he had been the one who was capable of truly caring about her.

Yet she hadn't realized then that she'd chosen the wrong brother. It was clear only now, with Yale's callous rejection still fresh in her mind.

Lexi was shaking her head; so Emmett had never mentioned her. Or, if he had, Lexi wasn't going to admit it.

Well, it didn't matter now.

Nothing mattered but getting her revenge against Yale for the way he had used her.

Meredith's hands were clammy. She kept them carefully hidden from view, not wanting Lexi to see them and realize that despite the storm, it was too warm out to wear black leather gloves.

Was she already suspicious? Did she wonder why Meredith wasn't wearing a trenchcoat or even a slicker?

No, instead, she wore this voluminous cloak whose folds concealed not just her hands, but the deadly knife as well. In a matter of moments, she would plunge the knife into Lexi's gut—or her heart; yes, that was more fitting.

And then she would leave her to die alone here on the floor of this shabby little house.

"What do you have to tell me?" Lexi was asking. "About Yale—you said . . ."

"Oh, yes." For a moment, she had almost forgotten the ruse she had used to get inside.

But now that she thought about it, why not tell Lexi the truth? Why not enjoy the look of shock and pain that would surely grip her the moment she realized that the man she loved had killed his own brother . . . whom she had, undoubtedly, also once loved.

"I'm afraid that what I have to say might be somewhat difficult for you to hear," Meredith said, looking around. "Maybe it would be better if we sat down . . ."

Yes, if we got away from this lit entry hall, where anyone driving by on the road could have to glance up and witness the bloody end of my mission.

But to her surprise, Lexi stood her ground, her jaw set stubbornly, fire in her eyes. "Just tell me," she said grimly. "I don't need to sit down. Tell me."

And then get out of here.

Her unspoken command was loud and clear.

Meredith contemplated overpowering her right here, right now. Despite the defiant gleam in her expression, Meredith knew she was defenseless. It would be so easy. The woman was tiny—she couldn't be much over five feet or a hundred pounds. Besides, Meredith had the weapon. It would all be over in seconds.

But first, she needed the pleasure of shattering

Lexi's vision of Yale. She wanted her to suffer emotionally before she suffered physically.

Meredith drew a deep breath. "I don't suppose Yale told you that he and I resumed our affair recently?"

The startled, hurt look on Lexi's face was her answer, and she was instantly filled with delight. Oh, yes, this was going to be fun.

"No," Lexi said, shaking her head. "I didn't know. But if that's what you came here to tell me—"

"It isn't," Meredith interrupted, eager to spill the rest.

"Then what is it?"

"You loved Emmett very much, didn't you?"

A shadow crossed Lexi's face at the mere mention of his name, and she nodded stiffly.

"Perhaps," Meredith said, enjoying herself immensely, "you're aware that his death wasn't an accident?"

She waited for another measure of astonishment to appear, but Lexi was nodding.

Jolted, Meredith wondered how much she knew. Could she possibly be aware that Yale was behind Emmett's death? If so, this had all been a colossal waste of time. She might as well just spill it and get it over with, then kill Lexi and be on her way.

"Do you know who murdered your fiancé?" she asked Lexi, who shook her head.

Hmmm. Maybe she was telling the truth. Maybe she really didn't know.

"Who did it?" Lexi asked in a shaky voice that wasn't just curious, but filled with dread.

She suspects the truth, Meredith realized. *She*

*doesn't want to hear it. She's terrified of what I'm
going to tell her.*

"I hate to be the bearer of terrible news," Meredith
said softly, "but Emmett's death was caused by his
own flesh and blood. Yale killed him."

Lexi went pale, her eyes fluttering closed and her
hands clenching into fists in front of her, as if to
fight off the grisly truth.

Meredith reached out and lay her left hand on
Lexi's shoulder in a comforting gesture.

Meanwhile, she moved her right hand, ever so
slightly, inside the cloak, closing her fingers over
the handle of the blade.

She was about to brandish it, taking advantage
of catching Lexi off guard, when a faint, sudden
sound made her pause.

It was coming from upstairs.

The wail of a baby.

And in that moment, Meredith's rage gave way
to a rush of despair.

The child was Emmett's.

Once, so very long ago, Meredith had carried this
little girl's half-sibling in her own womb.

She had known all along the baby she'd carried
was Emmett's, but that hadn't made her want the
child. Not then. No, she'd been relieved when her
body had rejected it the way her heart already had.

It was only later that she'd felt an occasional pin-
prick of regret. Of course, she'd become a master
at shoving those unwelcome, wistful feelings aside.
Never, until now, had she even acknowledged them
for more than a split second before moving on,
blithely, through her busy days and nights.

Now, though, her body was consumed by an over-whelming surge of maternal contrition. She ached for Emmett's child, the one he and she had created together, the child who had been expelled from her body in a painful, violent rush of blood and tissue, as if it had sensed she didn't want it. Or maybe it had sensed how she had tortured its father with her lie so that he hadn't even known he had created the brief life inside of her.

And she ached for Emmett's other child, the one who at this very moment was upstairs, sobbing for her mama.

The little girl had lost her father.

And now she would lose her mother as well.

Meredith's throat constricted around a hard lump that suddenly rose and took hold, refusing to budge. She tightened her grip on the knife in her cloak, commanding herself to make her move now. Now, while Lexi's head was turned toward the stairway, her head cocked, listening to the baby's cries.

"That's my daughter . . . I have to get her," she told Meredith distractedly. "Sometimes she has nightmares, I think . . . she won't calm down until I pick her up and rock her."

Nightmares.

Against her will, Meredith found her mind was filled with the image of Lexi cradling her child in her arms, her pale cheek nestled against downy baby hair, murmuring comforting words as she stroked her daughter's soft, dimply cheeks.

Who would chase the little girl's nightmares away when her mama was gone?

Was Emmett watching over his daughter from

wherever he was now? Did he know what Meredith intended to do to the child's mother, the woman he had loved?

"If you don't mind," Lexi said, clearing her throat and looking meaningfully toward the door, "I really have to get her."

Meredith swallowed.

The baby's wails grew more frantic, erupting into choking screams. She desperately needed her mommy.

Meredith couldn't rob her of that. She just couldn't, no matter how much she hated this woman for stealing Yale away from her, no matter how much she hated Yale for loving someone else.

Meredith's hands trembled. She let go of the knife and faced Lexi. "I . . . I'll leave," she said numbly. "I just wanted to . . . warn you about—"

Lexi cut her off with a terse, "Thanks. I'll stay away from him."

Meredith nodded and she turned toward the door. As she opened it, she said, "You take care of that baby of yours, okay? Emmett would have wanted her to grow up to be a good person."

"She will."

With Lexi's promise echoing in her ears, Meredith stiffened her chin and stepped out into the wet, windswept darkness.

The moment Meredith MacFee had closed the door behind her, Lexi let out an audible sigh of relief and rushed to bolt the door behind her.

Her entire body was shaking, she realized, and numb with fear.

She had been certain the woman was going to pull a gun on her. She had noticed the way she tried to keep her hands concealed by that black cloak she was wearing, but when they had fluttered nervously toward her hair, Lexi had seen that she was wearing gloves.

Gloves, in September.

And as Meredith had shoved her long black curls back over her shoulders, Lexi had seen a few telltale strands of red escaping around her forehead. The woman was wearing a wig. And her eyes kept shifting guiltily away from Lexi's.

Yes, she had instinctively known Meredith had meant to harm her.

But . . . why hadn't she?

Now she wondered if she had been paranoid to imagine Yale's lover brazenly coming to her home and gunning her down in cold blood. Had she misread the cold hatred in Meredith's eyes?

She didn't think so . . . but what, then, could have caused the woman to have an abrupt change of heart?

Emma Rose.

The moment the baby had started crying, Meredith had grown distracted.

Panic had coursed through Lexi. Until then, she had been thinking that even if Meredith attacked her, the baby would be safe.

When Emma Rose had started crying, all sorts of terrible thoughts had darted into her mind. She had been terrified that the squalling would agitate Meredith, that she would lash out at the baby, too.

Heaving another enormous sigh, Lexi turned and hurried up the stairs toward the nursery and her sobbing daughter. She swooped down over the crib and gathered Emma Rose into her arms, stroking her warm, downy head, cooing, "It's all right, sweetheart, it's okay. Mommy's here. Mommy's got you. Yes, it's all right."

Thank you, Em, she thought, squeezing her eyes shut tightly, *for waking and crying when you did. You might have saved Mommy's life . . . but we'll never know for sure, will we?*

Lexi rocked her daughter against her breast, and the cries subsided, giving way to sniffles and whimpers. Emma Rose snuggled her head against Lexi's shoulder with a final, wracking shuddering sigh.

"See, Em? I told you it would be all right. You're just teething, aren't you? Or maybe it really was a nightmare. Maybe the storm scared you."

Lexi walked to the window and looked out at the rain just as a loud clap of thunder sounded outside. She gasped, and the baby whimpered again.

"It's all right, sweetie. That's just thun—" Lexi's words were cut off by a sudden flash of light in the bushes in front of the house, and a sharp squealing sound.

Headlights . . . and tires peeling out as a car raced off down the road.

Lexi's heart pounded and she peered out into the night. It was impossible to see anything, thanks to the blowing trees and the driving rain.

Then a bolt of lightning illuminated the world

below for a brief second or two, and what Lexi saw
made her blood run cold.

A crumpled black-clad figure lay at the foot of
her driveway, at the edge of the grass, just inside
the stone pillar.

And even as she gazed at it, Lexi realized that
lightning came *before* thunder, not after.

What she'd heard, then, had been gunfire.

Someone had shot Meredith MacFee.

She pressed a hand to her open mouth, stunned.

I have to call the police, Lexi realized frantically,
turning from the window and hurrying toward the
hall, clutching the baby against her. *And an ambu-
lance.*

She was halfway down the stairs when another
thought struck her.

It was dark and rainy outside, which made it difficult to see clearly.

Meredith had been wearing a long, dark curly
wig, one that bore an uncanny resemblance to
Lexi's own hair.

Could whoever had fired at Meredith have thought
he was aiming at Lexi?

Could . . .

Oh, God.

Could it have been Yale? Could he think that she
had somehow found out he had killed Emmett?

Had he tried to kill her to keep her quiet?

No! Lexi's mind screamed.

She didn't want to believe Yale was capable of
harming her. But she hadn't thought he could harm
Emmett, either . . .

And he had killed him.

It added up, Lexi thought wildly, her mind running back over everything that had happened over the past week. He had seemed so edgy, as though he was hiding something. And he had lied to her . . .

That doesn't make him a killer, an inner voice protested; yet Lexi knew she had to face the truth.

Once before, she had believed in Yale . . . and learned that he could be a cold, uncaring son of a bitch.

He hadn't changed.

She had been caught up in his captivating charm once again, lost in her own undeniable attraction for him. Her judgment had been clouded so that she had allowed herself to lose touch with the pain he had caused her so many years ago. She had tried so hard to forget the lesson she had learned in the past.

She had wanted him, needed him so badly . . .

How could I have been such a fool?

Trembling, Lexi turned and scurried back up the stairs and into Emma Rose's room.

Reaching into the closet, she jerked the small hangers until she found a warm, hooded bunting and carried it over to the changing table.

She lay the baby down and said, "It's all right, sweetie. We have to get out of here . . . before he finds out I'm still alive."

A mile to go before he reached Lexi's house.

Yale kept his eyes on the slick, twisting, hilly road before him, aware that he was driving much too fast, but unable to allow himself to slow down. He had to get to her.

At every curve, as he struggled to stay right, he prayed that no one was coming in the opposite direction. Every time, his prayers were rewarded. The country roads were mercifully deserted on a stormy night like this. And the Lexus performed well, holding to the winding road as if it were a train on a track.

Finally, Yale rounded the last bend before the familiar low stone wall on the righthand side that bordered the estate where Lexi lived. He slowed the car and conjured one last prayer, uttering this one aloud.

"Please, dear God, let Lexi and the baby be all right. Please . . . I'll do anything if they're all right . . ."

The darkness ahead of him was pierced by a sudden flash of headlights.

A car was pulling out of the driveway in front of the carriage house.

As it emerged from behind the stone pillar, Yale recognized it as the one Lexi's parents had loaned her.

And there was no mistaking the driver. Her head barely topped the headrest, and her silhouette clearly showed a mane of long hair.

Lexi was all right.

Relief coursed over Yale.

Lexi was alive . . .

And she was leaving.

Where could she be going at this hour in this weather?

Yale speeded up as she turned out of the drive-way, headed in the same direction he was going. He saw her glance into the rearview mirror. He hit the brights and flashed his headlights at her to show her that it was him.

She promptly picked up speed.

She doesn't recognize the car, he told himself, pressing his foot against the gas pedal. He had seen Emma Rose strapped into her carseat in back. He knew Lexi would never drive so recklessly with the baby in the car unless she was frantic to get some-place . . .

Or away from someone.

Had Franco or his men gotten to her, threatened her?

The thought filled Yale with fury.

Again he flashed his brights, then turned on the interior light in the car, hoping she would see who he was.

She glanced into her rearview mirror once more, and again her speed increased.

Yale saw the old car swerve into the left lane as she rounded a sharp curve, and his heart leapt into his throat.

"For Christ's sake, slow down, Lexi," he mut-tered. "That old boat isn't going to hold the road."

But as he came around the turn he saw that she had made it, and her taillights were zooming off along the straight expanse ahead.

He floored the pedal, wondering what the hell had happened to spook her like this.

She must think someone dangerous was chasing

her, that one of Franco's thugs was after her. He had to let her know that it was just him.

But hadn't she recognized the Lexus? Hadn't she seen him when he'd turned on the lights inside the car?

Obviously she hadn't, difficult as it was to believe.

In the distance up ahead, her headlights illuminated a yellow sign. Yale saw it and its warning filled his heart with dread.

Dangerous curve.

He automatically slowed down and watched for Lexi's taillights to show that she, too, had hit her brakes.

But they didn't.

Oh, Lord, she was barreling forward as though she was being chased by the devil himself.

And the way the road was sloping downhill . . .

The big old car disappeared around the bend, and then, above the pouring rain and the curse that spilled from his lips, Yale heard it.

The high-pitched screech of brakes being slammed on too late.

Somebody was singing.

Emmett.

Yes, Emmett was singing, an old Welsh lullaby he'd once told Lexi had been sung to him by his grandfather when he was a little boy. It was the same tune that he used to croon to Lexi's belly in the months before the baby was born.

His voice came to her as if from across a great distance, and she realized that she was dead.

She had to be, if Emmett was here with her.

What had happened?

It came back to her then . . .

She remembered the frantic, yet curiously slow-motion moments when she'd realized that the road was swinging off sharply to the left, and that it was under a layer of rainwater. She had hit the brakes but the car had kept going, hydroplaning and rushing toward a thick patch of trees and bushes that loomed ominously in the misty yellow glow from the headlights.

That was the last thing she recalled.

And now she was dead, floating in gauzy darkness as Emmett's voice beckoned to her with a sweet lullaby.

Emmett is an angel, she thought, and smiled. *He's waiting for me . . .*

Then she was struck by a thought so devastating that she actually heard herself gasp.

Emma Rose!

Had she killed her baby, too?

Where was Emma Rose?

The singing had stopped abruptly, and now she heard Emmett calling her name.

"Lexi? Lexi, did you make a sound? Are you waking up? Come on, Lex, open your eyes. That's it . . ."

The darkness disintegrated, replaced by Emmett's face hovering over her, and a bright light.

This must be heaven, Lexi thought fuzzily, vaguely remembering that people who had had near-death experiences had described their loved ones waiting, and bright, beautiful white lights.

But the glaring beam overhead was harsh and yellow; it made her squint.

Still, there was Emmett. The expression in his eyes was unmistakably familiar. He was so happy to see her, and he loved her so much . . .

"Em—" She started to speak, but her voice came out a croak, and she broke off the moment she heard the sweet sound of her baby.

Yes, Emma Rose was nearby, her soft cooing unmistakable.

"Mommy's calling for you, sweetie," Emmett said in a baby-talk voice.

Lexi struggled to find her voice, to tell him that she had been calling *him,* Emmett . . . to ask what was going on . . .

"Don't worry, Lexi. Emma Rose is right here. She's fine. See her?" Now he was holding the baby in her line of vision, and relief surged through Lexi, along with a wave of confusion.

Her eyelids fluttered shut again.

Nothing made sense.

Where was she? What was Emma Rose doing here? Were they both dead? They had to be, since Emmett was here . . .

Unless . . .

Yale.

He had been chasing them just before the accident. Had she and Emma Rose survived? Was it Yale who was talking to her, who held her baby above her?

It had to be.

Yet something intimate in his gaze had told her so clearly that he was Emmett . . .

She forced her eyes open again and saw him there, looking down at her expectantly, holding Emma Rose against his chest.

It *was* Yale.

His hair was short, not long and flowing; he wore a trenchcoat, not a plaid flannel shirt, as Emmett would have.

Bitter disappointment swiftly overtook her, and on its heels came stark fear.

She struggled to raise herself up, to escape, but it was as though she was pinned down. Had he tied her up? As panic darted through her, Lexi found her voice again and said hoarsely, "What . . . what are you going to do to us?"

He blinked, looking bewildered.

"What are you talking about, Lex?"

You killed Emmett!

You killed Emmett!

She was very weak. It was difficult to speak, but she tried to force the words out. "You . . . Emmett . . . killed . . . you . . . killed . . ."

His eyes closed again, and this time they didn't open right away. When they finally did, she saw the pain and sorrow in his gaze.

"We need to talk, Lexi."

His simple, direct words and his resigned tone caught her off guard.

For a moment, he vanished from view, and she heard him gently say, "There, Em, you stay right in the middle of the bed, all right?"

Then he was hovering over Lexi again, tugging gently at her shoulders. "Here, can you sit up?"

She felt him propping something—a pillow—behind her, and realized that she hadn't been tied down at all. Her body ached all over; it was the weight of her pain and exhaustion that had kept her flat.

Now she saw that the glaring light came from a cheap overhead fixture. She was in a rectangular room with dark paneling and a door and window on only one wall, a bathroom through an open door . . . a motel room. There was a cheap desk and chair, and a bed covered in a gold-patterned spread. Emma Rose lay in the middle of it, gurgling happily and swinging her feet in the air.

Lexi was in the other bed, and Yale sat at her side.

She turned her attention back to him warily. "Where are we?"

"At a motel in Dutchess County. I stopped at the first place I came to when I felt like I was getting too tired to drive."

"What . . . ?"

"You drove off the road and down an embankment," he said. "You hit your head on the steering wheel. When I found you, you were unconscious. I put you and the baby in my car and got out of there."

"You were chasing us—"

"Because I wanted to save you, Lexi."

She started to shake her head violently, but dizziness and an excruciating throbbing in her temples made her stop.

"No . . ." she whispered.

"Yes. Lexi, I have something to confess to you."

He was going to tell her that he had killed Emmett. Hadn't she just told him that she knew?

She wasn't sure. Her head ached so badly, and she was still so disoriented . . .

"It's going to be a shock to you, I know," he was saying. "But I did what I had to do, Lexi."

"Yale—"

"No," he interrupted her. "I'm not."

What? *I'm not . . . what?* What was he talking about? Had she blacked out and missed something?

Lexi stared at him in confusion.

"What are you talking about, Yale?"

"That's what I'm talking about, Lexi," he said cryptically. Then he added three words that sent Lexi careening, in utter shock and denial, back into the silent darkness.

I'm not Yale.

Twelve

When Lexi woke again it was morning.

She glanced around, her initial disorientation swiftly replaced by recognition of the shabby quarters she had seen last night.

Filmy gray dawn filtered through the heavy rust-colored curtains at the room's one window, just enough light to outline the clothes tossed on the chair at the foot of the bed—a familiar trenchcoat, a dress shirt, and a pair of jeans.

Lexi turned her head cautiously and found that the pain had lessened. She could clearly see the two figures, one large and one tiny, on the double bed a few feet away.

The man lay on his side, facing her, his head was on a pillow, and his eyes were closed in slumber. Nestled in his strong, bare arms, her head tucked against his powerful chest, was a sleeping Emma Rose.

Lexi stared at them, wondering if there was any way that it could be true . . .

If this could actually be Emmett.

Then reality took over and she scoffed at her own gullible longing to believe Yale.

This was just another of his lies . . . a desperate

attempt by a desperate man to escape punishment for the heinous crime he had committed. She could imagine how the wheels in his shrewd mind had turned when he'd come up with this plot.

I'll just pretend that I switched places with Emmett before he was killed, and that someone wanted him dead, but they obviously got the wrong guy.

But that didn't make sense, Lexi realized. Yale thought she thought *he* had murdered Emmett. If he was going to claim that he hadn't killed his brother—that, in fact, he *was* his brother—who did he expect her to believe had supposedly killed Yale?

He'll come up with something.

She had no doubt that Yale had a story ready and waiting for her. And she had no desire to hear it.

She only wanted to take Emma Rose and escape, continuing on the blind journey she had begun last night. When she'd left the house, she'd had no idea where they were headed, only that she had to get away. She vividly recalled the stark terror that had seized her the moment she'd seen the headlights flashing behind her. She had recognized the black Lexus even before Yale had lit up the inside, waving frantically at her.

As though she were foolish enough to stop for him.

She'd done her best to outrun him.

Now here she was, right in his clutches, with her baby girl innocently sleeping in his arms. Seeing sweet, trusting Emma Rose lying there with him made her sick.

I have to get her away from him, Lexi thought. *We have to escape somehow.*

But if she confronted Yale, told him that she didn't buy whatever flimsy story he'd concocted, he might fly into a rage. A man who was capable of killing his brother would surely be capable of killing her.

But not Emma Rose.

Her gaze swept over the sleeping man and child and Lexi remembered how he had tenderly sung the lullaby to Emma Rose last night.

Again, she wondered . . .

Was it possible that he really *was* Emmett?

Then, once more, common sense won out. She realized that if old Geoff Bradigan had sung the lullaby to Emmett, Yale probably knew it, too.

She stared at him, loathing him, realizing that if something happened to her, no one would ever suspect Yale. He was cunning enough to cover his tracks the way he had with Emmett. And then . . .

And then he would surely win custody of Emma Rose.

The thought filled Lexi's mind with dread and her throat with bile.

She desperately tried to deny that it could possibly happen, but she couldn't. Her parents couldn't take Emma Rose, not with her mother's days numbered and her father an emotional wreck. Not with the courts far more likely to rule in favor of the young, dashing, rich uncle.

Lexi remembered what Yale had said—that Emma Rose was a part of his family, that she deserved to bear the Bradigan name. He would claim her as his own, and he would raise her.

That had been his motive all along . . .

It had been why he'd seduced her, made her think he'd changed, that he cared about her . . .

No! she protested vehemently, jerking herself to a sitting position. *I won't let him get his hands on her! She's mine!*

As if he had heard the voice screaming inside her head, Yale stirred. And when he moved, so did Emma Rose, spontaneously stretching and purring in his arms. He tightened his grip on her and opened his eyes, looking down at her, then shifting his gaze to Lexi.

"Hi," he said, watching her closely.

In that moment, she knew that the only way to get out of this alive was to pretend she believed him.

She took a deep breath, steeled her emotions, and said, "Hi, Emmett."

His stomach flip-flopped at the sound of her words.

"How do you feel?" he asked her, carefully concealing his emotions. "You fainted."

"I know. It was just that I was so surprised when you told me . . ."

"I know. I figured you would be shocked, but I couldn't think of a way to tell you so that you wouldn't be."

"It's okay."

"I thought you'd be angry, Lexi, that I'd kept it from you for so long . . ."

"No . . . I'm just really . . . I'm glad you're still alive, Emmett."

He smiled at her and sat up carefully, lifting the baby and cuddling her against his bare chest.

Last night, he'd discovered that the climate control knob on the wall beside the door was broken. The room had grown unbearably overheated. He'd stood it as long as he could, then finally, had taken off his clothes so he could sleep comfortably.

Now he wished he hadn't. He felt vulnerable, lying here wearing only a pair of boxer shorts and covered by the stiff polyester bedspread.

"I suppose you want to know how it happened," he said, looking at her.

She nodded. She was more pale than usual, and her hair was matted on top of her head, where he'd bathed her nasty bump with a cool washcloth while she was still unconscious. Her eyes were enormous and focused on him, bearing an expression he couldn't read.

She had been through so much, he thought. He wanted nothing more than to cradle her in his arms the way he was holding the baby. But instinct told him to move cautiously, not to expect too much.

Emma Rose twitched and cried out.

"She's hungry," Lexi said immediately, reaching out for her daughter. "Can I have her? And I packed some bottles in the diaper bag last night before we left . . ."

"I know. I found them. There's an ice machine in the front office, and I've been keeping them cold for her." He pointed to the desk where the nipples poked out of the motel's cheap plastic container like foil-wrapped champagne corks in a crystal ice bucket.

"Thanks," Lexi said briefly, glancing at the bottles, then at him.

"No problem. After all . . . I *am* her father."

She nodded, then asked again, sounding strained, "Can I have her?"

"Sure." Reluctantly, he threw the covers back and stepped out of bed, conscious of her eyes on his nearly-naked body. He handed her the baby and saw that her gaze was roaming down over his torso, lower . . .

She caught him looking and quickly turned away. She focused her attention down at the baby, obviously not wanting to acknowledge her blatant appraisal of him.

He stepped back, feeling heat rushing to his face and to his groin, and realized he was rapidly growing hard. He looked down and saw that his arousal was straining against the front of his boxers. Hurriedly, he turned his back to Lexi.

He crossed to the chair and grabbed his jeans and shirt, then considered going into the bathroom to shower and change.

No, not now. Not yet. They had too much to talk about.

He bent and pulled on his jeans, balancing on one foot and then the other and gingerly tucking his erection inside the stiff denim. Then he threw his shirt on, not bothering to button it or tuck it in, and turned to face her again.

She was looking at him expectantly.

He frowned, confused, then realized she was waiting for a bottle of formula. He grabbed one from the ice bucket and handed it to her.

"Thanks," she murmured. "Here you go, Sweetie . . ." She popped the rubber nipple into Emma Rose's searching mouth, and the baby began to suck greedily.

Finally, Lexi looked up at him again.

"She was hungry," he observed inanely.

She nodded.

He perched on the edge of the bed opposite her, and cleared his throat. "I'll tell you what happened if you want to hear it now," he offered, and waited for her response.

She hesitated, then nodded. "Tell me. But Yale—"

"Emmett," he corrected, and she flushed.

"I'm sorry. Habit," she said, not meeting his gaze.

"It's okay."

"I just wanted to know how long we're going to stay here, Emmett. I . . . I really want to go home."

Her voice had come out so plaintive, Lexi thought. Was he suspicious? Did he think it odd that instead of jumping all over him in an emotional reunion, she was asking him to take her home?

There was no way of knowing what was going on behind those guarded green eyes of his. And she couldn't risk letting him guess what she was thinking, either.

Not when she was plotting how she would escape . . . and not when she was marvelling at how much she wanted him, still.

It was preposterous, what the sight of his lean, almost-naked body had done to her. Here she was, thinking of how much she hated him, and she couldn't help ogling him, couldn't keep lustful thoughts from darting into her mind.

The best thing to do, Lexi decided, was keep her gaze fixed on Emma Rose, who was noisily gobbling down the formula. She stroked her daughter's cheek and was rewarded with a brief, milky smile before Emma Rose went back to sucking.

"We can head back in a little while," Yale said. "After I've made a few phone calls."

"Who do you have to call?"

"I'll tell you that in a few minutes. First, let me explain what happened."

She nodded. "Go ahead. I'm listening."

He paused, and she could feel him watching her. Again, she wondered if he was suspicious.

"Emmett?" she prodded, looking up at him.

As if her uttering that name had reassured him, he started talking. "You know, now, that I had a pretty serious problem with gambling, right Lex?" He didn't wait for a reply. "I always was an addictive personality, you know? I should have known better than to start betting, but I couldn't seem to help it."

He paused, and she realized he was waiting for her to respond. "What were you betting on?"

"You name it. I had a bookie, a friend of Joe's, down in the Village. I was nuts, Lex. I got in over my head, and when I couldn't pay off my debt, Joe set me up with another friend of his. A loan shark, just like you guessed."

"What a friend," she said dryly, wondering how much of this was true. All of it, she supposed. So far. But she knew he and Emmett had been in touch recently. Emmett could have told him everything he knew.

"Nah," he said, sounding just like Emmett. Gone were the proper, clipped speech and carefully thought-out words so typical of Yale.

"Joe's a good friend, Lex," he went on defensively. "He was trying to help. He even got me into gambler's anonymous, and I stopped for a while. But right after I borrowed the money, you and I split. And I got depressed. I started betting again. I was a mess . . ."

His voice faded and she looked up and saw him staring off into space.

"And then we got back together . . ." she nudged, watching him until he looked at her. She quickly glanced down at the baby again.

"Yeah," he said. "We got back together. And when you told me you were pregnant, I vowed I was going to straighten out. I wanted to be a dad a kid could be proud of. I stopped gambling, and I worked every job I could to keep up with the payments. But the guy started threatening me, Lex. He said he was going to hurt you."

The emotion in his voice took her by surprise. She found herself looking at him again, probing his face for signs that he was acting. There were none.

If she didn't know better, she'd believe that he really was Emmett, that he really did care about her.

But you do know better.

"I couldn't let anything happen to you and the baby," he went on. "So I swallowed my pride and went to my brother to ask him for money. He turned me down."

"Yale always was a cold-hearted son of a bitch," Lexi said, taking pleasure at the opportunity to jab him to his face.

"Yeah, he was." There was no evidence that he was stung by her comment. He was good. "But he ended up giving me the money."

"Why?"

"I blackmailed him. He was having an affair with this married woman, Meredith MacFee. I found out about it and took pictures. I told him that if he didn't come up with the money, I'd show them to Franco Di Pierro. That was all he needed to hear."

"Pretty lowdown of you, Emmett."

"I had to play his game, Lex. I was desperate. So he gave me some money, and I paid off the debt and got the guy off my back. Then I screwed up."

"How?"

"I started thinking about what a life I could give the baby—and you—if Yale would just loan me a little more money. I couldn't stand the thought of not being able to buy my kid shoes or toys, Lex. So I hit him up for more money. Just a loan. Just until I could get back on my feet . . ."

"And he refused you again, of course."

"Right. But this time, I was ready to play hardball. Thanks to Joe's smart thinking, I had bugged Yale's office at the gallery the first time I went to see him. Joe had said I might come up with some dirt I could use against him. I guess he knew my brother better than I did."

Lexi found herself hanging on every word despite her intentions to merely *act* interested. "And what happened?"

"I had found out that Franco Di Pierro and Yale were peddling fake art. That was how Yale became so rich, such an overnight success. He was in on the whole thing. And I have taped conversations to prove it. I kept the tapes, along with the negatives for those pictures of Yale and Meredith, in that metal box I stashed at your place. I, uh, was the one who stole it back," he added.

She scowled. "When?"

"While you were in the hospital, after the baby . . ."

"Oh," she said quickly. After Emmett had been killed.

"So anyway," he continued, his expression clouding over, "when I threatened to spill the dirt on the fake art, I guess it sent him over the edge. He gave me some money, and he told me he'd have to see about getting the rest. Obviously, he had no intention. I had thought Franco was the one who ordered the hit, but according to Meredith, it was my brother."

The room was silent except for the slurping sounds Emma Rose made on the bottle.

Lexi fought her impulse to believe that he really was Emmett, not Yale twisting parts of the truth in order to create the perfect alibi. He seemed so sincere . . . sounded so much like Emmett.

But then, Yale was cunning enough to have mastered his brother's speech patterns, thinking he could use that and his skillful acting to fool her into believing his distorted tale.

"How did Yale happen to be killed instead of you?" Lexi asked, carefully barring emotion from her voice, and still avoiding eye contact, though she desperately wanted to look at him, to see him boldly lying to her face.

"The night it happened, I had gone shopping with some of the money Yale had given me. I wanted to surprise you with some stuff for the baby. I was on my way to Macy's when I realized that I'd forgotten my beeper at home. I tried to call you to make sure you were all right, but I got a busy signal."

I was probably trying to beep him, Lexi thought, remembering how she had repeatedly dialed Emmett's beeper number after her water had broken.

"So I called my home machine, and I had a message from Yale. He sounded agitated, and he said he needed to talk to me, that it was really important. He said he was on his way over to my apartment, and not to open the door for anyone until he got there."

"You think he was coming over to kill you," Lexi said flatly.

"No. According to Meredith—who, by the way, had no idea I wasn't Yale—he'd ordered a hit. She called him—me—a coward. She said I didn't even have enough guts to do my own dirty work, that I'd had to find a hit man to do it for me."

"So if a hit man was going to kill you, why did he call you that night?" Lexi asked. The pieces of the big picture were starting to fall into place in her mind as she realized where Yale was headed with his story.

"I've been thinking about that," he said, rubbing his chin thoughtfully. "What makes sense to me is that he had ordered the hit, then couldn't go through with it. I think he changed his mind and he wanted to warn me. So he came over to my place . . ."

"And was murdered instead of you."

"Exactly. The killer must have been waiting for him in the apartment. He would have known I always kept a key under the mat—when we were younger, he used to tell me I was a fool to do that, that it was the first place a burglar would look. I guess I kept up the habit to spite him after all those years. Anyway, I figure he found the key and let himself in——"

"And the killer attacked him, thinking it was you."

"Exactly. Then he set things up to make it look like an accident, and set fire to the place. I showed up just as they were carrying the body out."

His voice faltered, and at last, Lexi looked up at him. It was nearly impossible to believe that the tortured look on his face wasn't sincere, that he was Yale and not Emmett.

Don't fall for his story, an inner voice warned, and she struggled against the urge to go to him, to lay a hand on his shoulder and comfort him.

"There was a big crowd on the street," he said, wearing a faraway expression as though he was lost in his memory. "I overheard someone say that they'd found the dead body of the guy who lived in the second-floor apartment. I started pushing my way to the front of the crowd, looking for a cop, when I saw something . . ."

"What was it?"

"The hand of the body on the stretcher had poked out from underneath the sheet," he said hollowly, and swallowed hard. "It was wearing a ring. I thought I recognized it . . . I got as close as I could, and I saw that it was the ring my grandfather had given Yale and me on our graduation day. I never took mine off. I knew he didn't, either. I realized that my brother was dead, that someone had mistaken him for me."

"Where did you go?"

"To Joe's. He cut my hair—he was a barber in prison—and I stepped into Yale's identity. I realized it was the only way I could find evidence that Franco Di Pierro had ordered a hit on me."

"So when you told me you had no idea who had killed Emmett—you," Lexi hastily corrected, "you were lying."

He shrugged. "I had a pretty good idea what had happened. I just never suspected that it was my brother, and not Di Pierro, who had murdered me. As far as I know, Franco doesn't know that anyone was aware of the art scam. But he apparently knows about us."

For a moment, Lexi didn't realize what he meant. Then it sank in. "You mean he knows Yale was cheating on Justine . . ."

"With you."

She struggled to banish the image of that passionate night they had spent together, not wanting to remember how it had felt to lie naked in his arms, to make love all night long . . .

"Someone shot Meredith MacFee out in front of your house." Yale's words shattered her reverie. "What did she say to you, Lexi? What did she do?"

"I don't know what you're talking about."

"You didn't—she didn't approach you?"

"Who?"

"Meredith." The woman my brother was sleeping with. I thought, since you went flying out of there like a bat out of hell, that she might have threatened you or something."

Or told me what you did to your brother.

"She must have been snooping around, spying on you," Yale was saying. "It makes me sick to think about it."

She kept her face carefully neutral, not wanting him to know about her conversation with Meredith. "What are you talking about, Yale?"

"Meredith was prowling around your house to-night, Lexi. I turned on the television while you were out cold," he said. "It's all over the news. Meredith MacFee's body was found near your house. At first they thought it was you. She was wearing a long, dark wig that could have made her look like you in the dark, with the weather so bad. Whoever killed her—"

"Was trying to kill me instead," Lexi finished for him. Her heart was pounding. She hugged the baby close against her. Emma Rose sharply protested be-ing jostled as she was drinking.

"It was Franco's hit men, of course," Yale said. "And now that they know you're still alive, you're not safe anywhere. I'm not, either. They think I'm Yale. Except . . ."

Lexi nodded, reading his mind.

It was so clever of him, she thought, to have come up with this plan. All he had to do now was step forward and claim to be his twin brother in disguise. Then Franco would believe that Yale Bradigan was already dead.

"So you're going to call Franco and tell him the truth," Lexi asked, but it was more of a statement than a question. "You'll tell him that you're really Emmett."

"No. Franco's no fool. He'll think I'm lying."

"Then what . . . ?"

"I'm going to take the evidence to the police. I got the box from my apartment right before I left for your place, Lexi. I'm going to take it to the police, and they can get Franco into custody. They've been trying to get something on him for years, but he always manages to stay clean."

"Won't you go down with him, since you were involved in the art scam?" she blurted, then realized what she was saying.

"No," he said, levelling a look at her. "Because *Yale* was involved. I'm not Yale. I'm Emmett."

"How are you going to prove it?"

"Witnesses," he said, looking perplexed, as though he didn't see why she was questioning him. "Joe. And you. You can tell them who I really am, Lex."

She nodded, unable to trust her voice.

If she didn't cooperate, he would go to jail with Franco . . .

Or would he? What if he managed to convince them, with Joe's help, that he really was Emmett?

Then what would he do to her?

She knew exactly what he would do. He'd manage to get rid of her somehow, and make it look like an accident.

And then what would become of Emma Rose?

She would be Emma Rose Bradigan, raised in Yale's cold, twisted world by a liar posing as her father. And Emma Rose would never know the truth.

Lexi closed her eyes and swallowed hard, wanting desperately to escape.

But she knew there was only one thing she could do.

Help Yale pull of his scam . . . on one condition.

He studied her, wondering what she was thinking as she sat for so long with her eyes closed, clutching her baby against her.

Again, he fought the urge to go to her.

Finally, she opened her eyes and looked directly at him.

"All right," she said. "I'll do it."

"You'll do what?"

"I'll tell them that you're really Emmett. I'll say I've known all along."

"But you haven't," he said, frowning. He had never considered that she might not help him. "I just told you now."

"If I say I've known all along, it'll be more believable to the police, and to Franco. Correct?"

He grinned and nodded, realizing she was right. "You're incredible, Lex. I knew I could count on you, but you had me going for a second there."

"Don't be so grateful. I'm not finished. I'll help you on one condition." For the first time in awhile, she looked him directly in the eye.

He saw the anger flashing in her gaze and felt a sickening thud in his stomach. "What's that?"

"That you stay away from me—and Emma Rose—forever."

For a moment, he couldn't speak. Her words were

so harsh, so unexpected, that he felt as though she had physically slammed into him, knocked him to the ground and left him dazed.

"What are you talking about, Lexi? Why would I stay away from you?" he finally managed to ask, shaking his head, wanting her to say that he'd heard her wrong, that what she'd really said was, *I want you to take care of me and Emma Rose forever.*

"Because," she said tautly, "I never want to see you again after what you've done."

"What have I done?"

"You know damn well."

"Okay," he said, throwing up his hands and pacing away. "I know you, Lex. I realized you'd be furious with me for not telling you right away that I was still alive. And I'm sorry, Lex. I know you've suffered terribly, and—"

"Don't you tell me you know how I've suffered!" she spat the words at him, and Emma Rose started crying immediately. Lexi clamped her mouth shut and put the baby over her shoulder, rubbing her and murmuring comfortingly in her ear.

"Just let me speak, will you, Lex?" he asked, struggling not to let his voice rise and startle the baby again. "Damn it, you always think you know everything. You never want to listen to what anyone has to say. Do you think I don't realize that I left you alone to have the baby? Do you think I wanted you to raise her during all these months without me? Do you think *I* wanted to miss any of that? Do you think I wanted to make you grieve, and struggle, and . . ."

Emma Rose was whimpering again. Lexi was

saying nothing, not looking at him, just rubbing the baby's back and rocking her back and forth. He couldn't tell if what he was saying was sinking in to her or not.

He took a deep breath. "Look. I'm sorry, Lexi. I never meant to hurt you. But don't you see that there was nothing else I could do?" He reached out to lay a hand on her arm.

She stiffened. "Don't you dare touch me."

He retreated, faced her from the end of the bed. "I did what I had to, Lex. I didn't want you involved until I figured things out on my own, but you came to me, remember? You needed money, and it was the only way I could help you, and——"

"Money," she said, venom in her voice. "That's all that ever mattered to you, isn't it, Yale?"

Yale.

He froze when she uttered the name.

She didn't believe him.

Rage boiled up inside of him, and he fought to keep from exploding as he stared at the hatred in her face.

"What's the matter, Yale?" Lexi kept her voice as calm as she could, not wanting to frighten Emma Rose. "Are you shocked that I'm not buying your acting job?"

"I'm not acting, Lexi. Jesus Christ, you think that I'm *acting?*"

"I know you, remember?" She glared at him, fully aware that she was treading on dangerous ground. She didn't want to risk his losing his temper, but she couldn't seem to help herself. "I know you're a liar, that you're a selfish jerk who only cares about himself. You've always been that way, and I don't think you've changed, any more than your brother ever could have."

"That isn't fair. I'm Emmett, Lexi, and damn you, I have changed. I wasn't ready before to settle down and be a husband, much less a father. But now I am. I want to take care of you and my daughter. I want to be with you forever. Can't you see that?"

"I don't doubt that you want to be with Emma Rose forever, Yale," Lexi said, telling herself that she had to stop, but unable to keep her mouth shut. "I know you want to raise her as a Bradigan. But she's not your daughter, and you'll be a part of her life over my dead body."

Her threat hung in the air, and a chill swept down her spine.

She held her breath, realizing she may have gone to far. If he lost it now, if he lashed out at her, there was little she could do to stop him. He was bigger than she was, and she was still so weak from the accident. He could kill her with his bare hands, right in front of her daughter.

Oh, God, please don't let him hurt me, she prayed.

He was walking toward her, his green eyes hardened and focused on her, his jaw set grimly.

She tensed, clinging to the baby as though she were a protective shield.

He won't touch me if I'm holding the baby, she told herself. Yale would never hurt Emma Rose. For all the terrible things she knew about him, she remained positive of that.

He stopped in front of her.

She trembled, but kept her head held high.

"Lexi," he said after a moment. His voice was hoarse, resigned. "I'm Emmett. I know you don't believe me. But I can convince you. I can tell you things that only I would know—"

"So Emmett told you details about our relationship," she said with a shrug. "You can't prove anything."

"Look into my eyes, Lexi," he said, crouching in front of her so that he was on her level. "What do you see?"

She turned away. "I see a man who thinks he can make me believe in the impossible. A man who thinks I'm still a naive fool. But I'm not. I'll never believe anything you tell me again, Yale."

He stayed there in front of her for a few seconds longer.

She refused to turn her head and look at him.

Finally, he let out a heavy sigh of resignation, and moved away, to the telephone.

"You might as well get the baby ready," he told her. "I'm going to call a lawyer, and then the police. It's time to get this over with."

She nodded. "Remember, Yale. I'm on your side . . . as long as you agree to my stipulation."

"Don't worry, Lexi," he said in a weary voice that sounded devoid of emotion. She guessed he had given up the charade. "You go along with my story, and I'll never have anything to do with you and Emma Rose again."

Thirteen

It was the coldest, most bitter December anyone in the tristate area could remember. Every day during the first three weeks of the month dawned bleak and gray, with storm clouds invariably moving in to dump freezing rain or snow on the miserable landscape.

But on the twenty-first, the morning of Kathleen Nealon Sinclair's funeral, the sky was a deep sapphire and the sun shone brightly. A wet, heavy snow had fallen all night, leaving the world sugar-frosted and the air crisply clean.

The service was held at red brick St. Theresa's church on Water Street in Cady's Landing, with Father Michael Mitchell presiding. He had married Kathleen and Scott, and baptized first Lexi, and then Emma Rose; and he mentioned all of those joyous occasions in his eulogy. Today his blue eyes were somber and his tone was subdued as he spoke of the woman who lay in the gleaming wooden coffin before the altar.

Lexi and her father sat numbly in the front pew, leaning on each other and quietly weeping throughout the service. As Lexi clutched the damp linen hanky she had taken from her mother's drawer just this morning, she tried to tell herself that Kathleen was in a better place, that she should be grateful her suffering was over.

And she was.

It was just that she missed her terribly.

Just that it was so unfair that everyone she loved had to leave her.

First Emmett.

Now her mother.

If anything ever happened to her father or Emma Rose, she wouldn't survive. She couldn't bear anymore grief.

Her mother's last days had been torture. She had been in the hospital since the day after Thanksgiving, having held out against the inevitable for as long as she could. She'd spoken of wanting to die at home, but in the end, it was more merciful for her to be in the hospital, where doctors and nurse kept her as comfortable as possible, and where Scott and Lexi had kept a bedside vigil throughout the somber, stormy weeks.

It was sadly ironic that neither of them had been with her when death came, in the wee hours of the morning.

Lexi would never forget the last words her mother had spoken to her before she'd left the hospital the night before. Kathleen's voice had grown weak and bleary from the drugs, but Lexi understood her.

"Don't let Daddy be alone, Lexi," her mother had said.

"I won't, Mom. I promise, I'll be with him, and Emma Rose . . ."

Kathleen had struggled to shake her head. "Not

what I mean," she'd said. "He should get married again. No one should be alone."

The idea of Scott with anyone but her mother had seemed obscene to Lexi then, though she'd patted her mother's hand and said, "Don't worry, Mom. Daddy won't be alone."

Now, though, as she saw her father's sorrow-racked face and the stark loneliness in his eyes, she wanted nothing more than to see him smile again. Maybe someday, someone nice would come along . . .

Oh, God, how can I be thinking this at my mother's funeral?

Lexi swallowed over the lump that had resided in her throat for weeks now, and told herself that it was understandable. She just wanted her father to be happy.

As for herself . . .

Well, it seemed impossible to believe that the oppressive dark cloud that had hung over her for months now would ever lift. But for her daughter's sake, she had to make an effort to go on, to make their life return to some semblance of normalcy.

Lexi was grateful that Anita had come up to stay at home with Emma Rose. At nine months, the baby was already so aware of what was going on around her. Lexi wouldn't want her to witness the profound grief of her grandmother's funeral.

Yesterday, her father's brother, Uncle Nat, had flown in from Florida with his wife, Aunt Lois. They sat directly behind Scott and Lexi.

Now, as Father Mitchell completed the closing prayer and the organist began playing Kathleen's

favorite hymn, "I Will Arise," Nat stood and ush-
ered Scott out. Aunt Lois took Lexi's arm, patting
her shoulder and handing her a fresh tissue for her
tears.

Lexi found herself leaning heavily on Aunt Lois's
arm, blindly going down the aisle, the faces in the
crowded church a blur.

Then she spotted a familiar figure.

Yale Bradigan, wearing a black wool overcoat,
stood with his head bowed in the very last pew.

Lexi turned her head to look at him as she passed,
and he looked up. His eyes were filled with sympathy . . . and tears, she realized, vaguely startled.

Then she had passed him, being swept out into
the chilly wind and helped into the sleek black
limousine that waited at the curb.

She turned to see if she could spot him exiting
the church, but the icy steps were filled with her
parents's friends and neighbors.

Just as well, she told herself. This wasn't the time
or place to start thinking about Yale again, after two
months of struggling to keep him out of her head.

And her father was breaking down in the seat
beside her, his big body heaving with uncontrollable
sobs.

"It's going to be okay, Daddy," she said, weeping
as she put her arms around him. Her heart ached
for him, and for herself, and shame filled her as
she realized she wasn't just crying over her mother's
death. Not now.

"No," he cried, shaking violently and gasping.
"It's not going to be okay, Lexi. What the hell am

I going to do without her? How am I going to be alone?"

Tears ran down her cheeks as she rested her head against her father's shoulder.

I don't know, she thought bleakly. *I don't know what you're going to do alone.*

She tilted her head and wiped at her eyes, staring vacantly out the window.

And there she saw Yale's tall, dark-clad form, scurrying away along the sidewalk with his head bent against the wind . . .

Or, she thought incredulously, in sorrow.

She watched him until he disappeared around the corner as the limousine began the long, slow procession to the graveyard north of town.

Emma Rose took her first steps on Ground Hog's Day.

It happened just after breakfast, as Lexi was rinsing the cereal bowls in the sink. Emma Rose had been standing, holding on to a chair, when the next thing Lexi knew, she heard footsteps behind her.

She turned and saw her baby toddling toward her across the floor. "Em!" she screamed out, stunned. "You're walking!"

The sound of her voice startled the little girl, who promptly sat down on her butt with a loud cry.

Lexi scooped her into her arms before she could start sobbing and kissed her chubby face. "Em, you did it!" she said excitedly. "Mommy is so proud of you, sweetheart."

Emma Rose smiled, and Lexi was struck, as always, by how much she looked like her father. Her eyes had softened from their newborn blue to a hazel-green that was just a shade darker than Emmett's had been. Her fine-boned features were so like his; and her gap-toothed smile melted Lexi's heart, just as Emmett's always had.

"I wish there was someone we could tell about what you did, sweetie," Lexi said wistfully, resting her cheek against Emma Rose's curling blond hair.

But her father was in Florida, staying with Nat and Lois at their condo in Vero Beach. It was a much-needed reprieve, not just from the terribly stormy winter the Northeast was enduring, but from the empty house and the constant reminders of Kathleen.

Before her father had left last week, Lexi had helped him go through her mother's clothes. Her father kept telling her to take things home with her, but she knew she'd never want to wear them. It would hurt too much.

She had talked him into giving nearly everything away.

Everything except Kathleen's wedding dress.

They had come upon it at the very back of her closet, zipped into a quilted brown garment bag and shrouded in layers of protective plastic.

When Lexi and her father had realized what it was, they had both found themselves sobbing, releasing the tears that had been building ever since they'd begun their somber task.

"She looked so beautiful that day," Scott had said, wiping his eyes.

Lexi knew. She had gazed at her parents' wedding

album so many times over the years, always dreaming of the day when she, too, would be a glowing bride, as her mother had been. Clad in silk, and with her veil caught into a pillbox hat that had been so popular in the mid-sixties, Kathleen was the epitome of bliss, gazing up at her handsome new husband with pride and joy.

"You take the dress, Lexi," her father said, removing the garment bag from the closet and offering it to her.

"No, Dad, you should keep it," Lexi had told him, shaking her head.

"Why? I can't wear it." He'd smiled, a shadow of the once-ready grin she missed so much.

"Well, I can't, either," Lexi had said, smiling back. "I mean, what am I going to do, crawl around the floor after Emma Rose in it?"

"You'll get married someday, Lexi. You'll see. And then you might want to wear it. For luck."

A lump had risen in her throat then, and it did now, at the mere memory.

She'd wanted to say, *Forget it, Dad. I'm never going to get married.*

But she hadn't.

No, she'd gone home that night and hung the dress in her closet under the sloping eaves of the carriage house. And when she'd gone to bed, she'd dreamed about it.

About wearing it.

In her dream, she was a bride, walking down the aisle of St. Theresa's. The same people who had been at her mother's funeral crowded the pews, only this time, none of them wore black, and they were all smiling instead of crying.

Emma Rose had been walking in her dream, toddling along the white runner, tossing flower petals from a little wicker basket.

Behind her, Lexi had floated along on her father's arm, her long silk train rustling against the floor. The walk had seemed endless. Every time she glanced up at the altar, it had seemed farther and farther away.

She'd been straining for a look at her groom.

But the people in the pews blocked her view of the altar until the very last minute, when she finally reached the front . . .

And then, there he was.

Emmett Bradigan.

He stood smiling at her, his blond hair shaggy and hanging past the collar of his black tuxedo.

"Come on, Lex," he'd called when their eyes met. "I've been waiting for so long. Hurry."

And she'd dropped her father's arm, hiked up her skirt, and gone running into his arms . . .

And then she woke up.

Now, the memory of that dream was as vivid as it had been last week. She could still see the expression of love and hope in Emmett's eyes.

Emma Rose squirmed in Lexi's arms, and she became aware of the water she'd left running in the sink.

"Okay, sweetie," she said, bending and putting Emma Rose on the floor so that she was sitting. "No more walking until Mommy gets the dishes done. Then we'll go into the living room and practice. I just wish there was someone around who we could share this with."

"Da-da," Emma Rose said.

Lexi's heart skipped a beat.

Then she realized that it was just baby babble, that Emma Rose hadn't really been trying to say "Daddy."

She turned back to the sink and picked up a bowl filled with the watery remnants of milk and cereal. "That's right, Em," she said softly, shaking her head. "Da-da *is* watching you. From heaven."

Nearly two weeks had passed since the day Emma Rose had taken her first steps. Now she was walking, on increasingly steady feet, everywhere Lexi would let her.

The slippery sidewalk in downtown Cady's Landing was not one of those places.

As Lexi hurried along Main Street toward the Hallmark store, Emma Rose squirmed and protested in her arms.

"No, sweetie," Lexi said, doing her best to keep a firm grip on her daughter, which wasn't easy since she was bundled from head to toe in a slippery quilted nylon snowsuit. "You can't walk here. It's too dangerous. The concrete is covered with ice, and it'll make you fall down and go *boom.*"

Emma Rose, it seemed, *wanted* to go boom, because she was really mad now, crying and doing her best to leap from Lexi's grasp.

"This is our last errand, Em," she said, reaching the door of the store. "I promise."

Poor kid. Lexi had rushed her all over town this afternoon. No wonder she was cranky and tired of being confined.

First, they'd had to drop off a new carload of baskets at the hospital gift shop. Lexi's business was moving briskly these days, and she had just received an order for a special Valentine's Day basket from Emma Rose's pediatrician.

He wanted it ready to give to his wife when he took her out to dinner tomorrow night. He'd given Lexi a list of things he wanted in the basket, which had resulted in her running all over the place, from the liquor store, where she'd purchased a specific bottle of French champagne, to the candy shop, where she'd bought a dozen chocolate roses, to the florist, where she'd picked up twelve of the real thing.

Now her last stop was the card store, where she was supposed to pick up the biggest, prettiest, most expensive card she could find.

Dr. Moriarty was sweet, she told herself, as she shoved the door open and walked into the store. Though if *she* were Mrs. Moriarty, she wouldn't want to know that someone else had picked out her Valentine's Day gifts.

The store was jammed with people.

Of course, Lexi thought, as she shouldered her way through the throng at the valentines display, with Emma Rose wriggling and babbling in anger. *It's the thirteenth. Thirteen is an unlucky number. Guess today is my unlucky day.*

No sooner had the thought slipped into her mind

than she turned a corner at the end of the aisle and bumped smack-dab into someone.

"Oops, sorry," Lexi said, stepping back and hoisting Emma Rose higher on her hip.

"It's—" The male voice broke off suddenly, and Lexi glanced up, startled.

Yale Bradigan stood in front of her.

Only, he didn't look like himself.

For one thing, he wore a baggy khaki-green coat. It was unbuttoned just enough to reveal the shirt underneath. It was a blue-and-green plaid flannel.

And his hair . . .

It was shaggy and tousled, not a long mane like Emmett had once had, yet not Yale's usual short conservative cut, either.

He was playing the role to the hilt, she realized, studying him. Would she expect anything less?

"Hi, Lexi," he said quietly, then turned to Emma Rose. He chucked her gently under the chin and grinned. "Hello there, kiddo."

"Da-da," the little girl said promptly.

"That's her all-purpose word," Lexi told him quickly. "It means hello, and, uh . . ."

She trailed off awkwardly, and stood there looking at him.

He kept his gaze focused on the baby. "She's getting big."

"She is. She's . . . she started walking two weeks ago."

"She did?" He grinned at Emma Rose. "Wow. You can get into all sorts of trouble now, can't you?"

"You'd have to see it to believe it. She's into everything."

"I'll bet." He glanced up at her at last, and his light green eyes collided with hers.

Her stomach was up to its old tricks, lurching about as highly inappropriate thoughts cascaded over her.

"What are you doing here?" Lexi asked, shifting uncomfortably. She was doing her best to muster the anger and loathing that had twisted her thoughts of Yale over the months. Yet somehow, unexpectedly seeing him in person again had left her so shell-shocked that she couldn't seem to think straight.

"I'm considering buying our old house back from the man Gramps sold it to," Yale was saying. "He's about to retire and move out west, and he's going to put it on the market. With the way real estate prices have soared around here, I'll have to pay a fortune for it, but it's a sound investment."

She felt as though she'd been socked in the gut. "You're thinking of moving *here?*"

He nodded and gave her a level look. "Don't forget, Lexi . . . Cady's Landing is my hometown, too. That old house was the only home I've ever really known."

"How . . . how can you afford it?"

He laughed, a bitter sound. "Yale's will named me heir to his estate. I guess he'd never changed it after everything that had happened."

She nodded numbly. "What about your apartment in the city?"

"I'm selling it."

"Oh." Her mind was swirling with confusion and denial. Yale, *here?* That couldn't happen. "What about the gallery?"

"Sold." He shrugged. "I couldn't stay in the business after what happened."

"Did everything turn out all right?" she asked. As if she didn't know.

Franco Di Pierro's case had been all over the local papers and news programs for months. It looked as though he was going to jail for a long, long time. Yale's involvement had been lost amid the colorful details involving Brooklyn's most notorious mobster.

Lexi had seen footage of Franco's family—including his daughter, Justine—loudly protesting his innocence on their way into and out of the courthouse where his trial was being held.

She had feared she'd be called upon to testify. But her father's lawyer had assured her that her involvement in the case had ended the day she'd sworn to the police that the man claiming to be Emmett Bradigan was, in fact, the man she had known and loved. It had made her physically ill to lie to the authorities that way. But she would do whatever was necessary to protect her daughter.

"Everything is going to be fine, as far as Franco is concerned," Yale said, and looked ill at ease. "I never did have the chance to thank you."

"For what?" she asked, though she knew damn well.

He glanced over his shoulder at the busy shoppers browsing through the cards, then said in a low voice, "For helping me out like you did, Lexi."

"Oh. You mean, for lying on your behalf."

She saw the muscles working in his jaw, saw the flinty expression that hardened in his eyes. "You weren't lying, Lexi. I really *am* Emmett."

No, you're not! Emmett's dead, and you killed him! a voice screamed in her head. Suddenly, she felt as though her face was on fire, as though she were burning up in this too-warm store, wearing her heavy coat and holding a heavy baby.

She said nothing to Yale, just turned and started for the front of the store, moving as quickly as the crowd and the fidgeting baby would let her.

She would worry about the card for Dr. Moriarty's wife later. Right now, all she wanted to do was get away from that lying scoundrel Yale Bradigan.

But what if he's telling the truth? a gullible, irritating inner voice asked.

Of course he's not telling the truth. I can't believe anything he says. He knows how badly I want to believe Emmett's still alive. I'm not going to let him use that against me. I'm not going to let him hurt me, not ever again.

She rushed out into the street. It was starting to snow again, fine, white, grainy flakes that came down with a sifting sound and stung Lexi's cheeks. She gulped the cold February air as she hurried toward the municipal parking lot, shielding Emma Rose's face against the wind.

She had nearly reached her car when she heard footsteps running behind her.

She turned and saw Yale.

"What do you want?" she called out, her voice taut with tension and emotion that she could no longer fight back.

"Please, Lexi," he said, stopping a few feet away. "I just want to talk to you."

"You promised," she said, fumbling in her pocket

with icy fingers for her keys. "You promised you'd stay away."

"I know," he said, nodding, "but I can't. Please, Lexi, just look at me. Just look at me. If you do, you'll see who I really am."

"I know who you really are, Yale. And I don't want anything to do with you."

"I'm not Yale, Lexi. I swear to you, I'm Emmett."

"Oh, yeah?" She spun to look at him. From here, with snow swirling around them and the wind whipping her hair across her eyes, she couldn't see his expression. "If you really were Emmett, you wouldn't be here."

"I told you, I'm not dead. They got my brother instead, Lexi."

"That's not what I mean. If you were Emmett, and you were alive, you'd be as far away from me and Emma Rose as you could get. Because I never could count on him. He didn't want to marry me, and he didn't want us to be a family. He wasn't ready for any of that. And Emmett would never fight for me, to win me back. That's what's giving you away, Yale."

She was sobbing now, damn it. Emma Rose was quietly watching her. After a moment, she pulled off one of her mittens and tentatively touched the wet tears on Lexi's cheeks.

"No, Em," Lexi said, sniffling. She bent to retrieve the mitten and tried to get it back onto the baby's hand.

"Let me help you," Yale said, and stepped closer to them. He took the mitten from her and tucked Emma Rose's hand inside. Then he took the keys from Lexi's shaking fingers and opened the driver's side door for her.

"There," he told her quietly, stepping back. "Get her inside, out of this weather."

She nodded and reached around to pull the lock button on the back door. She opened it and strapped Emma Rose into her car seat, then, aware that Yale still stood there, slipped into the driver's seat.

"Lexi," he said, putting a hand on the door as she reached out to close it, "you're right. I was never there for you in the past. And maybe I don't deserve a second chance. But I'm telling you that I've changed. I'm telling you that I love you. And I'm going to fight for you if I have to. Please, Lexi . . ."

She stared up at him. Her heart ached, physically ached, with the need to get out of the car and throw herself into his arms. She wanted so desperately to believe him, to believe that Emmett wasn't really lost to her after all, that her impossible dreams might come true.

"Please," he said again, quietly, his breath puffing from his mouth in a frosty cloud. "The reason I was in that card store was to buy a valentine for you. I was going to send it, even though I knew you didn't want anything to do with me, because I had to give it one more try. I was going to try to write everything I wanted to say . . . everything I'm trying to say now. I can't let you slip away from me this way, Lexi."

She swallowed hard and shook her head. She wanted to convince herself that he was a liar, that the sincerity she heard in his voice was as carefully manufactured as his ridiculous claim that he was actually his brother.

And yet . . .

Somewhere, deep inside, in a place Lexi had thought would be cold and barren forever, she felt a flicker of emotion.

Then, from the back seat, Lexi heard Emma Rose say, around chattering teeth, "Da-da."

Abruptly, she shook her head and pulled the car door closed.

What could she have been thinking?

She was shivering as she started the engine; her entire body convulsed with a chill so profound, so deep-seated, that she honestly didn't believe she would ever be warm again.

The next morning, when Emma Rose was finally fed and contentedly sitting in front of the Barney program on television, Lexi went into the dining room to work on the basket for Dr. Moriarty.

She had meant to do it last night, but the encounter with Yale had left her so out of sorts that she could do little but wander around the house aimlessly. She had struggled not to think about him, but had been unable to do anything but.

She knew, with every ounce of common sense she possessed, that she shouldn't trust him. And yet her impulsive, lonely heart wanted desperately to find some grain of truth in what he'd said.

But for once, her head was going to rule her heart.

She found the big heart-shaped white wicker basket she'd bought, and arranged the items that would go inside on the table.

Something was missing, she thought, frowning.

What was it?

Then she remembered.

Uh-oh.

The roses.

Where were the roses?

She went into the kitchen, thinking she might have left them on the counter in a vase, as she'd been planning to do when she'd left the florist's.

But she didn't remember finding a vase or filling it with water . . .

In fact, she didn't remember taking the long white florist's box out of the trunk.

Uh-oh.

Lexi hurriedly slipped into her black boots that lay on the mat in front of the back door, then dashed out across the snowy yard to the car parked at the side of the house.

Sure enough, there, on the floor of the back seat, were the dozen red roses.

Ruined.

"Damn, damn, damn," Lexi muttered, hurrying back to the house. She tossed the box onto the counter. It fell off, spilling dying, purple-black rose petals all over the floor. Cursing, Lexi kicked off her boots, then poked her head into the living room. Emma Rose had fallen asleep in front of the television set, clutching her raggedy blanket, her thumb in her mouth.

Lexi returned to the kitchen and found the phone

book in a drawer. She quickly dialed the number
for Blakely's Blooms.

"I have an emergency," she told the harried voice
that answered. "This is Lexi Sinclair, and I need a
dozen red roses because—"

"No red roses, Lexi," the woman told her. "We're
all out."

"You're all out?" she echoed.

"Completely. What do you want? It's Valentine's
Day. How about pink?"

"I need red."

"Good luck, honey."

Lexi hung up feeling irritated. You'd think a florist would know enough to stock extra red roses on
this particular holiday.

She dialed the only other florist in Cady's Landing.

"Red roses?" the owner repeated. "We're all
out."

"How can you be all out?"

"It's Valentine's Day."

Lexi slammed down the phone and turned to the
Yellow Pages.

She spent the next half hour dialing every florist
in a twenty-mile radius. No one, it seemed, had a
single red rose in stock.

Finally, in desperation, Lexi called Blakely's
Blooms and ordered a dozen pink roses. Dr. Moriarty would just have to understand, she told herself
darkly.

Then she remembered that she still hadn't bought
the biggest, prettiest, most expensive Valentine's
Day card for his wife.

With a heavy sigh, she returned to the living room to see if Emma Rose had awakened from her nap yet. It was going to be another long, unlucky day.

Dr. Moriarty was so pleased with the basket—pink roses and all—that he handed Lexi a twenty-five-dollar tip.

"Here," he told her. "Treat you and your valentine to something special."

And so she had.

She and Emma Rose had dined at Elmo's Pizzeria, a charming restaurant on Water Street where the waiters all knew Lexi by name, and kept stopping by their table to play with Emma Rose.

Lexi knew babies weren't supposed to eat pizza, but it was a special occasion. She fed Emma Rose bits of cheese and crust, trying to avoid the spicy tomato sauce. And she fed quarters into the mini-jukebox at their table, allowing Emma Rose's chubby fingers to select the songs.

The restaurant was filled with lovey-dovey couples, of course, and a collective groan went up when Emma Rose's first selection came on: Michael Jackson's *Thriller.*

"Not very romantic. Good going, Em," Lexi said with a laugh.

The last thing she wanted on this Valentine's Day was to be reminded of romance.

But the second song Emma Rose had selected was "Lady in Red."

"Great," Lexi muttered.

She and Yale used to make out in his vanilla-colored Mustang with this playing on the car radio.

Emma Rose started rubbing her eyes before the song was over.

Lexi had the waiter box the rest of the pizza to take home, then loaded Emma Rose into the car.

She could hear her snoring from her car seat in the back as she drove along the winding road toward home.

It hadn't been such a bad Valentine's Day, she thought, carefully guiding the big, old car around a bend. At least she wasn't alone. She had Emma Rose. And her daughter would never leave her.

Not like a man would.

Not like Emmett would have, she told herself.

Again, she thought of what Yale had said to her yesterday in the parking lot.

His words had been ringing through her mind ever since, haunting her dreams last night when she'd finally managed to drift off to sleep.

"I've changed . . . I'm going to fight for you . . . I love you . . ."

Lies, she thought stubbornly, lifting her chin as she rounded the last curve before the carriage house. Everything he said had always been a lie.

And yet, there was still the tiny part of her that wanted to believe him.

She pulled into the driveway, noticing that the tire tracks in the snow looked fresh. That was odd, since it had been snowing ever since she'd left the house late this afternoon.

She pulled up in front of the house . . . and saw it.

The shiny black Lexus parked in her usual spot. It was empty.

Where was Yale?

She hadn't bothered to lock the back door. She rarely did, lately, having gone back to her casual old ways.

He must be inside.

Rage boiled up inside her, and she wondered, only for a moment, what to do.

Then, spontaneously, she opened the door and stepped out into the frigid night. She carefully took Emma Rose from her car seat, and the baby went right back to sleep, her head nestled on Lexi's shoulder.

"Don't worry, Em," she muttered, as she stomped across the dark, snowy yard. "I'll kick him out, and he'll never bug us again."

It didn't occur to her to be afraid until she had yanked open the back door and stepped inside. That was when she realized that the entire house was dark.

For a moment, she stood just inside the back door, contemplating the situation.

Was Yale lying in wait for her, planning to jump out and attack her?

He must be, her head said, but her heart told her not to be afraid.

How can I not be afraid? He killed Emmett, Lexi argued with herself.

And yet, inexplicably, she found herself moving forward, turning on lights as she went.

The roses she had carelessly dropped on the floor

earlier lay scattered there still, and their pungent, sweet scent seemed to permeate the air, stronger, if possible, than when they had been fresh.

She didn't find him in the kitchen, or in the dining room, or in the living room.

The house was silent.

And yet he was there. She felt his presence as surely as she had seen that familiar black car parked outside.

She turned on the light at the foot of the stairs and started up tentatively, clasping the sleeping baby against her shoulder.

At the top of the stairs, she found her bedroom door closed.

He was in there, she knew, waiting to confront her.

She hesitated a moment, then turned toward the nursery. She would put Emma Rose down in her crib first. She didn't want the baby awakened by another angry confrontation.

And this would be the last, Lexi added, as she settled her daughter in the crib. After this, she would make certain she never came into contact with him again. If he moved to Cady's Landing, she and Emma Rose would leave. It was that simple.

"Goodnight, sweetheart," she whispered, pulling a blanket over her sleeping baby. She bent to turn on the nightlight, then pulled the door closed all but a crack.

It was time to face Yale Bradigan.

Lexi turned toward the master bedroom door, took a deep breath, and braced herself, stiffening her shoulders as she reached for the knob.

The first thing that captured her attention as she opened the door was the candlelight. The room glowed with what seemed like hundreds of tiny white lights, and she realized, as she glanced around, that glass globes holding flickering votive candles covered every surface in the room.

Frowning, she stepped over the threshold.

And in that split second, everything changed.

The overpowering sweet, familiar scent of roses rushed at her, sweeping her off to another time, another place.

Maybe I can make your life a bed of roses after all, Lex . . .

"Oh, my God." She clasped her hands to her mouth and stared at the bed, covered in thousands of slippery-soft red petals.

"Lexi . . ."

He stepped from the shadows and a sob caught in her throat.

Emmett . . .

His name echoed over and over as she stared at him, beyond shocked, her mind whirling crazily.

And yet somehow, her heart had already known, long before she had opened the door to this room. Maybe her heart had known all along.

"I told you it was me," he said, moving toward her, his voice hushed. "Please, Lexi, I love you so much."

"Emmett," she breathed, as he came to her. She reached out with a shaky hand and brushed his cheek with her fingertips.

"It's me, Lex. I swear it's me."

"I know it's you," she said, and tears were rolling down her cheeks and his. "I know it's you."

"I really have changed, Lexi. I want to get married, and I want to be Emma Rose's daddy, and I want a bunch more kids . . ."

She smiled and glanced at the rose-petal-covered bed. "Well, the roses worked the first time," she said, slipping her hands beneath his soft flannel shirt.

She felt his heart beating beneath the warm flesh against her fingers. Emmett's heart, beating rapidly, alive . . . *alive* . . .

Joy surged through her.

"Why are you laughing?" he asked, touching her lips.

"It's just . . . roses," she said, her own heart so light it threatened to burst from her chest. "I've been trying to get my hands on red roses all day, and every florist is sold out. Now I know why."

He smiled tenderly, ran a hand over her hair. "I promise I'll never leave you, Lexi. Never, ever again."

"I thought you didn't make promises," she said, her lips inches from his.

"I only make promises I can keep," he told her, just before his mouth came down over hers.

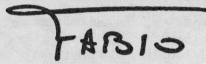

WIN YOUR FANTASY-COME-TRUE DATE with *Fabio*

Join Fabio for a day and evening of fabulous fun in Los Angeles. In 25 words or less, describe your fantasy date with Fabio—and you could be on your way to L.A. One lucky winner will be chosen by a panel of judges including Fabio.

OFFICIAL ENTRY FORM

Please enter me in the FABIO FANTASY-COME-TRUE DATE contest.
My fantasy date with Fabio would include:

(25 WORDS OR LESS)

_____

_____

_____

_____

_____

_____

(ATTACH ADDITIONAL PAGES IF NEEDED).

Name_____

Address_____

City_____State_____Zip_____

Tel. # (optional)_____

Mail to: FABIO FANTASY-COME-TRUE DATE
c/o Kensington Publishing Corp.
850 Third Ave., NYC 10022-6222
CONTEST ENDS 9/30/96.

OFFICIAL RULES

1. To enter, complete the official entry form. No purchase necessary. You may enter by hand printing on a 3" x 5" piece of paper, your name, address and the words "Fabio Fantasy-Come-True Date". Mail with essay to: "Fabio Fantasy-Come-True Date", c/o Kensington Publishing Corp., 850 Third Ave., New York, NY 10022-6222.

2. Enter as often as you like but each entry must be mailed separately. Mechanically reproduced entries not accepted. Entries must be received by 9/30/96.

3. Winner selected in a random drawing on or about 10/31/96 from among all eligible entries received. Winner may be required to sign an affidavit and release which must be returned within 14 days or alternate winner will be selected. Winner permits the use of his/her name/photograph for publicity/advertising purposes without further compensation. No transfer of prizes permitted. Taxes are the sole responsibility of prize winner. Only one prize per family or household.

4. Winner agrees that the sponsor, its affiliates and their agencies and employees shall not be liable for injury, loss, or damage of any kind resulting from participation in this promotion or from the acceptance or use of the prize awarded.

5. Contest open to residents of the U.S. except employees of Kensington Publishing Corp., their affiliates, advertising and promotion agencies. Void where taxed, prohibited or restricted by law. All Federal, state and local laws and regulations apply. Odds of winning depend upon the total number of eligible entries received. All prizes will be awarded. Not responsible for lost, misdirected mail or printing errors.

6. For the name of prize winner, send a self-addressed, stamped envelope to: "Fabio Fantasy-Come-True Date" Winner, c/o Kensington Publishing Corp., 850 Third Ave., NYC 10022-6222.